A MATTER OF MARTYRDOM

Also by Hugh Ross Williamson

Historical Novels
THE MARRIAGE MADE IN BLOOD
THE BUTT OF MALMSEY
THE SISTERS
CAPTAIN THOMAS SCHOFIELD
THE SILVER BOWL
JAMES, BY THE GRACE OF GOD

Historical Plays
HEART OF BRUCE
ROSE AND GLOVE
THE CARDINAL'S LEARNING
HIS EMINENCE OF ENGLAND
QUEEN ELIZABETH
TERESA OF AVILA
GUNPOWDER, TREASON AND PLOT

Historical Biography
SIR WALTER RALEIGH
KING JAMES I
GEORGE VILLIERS, FIRST DUKE OF BUCKINGHAM
JOHN HAMPDEN
CHARLES AND CROMWELL
FOUR STUART PORTRAITS
JEREMY TAYLOR

Historical Occasions
THE DAY THEY KILLED THE KING
THE DAY SHAKESPEARE DIED

Historical Mysteries
HISTORICAL WHODUNITS
ENIGMAS OF HISTORY

Historical Places
CANTERBURY CATHEDRAL
THE ANCIENT CAPITAL (WINCHESTER)
THE FLOWERING HAWTHORN (GLASTONBURY)

History
THE GUNPOWDER PLOT
THE BEGINNING OF THE ENGLISH REFORMATION

HUGH ROSS WILLIAMSON

A Matter of Martyrdom

London
MICHAEL JOSEPH

First published in Great Britain by
MICHAEL JOSEPH LTD
26 Bloomsbury Street
London W.C.1
1969

7181 0650 4

Set and printed in Great Britain by
Northumberland Press Ltd., Gateshead,
in Granjon eleven on twelve point

To

my brother Allsebrook

CONTENTS

'I pray you, recommend me unto my good lady of Salisbury, and pray her to have a good heart, for we never come to the kingdom of Heaven but by troubles.'

Catherine of Aragon in a letter to her daughter

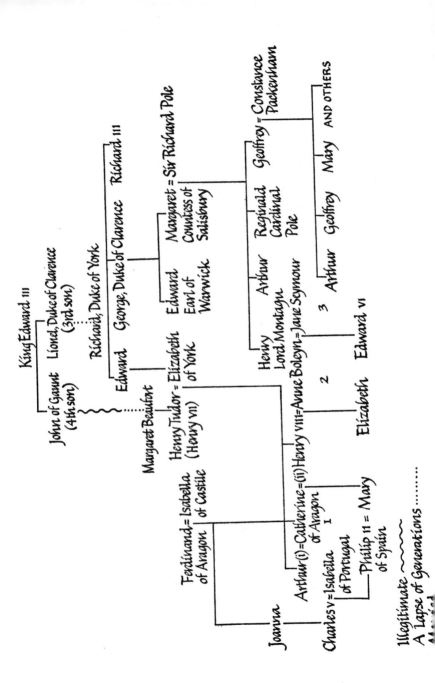

King Edward III

Lionel, Duke of Clarence (3rd son)

John of Gaunt (4th son)

Richard, Duke of York

Edward   George, Duke of Clarence   Richard III

Edward Earl of Warwick   Margaret = Sir Richard Pole Countess of Salisbury

Margaret Beaufort

Henry Tudor = Elizabeth of York (Henry VII)

Henry Lord Montagu   Arthur   Reginald Cardinal Pole   Geoffrey = Constance Packenham

Ferdinand = Isabella of Aragon of Castile

Arthur (i) = Catherine = (ii) Henry VIII = Anne Boleyn = Jane Seymour of Aragon
                    I   2   3

Arthur   Geoffrey   Mary   AND OTHERS

Joanna

Charles V = Isabella of Portugal

Philip II = Mary of Spain   Elizabeth   Edward VI

Illegitimate ～～～
A Lapse of Generations ·········
Married

I

The Countess goes to Ludlow

Margaret Pole, Countess of Salisbury, violently disapproved of the proceedings. She said nothing, since any protest would only have made things worse, but her white bleak face, her contemptuous eyes and her pursed mouth left no doubt of her feelings. However interpreted, the occasion was an insult to her friend, the Queen, who, on that account, had pleaded illness and refused to attend it. Margaret would have preferred to absent herself also, but, as Governess to the Princess Mary, heir to the throne, she had a duty to be, almost defiantly, there.

The occasion was King Henry VIII's official recognition of his six-year-old bastard, Henry Fitzroy. The immediate implication of the ceremony was that, as Queen Catherine was now too old to give the King the male heir he so passionately wanted —their four sons had all died in infancy—he would, in certain circumstances, be willing for Fitzroy to succeed. There were others, however, who saw this merely as an interim move which would lead ultimately to the putting away of the Queen.

The scene of the investiture was Henry's new palace of Bridewell which had been completed three years earlier for the reception of the Queen's nephew, the Emperor Charles V, when (brought by a fleet of 180 ships and accompanied by 2,000 retainers) he came to England to be affianced to Princess Mary.

In the event, Charles had not occupied Bridewell but had stayed in the great monastery of Black Friars, just across the River Fleet, with which Bridewell was connected by a 'gallery' or bridge, passing through an opening in the city wall near the Lud Gate.

The recognition of Henry Fitzroy was thus the first important occasion for the use of the palace, and the King was not undeliberate in the choice. It had historic overtones. The site had been occupied by the remains of a building supposed to be Roman and said to have been a palace of the Saxon kings before the Conquest. Henry I had given stone for the rebuilding of it, but in later centuries it had fallen into decay. And now Henry, upon the site of the old Tower of Mountfiquit, had 'built a stately and beautiful house giving it the name of Bridewell because of the parish and well there'. Here he would honour his only son.

First, the boy was knighted. Then he was led out of the royal presence to return shortly, garbed as an earl, between the Earls of Arundel and Oxford. After he had been created Earl of Nottingham, he retired again and returned again, this time in the robes of a duke, between the only two English Dukes, Norfolk and Suffolk, the latter the King's brother-in-law. He was then created Duke of Richmond and Somerset.

The procession formed to go into the King's chamber to hear the patents read where Henry 'stood under the cloth of estate, well accompanied by lords spiritual and temporal and my lord Cardinal. The young lord then kneeled to the king, who commanded him to stand up'. Sir Thomas More, the chancellor of the Duchy of Lancaster, read the patents aloud and when he reached the words *gladii cinctorum*, 'the young lord kneeled down and the King put the girdle about his neck'.

The boy in addition to his knighthood, his earldom and his dukedom, was proclaimed Lord Admiral of England, Wales and Ireland, of Normandy, Gascony and Aquitaine, Knight of the Garter, Keeper of the City and Castle of Carlisle, and first peer of the realm. Nothing was wanting except Princess Mary's title of Wales.

In the course of the festivities that followed, Margaret's eldest son, Henry Viscount Montagu, and her youngest, Sir Geoffrey Pole, took her lightly to task.

'Madame my mother,' said Montagu, 'dare I say that this is hardly the occasion for so sour a countenance?' He said it hesitantly because, though he was thirty-three, he was still in considerable awe of his mother. But he felt it his duty to warn her. Brought up as one of the younger set at court—he was a year younger than the King—he was particularly sensitive to the royal moods, and he had noticed Henry's small, hard eyes watching her from time to time during the ceremony.

Before she could reply, his brother said: 'Even the saints smile.' Geoffrey, as the Benjamin of the family, could safely make remarks which the others could not. Indeed this was why Montagu had insisted that they should approach their mother together. The reference was to the King's recent description of the Countess as 'the saintliest woman in England', which she had deprecated but which had passed into court currency. On this occasion she was not amused.

'Sons,' she said, 'I thank you for your care of me, but both my conscience and my face are my own.' If her words and, even more, her tone had not made the situation clear, her next remark underlined it.

'No doubt you will wish,' she said, 'to make your felicitations to Tom Boleyn on his new honour, but I pray you hold me aloof from them.'

In the distribution of honours to grace the new Duke, Sir Thomas Boleyn had been made Viscount Rochford. The promotion of this mean, suave Treasurer of the King's Household was, as everyone knew, due not to his undoubted financial gifts but to his accommodating paternity. His elder daughter Mary was Henry's present *maîtresse-en-titre* and the more epigrammatic courtiers found it fitting that the King should honour the father of his present fancy on the same occasion as he honoured the son of her predecessor.

Mary Boleyn—she was Lady Carey, having been married, as soon as the *affaire* started, to an obliging nonentity who had been given a small post in the Household and a large fortune for his pains—was a weak, amorous, amiable creature who seemed unable to say 'No'. As a Maid-in-Waiting at the French Court, she was known by the time she was 17, as the 'English mare' and, after some trial attempts with courtiers, became mistress of the King, Francis I, who, when he heard that she had passed over to Henry VIII, referred to her (though whether nostalgically or not it was impossible to determine) as '*My* hackney'.

She was generally blamed not for her complaisance but for her failure to secure better terms from either of the monarchs whom she obliged and by no one was she more bitterly criticised than by her younger sister Anne, who had just returned from the French court unscathed.

Mary was pregnant and, lazily watching the ceremonial, wondered if her child, were it a boy, would be similarly honoured.[1] Anne had eyes only for young Henry Percy, son of the Earl of Northumberland, who was one of Cardinal Wolsey's household. They were sufficiently in love for the matter to be remarked. The youth managed always to be in attendance on the Cardinal on his visits to court, but at the moment he was more concerned with congratulating the father than in wooing the daughter.

Wolsey himself was preoccupied with affairs of state. At fifty, this preposterous butcher's son who ruled England and the King was, despite his power and wealth and splendour, still the unsparing worker he had been when, years ago, he had

[1] The child was Henry Lord Hunsdon who played a considerable part at the court of his half-sister, Queen Elizabeth I.

14

first attracted the attention of the King's father by managing to return from a successful mission to the Continent before anyone thought he had set out.

Now that he had weathered all storms and was indifferent alike to the hatred of the older nobility who despised him as a parvenu and to the cringing of the younger who recognised him as a power, he had only one ambition left—the Papacy. When he had been made Cardinal, he had seen to it that the Hat which the Pope had sent him by an ordinary messenger was officially met at Blackheath and conducted in solemn procession to Westminster where 'it was then placed on a table with tapers around it and the greatest duke in the land was compelled to make a curtsy to it'. This formal recognition of the superiority of the Spiritual Power had the incidental advantage of demonstrating Wolsey's status as Papal Legate, in which capacity he considered himself above the King. As Pope, he would be above all the kings. In the meantime, there was the international situation to be manoeuvred to his—and, by definition, England's—advantage.

But earlier that year, 1525, the balance of Europe had been violently upset. The two great powers, France under the Valois Francis I and the Empire under the Hapsburg Charles V strove for hegemony by intermittent warfare in Italy, to portions of which they advanced rival claims. By skilful diplomacy, therefore, wavering between one and the other, Wolsey could retain the balance of power. Recently, however, the Constable Charles de Bourbon, whose great holdings in the heart of France— La Marche, Bourbonnais, Auvergne, Forez, Beaujolais—made him almost an independent prince, deserted to the Emperor on the promise of the addition of Dauphiné, Provence and Lyonnais.

It was the treason of the century. When Bourbon recognised on a battlefield the dying Bayard, 'le chevalier sans peur and sans reproche', and expressed his sorrow, Bayard retorted: 'I have no need of pity, for I die an honest man; but I pity you, since you are serving against your prince, your country and your oath.'

The immediate effect of the desertion was so to tip the scales in favour of the Emperor that, at the battle of Pavia, the French suffered a crushing defeat and their king, Francis, was taken prisoner and sent as a captive to Madrid.

The result of Pavia was so overwhelming and unprecedented that Wolsey was apprehensive. It was not the vanquished Francis (whose message, 'Everything is lost but honour' was to ring through the centuries) who troubled him. It was the victor, Charles. For, palpably, Charles had now no need of England's friendship. And Charles, the nephew of the Queen of England, the affianced of her daughter, Princess Mary, was, so Wolsey's spies informed him, about to repudiate the match. But until he had some certainty in the matter, the Cardinal was at a loss how to proceed.

In April he had consulted the King and Queen and the Countess of Salisbury—who, as Princess Mary's Governess, was usually referred to in matters concerning her—as to the most tactful means of finding out Charles's intentions. It had been decided that Mary—who was nine—should send to Charles—who was twenty-five—an emerald ring, with the message that 'Her Grace has sent this token for a better knowledge whether His Majesty keeps constant to her as, with God's grace, she will to him'. It was a pretty conceit, of which the child had in fact approved; for the emerald, whose colour is the symbol of constancy, is supposed to fade and pale its brilliant green if the heart of the betrothed swerves in loyalty to his lady.

That very morning, June 18, Wolsey had at last received the reply from the envoys in Toledo, describing the Emperor's demeanour on receiving the ring. Charles had stuck it on his little finger as far as it would go and told the ambassadors to say 'he would wear it for the sake of the Princess'. At the same time he had asked after her health. This struck the Cardinal as unsatisfactory and inconclusive and he now wanted the Countess of Salisbury's interpretation of it.

Between them there had always been sympathy and understanding. Two years his senior, Margaret had never despised him for his plebeian birth if only because, as a Plantagenet, she considered him only a little less lowly-born than most of the nobility. She had, in the days before his leap to power, employed him as her man of business for no other reason than that he was the most competent one she knew. Later, as his power commenced, he had done her several favours, especially in connection with her best-loved son, Reginald, who was now in Italy, and she was constant in her gratitude.

On his side, he trusted her judgment as that of one who, if not altogether above the battle, had at least inherited some of the innate statesmanship of her house which, until her uncle was killed at Bosworth forty years before, had ruled England for more than three centuries. And, as regards Princess Mary, he and she were the child's godparents and were both genuinely concerned, in their different ways, for her welfare and happiness.

'What does it mean, my Lord Cardinal?' said Margaret in answer to his report and question. 'No more and no less than it says. It may be the Emperor was unwilling to hurt Mary.'

'He is not such a fool as to miss the meaning of the question.'

'He may have thought us not such fools as to have asked the question that way.'

'Your Ladyship concurred in it.'

'When you and the King and the Queen and the Princess were all agreed, it was not for me to protest. Besides, it did no harm.' She paused for a moment, not sure of her ground. Then she said: 'This is the harm.'

'What?'

'This ceremony. Do you encourage the Emperor to marry the Princess by honouring her bastard brother?'

'Affairs in the North,' said Wolsey, 'make it necessary to strengthen the Council at York. The boy is a good figurehead for it, if we make him so. As for the Princess, I have already arranged that she should hold her own court in the West.'

Yet it was ten weeks before, in the early days of September, Mary and her Governess set out for Ludlow, 'the Windsor of the West' and in that interim the Emperor Charles, in a letter written in his own hand, had repudiated his engagement to the Princess. It was done elegantly and as tactfully as possible—he merely asked permission to marry instead Isabella of Portugal[2] —a match which would consolidate his Spanish kingdom— and there was an adequate financial arrangement.

Mary herself who, for three years, had dreamt of her destiny as Empress and had studied, under her Spanish tutor, to prepare herself for it, went white and faint—so the Court noticed—at the hurt of the news. They attributed it to a fantasy of jealousy, encouraged by the Maids-of-Honour's chatter about love. But they were wrong. The hurt was to her pride. The very young are less equipped than the old only to mask misery, not to feel it, and her creation as Princess of Wales—a unique distinction— was little consolation. Yet outwardly after the first shock she showed no sign. It was, even at nine, her way. When she was a baby, her father had once proudly shown her to foreign ambassadors as 'the child who never cries'.

Margaret Pole's reaction was, inevitably, conditioned by the remembrance that, at Mary's birth, she and Queen Catherine had decided that the child should marry Reginald Pole and so, restoring the true Plantagenet blood to the Throne, atone for 'the marriage made in blood'.[3] Both the Countess and the Queen had, as events ruthlessly shaped destinies, recognised

---

[2] It was their son, Philip II of Spain, who eventually married Mary.

[3] As a pre-condition of Catherine of Aragon's marriage to the then Prince of Wales, her parents, Ferdinand and Isabella, had insisted on the execution of Margaret Pole's elder brother, Edward, who was the true Plantagenet heir to the throne after the Tudor usurpation. The story is told in *The Marriage made in Blood*.

it as a dream unlikely of fulfilment; and when Catherine's favourite nephew, Charles (who was exactly a week older than Reginald Pole) was affianced to Mary, it dissolved in the harsh daylight of political realities. Now that Mary was again free, Margaret could not help a momentary speculation, but immediately dismissed it as her intelligence told her that in all probability Wolsey, who had to switch his alliances, would arrange a French marriage for Mary.

Meanwhile practical matters demanded attention—first and most importantly, to comfort the child not by showing any sympathy but by assuming she did not need it; secondly to see to the ordering of the expedition to the West. In the instructions which Wolsey had drawn up and the King had signed, it was set out how, on account of the long absence of the monarch, the tranquillity of Wales and the Marches had been disturbed and justice imperfectly administered, and the King had now determined 'to send at this time our dearest, best beloved and only daughter, the Princess, accompanied and established with an honourable, discreet and expert Council to reside and remain in the Marches of Wales, furnished with sufficient power for the better administration of justice.

The selection of the Council was Wolsey's affair. Margaret's was more personal and, since it involved the Heiress, ultimately more influential.

'First, principally and above all things,' the document ran, 'the Countess of Salisbury, being Lady Governess, shall, according to the singular confidence that the King's Highness has in her, give most tender regard to all such things as concern the person of the Princess, her honourable education and training in all virtuous demeanour. That is to say, at due times to serve God, from Whom all grace and goodness proceeds. Also, at seasons convenient, to use moderate exercise for taking open air in gardens, sweet and wholesome places and walks, which may confer on her health, solace and comfort, as by the Lady Governess shall be thought most convenient. And likewise to pass her time at her virginals or other musical instruments, and without fatigation or weariness to attend to her learning of the Latin tongue and French. At other seasons to dance and, among the rest, to have good respect unto her diet, which is to be pure, well-prepared, dressed and served, with comfortable, joyous and merry conversation in an honourable and virtuous manner. Every thing about her is to be pure, sweet, clean and wholesome and, as is proper to so great a princess, all corruptions, evil airs and things noisome and unpleasant are to be eschewed.'

Wolsey also ordered that every day at least two gentlemen ushers, two gentlemen waiters, two yeomen ushers, twelve yeomen and two grooms should be in attendance in the Presence Chamber—the number to be increased on the visits of strangers and on state occasions.

But before the impressive retinue set out for Ludlow—over three hundred of them, with the servitors in their new damask liveries of the Princess's colours, blue and green—there were farewells to be made. The King was staying at King's Langley on one of his regular hunting expeditions; the Queen had gone to Woburn Abbey that, in its religious peace, she might find some solace for the sadness of this first parting with her only child.

Catherine was now forty, a squat, solid Spanish wife and mother whose protuberant blue eyes gazed placidly from an oval face so curiously proportioned that the high forehead occupied half of it. What beauty she had had in her girlhood had gone, all but her celebrated auburn hair; but that was flecked with grey and she hid it under her hood-cap.

The strains and disappointments of her life had served only to strengthen her religious faith. She rose in the night to keep the conventual hours of prayer; she dressed herself for the day at five in the morning; next to her skin she wore the coarse habit of the Franciscans of whose Third Order she was a member. She had finery and jewels enough for state occasions, but she was accustomed to say that she considered no part of her time so wasted as that spent in dressing and adorning herself.

Erasmus had once written to Henry: 'Your noble wife spends that time in reading the sacred volume which other princesses occupy in cards and dice' yet, for Henry's sake and because it was her wifely duty, she had joined him in his amusements and a court versifier had noted:

> With stole and with needle she was not to seek
> And other practisings for ladies meet
> For pastimes—as tables, tric-trac and cleek[4],
> Cards and dice.

But these days, as she seldom saw Henry, she played seldom.

When Margaret and Mary arrived at Woburn, she said to the Countess: 'So time goes back on itself. I pray Our Lady that now Ludlow prove propitious.'

'It must be so,' said Margaret. 'The Princess of Wales has paid the stake.'

'Does the credit last so long?' said the Queen. 'I pray you, dear friend, use every care.'

The past was vivid for them. Twenty-four years earlier, Catherine had come to Ludlow as the bride of Arthur, Prince of Wales, Henry's elder brother and before a year was out he had died there. Then, as now, Margaret Pole was in charge of the household.

Looking back on this beginning of her tragic life in England when she was sixteen, Catherine found only one consolation in it—that she had met Margaret, who had at once taken her to her heart and had kept her there in all the bitter years between. Yet even this could not completely erase her instinctive fear of Ludlow which was for her associated for ever with death. And into this danger her only daughter and her dearest friend were being sent at a time when she was at her nadir.

Margaret understood her mood and said: 'I will bring the Princess back to you as soon as her Progress in the West is over.

[4] Chess, backgammon and whist.

It will take less time than you fear and Dr. Wooton will be with us even on the shortest journey.'

'He is the one physician I trust.'

'That is why he has been chosen,' said Margaret, without mentioning that it was she who had persuaded Wolsey to make the choice.

As soon as Mary had kissed her mother, they left her, making a formal reverence, and the Queen went into chapel and fell to her prayers.

The King's farewell was boisterous with laughter. Henry, however he might long for a son, adored his small daughter. Ambassadors had noted his habit, when she was a baby, of carrying her about in his arms in public and making Wolsey kiss her hand. When she was older and could dance with him, he would suddenly play some small trick on her, as during a Court Masque pulling off her hood so that her red hair—the same colour as his—tumbled about her shoulders; and they would both laugh uproariously. He, with whom music was a passion—he played the lute, the cornet, the flute; practised the organ sometimes 'day and night'; composed songs and never travelled anywhere without his chief musician, Dionysius Memo —was particularly proud that Mary, inheriting his taste and enthusiasm, was a musical infant prodigy, composing a tune and playing it on the virginals at the age of four; and she, basking in his affectionate encouragement, practised the harder.

Henry was now thirty-four but, beardless still, looked younger, except that, as he could no longer take the violent exercise to which he had been accustomed in his teens and twenties, he was showing the first signs of a double-chin. But, once a very notable athlete, he still gloried in his strength and his greeting to his daughter was to throw her in the air and catch her. Though Mary secretly considered herself, at nine, too old for such treatment, she made no demur and had no fear whatever that he would drop her. Father and daughter saluted each other with their usual laughter and even the Countess of Salisbury smiled.

As, late in September, the company approached Ludlow, Mary asked Margaret: 'Are the Welsh as great singers as my father said?'

'As I remember them, they are good-voiced,' the Governess answered.

'And he said that I must sing too.'

'You must indeed,' said Margaret. 'That may be the charm that Ludlow needs.'

2

The King falls in love

It was during the Easter season of the following year when the Princess and the Countess were in residence at Worcester Priory for a month, that Lord Montagu and Sir Geoffrey Pole came to visit their mother. Both had been born in that part of the country—at Stourton Castle—when their father was Warden of the Marches and they could combine with filial piety a pleasant round of visits to their friends; but, chiefly, they wanted to discuss with the Countess certain happenings at court. Gossip there had it that the King was about to take a new mistress, though there was no more solid basis for the belief than the fact that Henry no longer troubled to visit his wife—and the curious affair of Henry Percy. The first, Margaret knew, for Catherine had written to Mary: 'The long absence of the King and you troubles me.' The second, her sons now told her of.

Henry Percy and Anne Boleyn had secretly plighted their troth, but not so secretly that it had evaded Wolsey's ears, and, so, the King's. The result was that, one evening after the Cardinal had returned from a visit to Court during which the young lovers had made no attempt to disguise their feelings, he sent for Percy and, without any preliminaries, barked at him: 'I am amazed at your insufferable folly in getting entangled with a foolish girl at court. I mean Anne Boleyn.'

Before Percy could protest, he continued: 'Don't you consider the estate God has called you to in the world? When your noble father dies, you will inherit one of the greatest earldoms in the realm.'

'That is true, but—'

'The King and your father would have found you a wife who matched your estate and honour. Now, by your wilfulness, you have offended not only your father but your most gracious sovereign lord and secretly engaged yourself to one whom neither the King nor your father will agree for you to marry. I am going to send for your father and he will disinherit you if you persist in this.'

Percy's lip quivered and he started to cry. The Cardinal continued inexorably.

'The King's majesty himself will complain to your father of you. Already he has made arrangements for Anne Boleyn to marry another person and, although she knows nothing of it yet, I have no doubt that she will be glad and agreeable to do as he arranges when the time comes.'

This was not strictly accurate. No arrangements had yet been made, but both King and Cardinal had agreed that it would save much trouble if Anne Boleyn married the young Earl of Ormond. Anne's father had some claim to the Ormond estates and such a marriage, uniting the two branches of that family, would obviate possible Irish disturbances.

Percy, realising that pressure was about to be put on his love, regained some of his courage, bit back his tears and said: 'I knew nothing of the King's pleasure in this matter. If I have displeased him I am very sorry. But I am of age and I thought that I could choose such a wife as love should show me and that my father would have been persuaded to approve.'

'He is not yet in his dotage,' said Wolsey, reflecting that the Earl of Northumberland was some years younger than himself.

'Sir,' said Percy, 'though Anne is only a simple maid with a knight for a father, yet she is descended of noble parentage.

25

By her mother she is of Norfolk blood and on her father's side she is descended from the Earls of Ormond. Why should I then not marry her when her descent is equivalent with mine in dignity? Therefore, I most humbly desire Your Grace, of your especial favour, to entreat the King's Majesty on my behalf in this matter.'

The Cardinal, who had expected instant obedience, threw up his hands and shouted to the rest of his household standing round: 'Look, sirs, at a wilful, foolish boy.' Then, without lowering his tone, to Percy: 'I thought that when you heard me declare the King's intended will you would have submitted yourself to his royal pleasure.'

Percy, realising the implicit threat, said: 'Sir, so I would, but in this matter I have gone so far and taken my oath in troth-plight that I do not know how to withdraw in conscience.'

Wolsey looked at him in surprise. The Cardinal was so accustomed to regard the most sacred oaths as diplomatic counters to be discarded at convenience that he could hardly believe Percy's ingenuous sincerity.

'Do you suppose,' he said, 'that the King and I have not considered that?'

Then he who, as Papal Legate, could dispense almost any-thing became suspicious. Percy could not be such a fool as he seemed. He must be playing for time. In a voice sterner than any he had yet used, he said: 'I can see no trace of submission in you.'

Imploringly now, the youth replied: 'If it please Your Grace I will submit myself wholly to the King's Majesty and to Your Grace in this matter if my conscience can be cleared of the burden of my promise.'

The Cardinal allowed himself to be mollified. He said that he would see himself to the clearing of the conscience and added: 'I will send for your father from the North and we will take what measures we can to reduce the consequences of your folly.'

Percy thanked him, though the last person he ever wanted to see was his father, a man in whose cold heart and narrow mind the extremes of pride and meanness met.

'In the meantime,' the Cardinal concluded, 'I command you in the King's name never to attempt to see the girl again, if you wish to avoid the King's high indignation.'

Percy knew that, in the circumstances, it would be impossible for him to see her. To an older friend who had some influence with the Boleyn family, he wrote, telling him of his enforced absence and saying: 'I pray you that you do not suffer her in my absence to be married to any other man. Commend me to her and bid her remember her promise which none can loose but God only.'

The Earl of Northumberland, when at last he arrived, had a long conversation with Wolsey and after he had drunk deeply of the Cardinal's best wine, strode to the end of the gallery and rated his son before the servants.

'Son,' he said, 'you have always been proud, presumptuous, disdainful, and a very unthrifty waster. You have now showed yourself licentious and unthinking, having regard neither for me nor for the King, whose disfavour is able to ruin us and our posterity. Yet he, of his goodness, as also the Cardinal, your master, has excused me for your foolishness and, instead of maligning me, pity me for having such a son. Unless you now submit yourself wholly to them I shall so order my succession that one of your brothers, who are wiser than you, shall take the place that by right should be yours.'

Then, unpardonably, he turned to the servants and told them they had his authority to tell his son his faults on any occasion they might think it necessary; and, in high dudgeon, departed in his barge.

The immediate upshot was that Percy was betrothed to Mary Talbot, a daughter of the Earl of Shrewsbury, who hated him almost as much as he hated her; and Anne Boleyn was banished from court and sent to her father's castle of Hever, in the Kent countryside, there to await the provision of whatever bridegroom the King and the Cardinal determined on.

When Montagu and Geoffrey Pole had finished their recital of these facts, their mother asked: 'Who told you these things?'

'By Our Lady,' said Montagu, 'it was all public enough.'

'I happened to be there myself,' said Geoffrey, 'at the Cardinal's first shouting at him. I missed only a few words and afterwards others who had been nearer gave them to me.'

'I do not see how it concerns us,' said Margaret, 'except that the Talbots are in the Marches and we shall be bidden to the marriage.'

'What concerns us all,' said Montagu, 'is that rumour has it that it is the King himself who wants Anne in place of her sister Mary.'

The rumour happened to be true. Henry had fallen in love with his mistress's younger sister. It was Anne's vivacity, more than anything else, that attracted him. She was not particularly beautiful. She was, an Italian observer noted, a year or two later, 'of a middling stature, swarthy complexion, long neck, wide mouth, bosom not much raised and, in fact, she has nothing but the English King's great appetite and her eyes which are black and beautiful'. She had the additional drawbacks of a projecting tooth under the upper lip, a small extra finger on her right hand and a mole on her neck below her chin, which she covered either by a jewelled necklace or by a high dress. But her glossy raven hair was generally admired; and—sure ways to Henry's interest—she played the lute well and was a good dancer. She was eighteen.

At first she was unaware that Henry had particularly noticed her. Her early training at the French Court had accustomed her to the monarch's conventional dalliance with maids-of-honour, and if, now, the English king paid more attention to her than to the others, she attributed it to the fact that she was Mary's sister. She was too much in love with Henry Percy to think of any other man and, even if she had considered the

King in that guise, she would have found him, twice her age, sexually unattractive and not particularly likeable.

When her betrothal was broken, her heart was almost broken with it and for Wolsey, whom she regarded as the villain of the piece, she conceived an implacable and enduring hatred. Though both her sister and her father insisted that the King had been the prime mover in the matter and that his jealousy was the reason for it, she refused to believe them. But soon Henry's continual visits to Hever left her in no doubt and she transferred some of her bitterness to him. Her vivacity, which so attracted him, was now tinged with an insolent wit, which prostrated him.

Yet in spite of Mary's placid complaisance and their father's pressure—he could hardly believe his good fortune that, just as Henry was tiring of the elder daughter he should be attracted by the younger so that the royal mistress-ship would remain in the family—Anne refused absolutely to go to bed with Henry. Everyone assumed it would be merely a matter of time. But she remained unalterable and eventually the King was reduced to writing to her: 'If it shall please you to do me the office of a true, loyal mistress and friend, and to give yourself up, body and soul, to me who will be and have been your very loyal servant (if by your severity you do not forbid me) I promise you that not only shall the name be given you, but that also I will take you for my only mistress, rejecting from thought and affection all others save yourself, to serve you only. I beseech you to make an absolute answer to this, how far and in what I may put my trust; and if it does not please you to make an answer in writing, assign me some place where I may have it from your own mouth and, with well-willing heart, I will be there. No more, for fear of wearying you. Written with the hand of him who would willingly remain your H.R.'

He composed a song for the lute which began:

> Now unto my lady
> Promise to her I make.

From all other only
To her I me betake.

for which she thanked him, but remained adamant.

He wrote again: 'Although, my mistress, it has not pleased you to answer my last letter, nevertheless I think it is the part of a true servant (seeing that otherwise he can hear nothing) to send to enquire of the health of his mistress; and so, to acquit myself of the office of a true servant, I send you this letter, praying you to tell me of your well-being, which I pray God may endure as long as I would mine own. And, so that you may the more often remember me, I send you by this bearer a buck, killed by my hand late yester night, trusting that, as you eat of it, you will remember the hunter.'

He found a new signature for his letters (which were usually in French) which ran: H. autre Ⓐ⒝ ne cherche R.

When state affairs prevented visits to Hever, he protested that 'absence has so grieved my heart that neither tongue nor pen can express the hurt'. When Anne refused to come to court with her father, Henry told her to admonish him that 'he will not serve a lover's turn, as was his promise'. He sent many gifts, including 'my picture set in a bracelet and wish myself in their place when it shall please you'. The summer days suggested comparison: 'The longer the days are, the farther off is the sun and yet, notwithstanding, the hotter; so it is with our love, for we by absence are far sundered, yet it nevertheless keeps its fervency, at least on my part and I dare to hope it is the same on yours.'

Anne was at last so certain of her strength, rooted in his distracted passion for her and her cool indifference to him, that she allowed him peripheral intimacies. But she refused, even for an instant, to consider full possession; and nothing would induce her to succeed her sister as his *maîtresse-en-titre*.

She had decided, since this was how things were, to play for the Throne.

Wolsey, that summer and autumn, was absorbed in refashioning his alliances. Francis I had been released from his Madrid captivity by Charles V and diplomatic activity was intense. Italy and the affairs of the Pope provided the focus of it and so combined the Cardinal's public and private policies.

Italy, which had been the scene of war for thirty-two years, was now, after the battle of Pavia, the helpless victim of mercenary bands, living by pillage and ordering rather than obeying their generals. The case of Milan was a microcosm. Charles V's Spanish army[1] had been quartered on that unfortunate city and there were few soldiers who held aloof from the approved sport of binding their hosts to the foot of the bed or in the cellar in order to have them daily at hand to torture into satisfying some new caprice. The horror of it was a byword throughout Italy. Venice, Florence and the Swiss had united with the Pope in proclaiming a Holy League for the liberation of the Italian States from the Emperor and both France and England were invited to join. Francis agreed and thereby gave Wolsey the opportunity he was seeking to change sides. As fellow-members of a League formed to support the Pope, it would be easy enough for the Kings of England and France to bind themselves in alliance against the Emperor and for himself, as the militant champion of the Papacy, to demonstrate his credentials as the next occupant of Peter's Chair. Henry was named Protector of the League, in the hope that he would be flattered into sending substantial support. But he only sent 25,000 ducats which, as the Pope said on acknowledging it, would not go far and was, he hoped, 'only the presage of greater liberality'.

It proved not to be so and the King and the Cardinal devoted themselves to the matter of the French alliance. They decided that, in the first place, Princess Mary should cement it. She should marry Francis I, who was now a widower. He was thirty-two and the most notable debauchée in Europe. Henry, thinking of his small daughter as an actual person, suddenly insisted

[1] The Emperor, it will be remembered, was also the King of Spain and was thus served by Spanish as well as by German troops.

that the offer should be to marry either Francis or his son, Henry, who was seven. In any case, the Princess must return to London to meet the French Ambassadors and messages were sent to Ludlow that as soon as the Christmas festivities were concluded they were to leave the Marches.

The Countess wrote to Wolsey asking that, as there was likely to be 'a great repair of strangers to the Lady Mary', they might be provided with 'a ship of silver for an alms dish' and 'spice plates' and trumpets and a rebeck and enquired whether they might this Christmas have a Lord of Misrule, as well as 'interludes, disguisings and plays' and a banquet on Twelfth Night.

The Cardinal allowed everything, thinking that the child might as well have a memorable last Christmas in her own country, and ordered considerably more complicated and expensive entertainments to be prepared for the French Ambassadors.

When the English envoys to France presented Francis with Mary's portrait and, describing her as 'the pearl of the world and the jewel her father esteems more than anything else on earth', launched into the expected hyperbole about her virtue and beauty, he interrupted them with: 'I pray you repeat to me none of these matters. I know well her education, her form and her fashion, her virtue and beauty and what father and mother she comes of.' Privately, his own ambassador had sent him a message that Mary was 'so thin, spare and small as to make it impossible to be married for the next three years'.

The special envoys, the Bishop of Tarbes and the Vicomte de Turenne, duly arrived and were appropriately entertained at the St. George's Feast at Greenwich. After dinner, the King led them into the Hall and presented them to the Queen and the Princess. In the dancing that followed Henry partnered his daughter, which prompted a court versifier to utter:

32

> I saw a King and a Princess
>   Dancing before my face
> Most like a god and a goddess
>   (I pray Christ save their grace!)
>
> This king to see whom we have sung,
>   His virtues be right much,
> But this princess being so young
>   There can be found none such.

The Bishop and the Vicomte were—or at least expressed themselves as being—of much the same opinion. Henry urged them to speak to Mary in French, Latin and Italian. When they had done so and also heard her play the virginals, they said she was the most accomplished child they had ever seen.

Negotiations and entertainments continued. There was a great masque in the Queen's apartments, in which Mary was discovered, surrounded by ladies of the court, in a cave made of cloth-of-gold. To the sound of trumpets and accompanied by gentlemen bearing torches, she came down into the Hall, a jewelled garland about her head. Then the King, with Turenne and others, masked in gold and black satin, came in and the dancing continued till morning.

In one of the dances, Henry was partnered by Anne Boleyn.

Henry always insisted that it was the Bishop of Tarbes who first raised the question of Mary's legitimacy. Wolsey, who considered this to the last degree improbable, understood the King's real drift and was prepared to encourage it.

Some theological doubt had always existed about the propriety of Henry marrying his brother's wife. Such a marriage had obviously to be dispensed, yet, as it was actually forbidden by Holy Writ, it was arguable whether even the Pope could dispense it. Before Julius II had given the dispensation enabling Henry to marry Catherine, there had only been one previous case, which the validity of was regarded by theologians as open to discussion.

If, then, the Pope's Bull had been invalid, the marriage of Henry and Catherine was no marriage. Their daughter was illegitimate and the long, sad succession of deaths and miscarriages of the other children could be taken as evidence of God's wrath at the breaking of a Divine law.

It was now no secret that Henry wished to be rid of Catherine so that he might marry again and have a son. The pronouncement of the nullity of his existing union would leave him free to do so. But it was hardly diplomatic to endeavour to betroth his daughter to France at the moment when, by implication, he was considering trying to get her proclaimed illegitimate. Any steps in that direction must, therefore, be taken at some one else's instigation. And who, in the circumstances, more suitable than the French Envoy?

Wolsey, to whom the French alliance was an urgent necessity, did not demur, because he assumed that Henry, once free to do so, would himself marry the French King's sister. Henry encouraged him in that belief. The last thing he wanted the Cardinal to suspect was that the goal of the exercise was Anne Boleyn.

As the first step to freeing the King from the bonds of matrimony an elaborate comedy was secretly staged at Wolsey's London palace, York House. The Cardinal summoned the King from Greenwich and, in the presence of the septuagenarian Archbishop of Canterbury, William Warham, solemnly warned him that, as Legate of the Holy See, it was a part of his duty to correct offences against the marriage law. The King, he complained, had for the past eighteen years been co-habiting with Catherine, his brother Arthur's widow. Would the King graciously consent to the situation being thoroughly investigated?

The King, who admitted that he himself had in fact suffered pangs of conscience about the matter, welcomed a court of enquiry in which learned theologians should decide the validity of Pope Julius II's original dispensation—and, so, of the marriage—provided that he need not attend all the sittings but might be represented by a proctor.

This was granted and the investigation started. It would take a very short time, so they thought. Wolsey would pronounce the marriage invalid; the present Pope would ratify his judgment; Catherine would be given the status of Princess-Dowager as the widow of Arthur and Henry would be free to marry again and provide England with an heir. The whole proceeding would be a triumph of speed, secrecy and efficiency. So they thought.

They could not be expected to foresee that the matter would take six years and would shake Europe.

3

Thomas Cromwell visits Italy

While the 'collusive suit' (as history was to call it) was proceeding scrupulously on its theological way, the Cardinal heard a rumour that the Pope was inclining once more to the side of the Emperor and that the military affairs of the newly-formed League were in an unsatisfactory condition. Before he committed himself irrevocably to France, he therefore thought it wise to provide himself with some first-hand information from Italy.

Letters from his envoy at Bologna, Sir John Russell, the Knight-Marshall of the Household—a hardened, forty-two year old soldier who had, four years earlier, lost his right eye in a battle against the French—either had not been despatched or had been lost in the chaos which was Italy. He would now send one of his own household who, by his thoroughness, his experience of soldiering and his knowledge of Italy, would be able to provide an adequate report—Thomas Cromwell.

Thomas Cromwell, the son of a Putney armourer, had been a wild, brawling youth who had had to flee from England to escape trial for murder and had fought in Italy on the French side in the earlier war of 1503. His days with the common soldiery—'What a ruffian I was then!' he reminisced in later life—assuaged, at least temporarily, his passion for blood-letting and he drifted to Venice where he became book-keeper to a cloth-merchant and discovered that he had a natural aptitude, not only for fighting, but for business. When he had learnt all he could in Italy, he went to Antwerp and there set up as a cloth-merchant and moneylender. Eventually he returned in the same capacity to London where, his past forgotten, he started to study law as a necessary aid to questionable business deals and augmented his already considerable fortune, gained from loot, usury and overcharging, by marrying a wealthy wife who survived only a very few years of marriage.

The thick-set frame, the bull neck, the tight cruel mouth, the prognothic jaw, the cold merciless eyes set closely together and the heavy plebeian hands proclaimed the man. That he was tirelessly energetic and of brilliant business acumen recommended him even to those who disliked and despised him for his coarseness and unscrupulousness. Every great man, it has been said, keeps one underling to do jobs too dirty for anyone else; and before Cromwell became Wolsey's, he had served, in his legal capacity, a variety of aristocratic clients who needed a go-between to browbeat the timid, to ruin the resourceless, to break down the evasive or in some capacity to act as they would not themselves wish to be known to have acted.

The cynical realism which led him to judge men by their cries for mercy on the battlefield, by their cringing in the backroom of the usurer, by their gullibility or their ignorance or their cowardice, made religion a closed book to him. For the clergy he had a contempt as extensive as his knowledge of their weaknesses.

Consequently, when Wolsey decided to suppress six monasteries which were no longer fulfilling their charitable functions and which each contained less than a dozen inmates and to devote the proceeds to the founding of a new college—Cardinal's College—at Oxford,[1] Thomas Cromwell was his obvious instrument.

[1] The present Christ Church.

37

Cromwell had come to Wolsey's notice in 1520. A law suit between Canterbury and the Prioress of Cheshunt had been referred to the Papal Court in Rome. Wolsey, as Papal Legate, soon received a copy of the citation and inhibition 'with other information by the letters of Thomas Cromwell', and the Cardinal had been so impressed by the clarity with which the lawyer expounded the rights and wrongs of the case and by his suggestions as to the best method of handling it that he sent for Cromwell and, shortly afterwards, offered him a post in his household.

Five years later, in the January of 1525, he appointed him, with two assistants, to survey the six monasteries and their possessions and to carry through the complicated legal business connected with their dissolution. This involved surveying and estimating the value of the property, making inventories and stripping them of all their riches—altars, vestments, furniture, bells and tapestries—while their lands and permanent possessions were sold or leased on the spot. The transfer of property, the settlements with tenants and the adjustment of claims were tasks of greater intricacy than Wolsey had allowed for and Cromwell's success in carrying them out was impressive. Usually he was himself present to supervise the surrenders and dissolutions, if only to make sure of the bribes, to which he was notoriously accessible, in the disposal of the monastic leases.

Now, in the spring of 1527, the major part of the work was done and, for his pains, Wolsey had appointed him Receiver-General for Cardinal's College. After the spell of concentrated, if rewarding, work, Cromwell was by no means averse to a journey to Italy. Things would run smoothly enough in his absence, with his brother-in-law, John Williamson, in charge of his legal practice, and it was possible he could combine with his official duties some lucrative business on his own account with old acquaintances in Venice. But, in the first place, he went straight to Bologna.

On the way he came on the Imperial army which was encamped at Piacenza under the command of the renegade Charles de Bourbon; but he caught no sight of the army of the Holy League, whose commander, the Duke of Urbino, proclaiming that he was a pupil of Fabius Cunctator, carried his delaying tactics so far that he never came in sight, let alone within battle-distance, of his enemies.

The Imperial army was, indeed, a sight to strike terror into the stoutest heart. It was a rabble of 25,000 men, pillaging and terrorising the countryside. There were renegade Italians, outlaws, vagabonds, cut-throats from the cities. There were the Spaniards who, having sucked Milan dry, were anxious to quarter themselves for similar purposes on Florence. The Emperor, though he had engaged them, still showed no inclination to pay them and, as part of his policy, left them to live on plunder and to ravage the countryside wherever they might be stationed.

And there were the Germans, 13,000 of them, (who had offered to serve without pay provided they were allowed to pillage), under their leader, the *condottiere*, Georg von Fründsberg, notorious for his cruelty and hatred of the Church. He always wore a heavy gold chain round his neck with which, he said, he intended to strangle the Pope when they reached 'that sacrilegious Babylon, Rome.' As the *landsknechte* were Lutherans, religious fanaticism gave an interesting edge to their enthusiasm.

When news had arrived that the Pope had made an eight-month truce with the Emperor and had paid 100,000 ducats for it—a laughable sum considering Bourbon's needs—the Germans, all ill-fed and mostly shoeless, mutinied and von Fründsberg died of an apoplectic stroke trying to quell the outbreak. Bourbon, left alone in the leadership—which had become merely nominal—had no option but to obey the led and promise an advance on Rome.

As soon as Cromwell reached Bologna, the place of residence of Francesco Guicciardini, the Pope's vice-regent for the Papal States beyond the Apennines, where the English envoy was based, he sought out Sir John Russell, explained his mission and demanded his assessment of the situation. Did the Pope's conclusion of a truce with Charles V mean that he intended to repudiate his French and English allies?

'The Holy Father can hardly repudiate what does not exist,' said Russell. 'What help has he had from either but fair words? I speak plainly to you, sir, though I would not put it so baldly to the Cardinal.'

Cromwell approved his directness and said so.

'And the truce?'

'Will not be honoured.'

'So I construe it. Twenty treaties would not bind that rabble.' And Cromwell described the Imperial army he had passed.

'You saw Bourbon?'

Russell had a personal interest in this question because, a few years earlier, he had been sent on a mission to that renegade Prince of the Blood to try to discover his intentions. He had liked him.

'No,' said Cromwell. 'It was better to remain incognito till I had seen you.'

What he did not explain was that, at the edge of the army, he had unexpectedly found the sudden excitement of the camp, with its companionship and songs and bawdiness and tales of blood and loot in the past and the prospect of even greater things to come, too heady for safety. His youth surged back on him. It would have been only too easy for him to forget the present and immerse himself in it, to imperil at a stroke the position and the responsibility so hardly won. So he had contented himself with exchanging obscenities—in Italian—with a group engaged in slitting the throat of a pig they had taken from a cottager and anticipating the ensuing meal with more enthusiasm than they would have displayed even for the owner's daughter who had, for the moment, escaped them.

'Tonight,' said Russell, 'we will present ourselves to the Vice-regent, who will be as direct with you as I have been.'

'The Cardinal,' said Cromwell, 'will be in your debt.'

40

Francesco Guicciardini welcomed Cromwell with unmasked enthusiasm. As Lieutenant-General of the Papal army, in addition to his other offices, he knew better than anyone how critical was the situation and he had some hope that the Cardinal's servant might have brought, if not money, at least a firm promise of help. When he found that Cromwell was on an exploratory errand only, his courtesy increased as he pleaded the necessities of the Holy League. He was seconded, urgently, by his guest, who had just arrived from Pope Clement, Niccolo Machiavelli.

Guicciardini, Machiavelli and Clement VII had one thing in common. They were all Florentines and the fate of Florence, which Bourbon's barbarians might at any moment decide to attack, was of extreme importance to them all. A year earlier Clement had sent Machiavelli to inspect the state of that city's defences and, having received his report which was more encouraging than had been feared, he had seconded him to Guicciardini, who had sent him to Venice in an attempt to stir the Venetians, as members of the League, to an activity which might a little counteract the inertia of England and France. Now Machiavelli was back again in Bologna to spend some time with Guicciardini before reporting back to the Pope.

From the conversation between the two Florentines, Cromwell obtained a very clear picture of the third—a cold, small-minded, indecisive man, lacking in courage, quite unfitted to fill his great office in such a time of crisis.

'You have to remember,' said Machiavelli, 'since he can never forget it, that he is a bastard.'

Clement VII was born Giulio de' Medici, the natural son of Lorenzo the Magnificent's murdered brother. Lorenzo had brought the boy up with his own son, Giovanni, three years his senior. When, in 1513, Giovanni had become Pope Leo X, his first action had been to appoint his cousin-foster-brother, who was then thirty-five and a layman, Archbishop of Florence. For the whole of his reign, Leo had been content to leave the main conduct of public business in his hands. His success was un-

41

questioned and his ability and his tact, his sagacity and his prudence, had won him golden opinions. But once he himself became Pope, all these seemed to desert him.

'I know no man,' said Guicciardini, 'who so perfectly illustrates Tacitus's judgment on Galba.'

As it was quite clear, despite their polite nods, that neither Englishman knew what that was, Machiavelli tactfully supplied the classical allusion: 'Had he never ruled, everyone would have agreed that he would make a great ruler.'

'In war and statecraft,' Machiavelli added, 'few things are more important than knowing which lieutenants are capable of captaincies.'

'That is very true,' said Russell. 'I have seen a battle lost for that mistake.'

Cromwell said nothing, but fell to wondering how well he could fill Wolsey's place. It was one of his day-dreams and for a moment he allowed himself to lose the thread of the conversation.

When he recovered it, they were speaking of power in the Church.

'No one,' said Guicciardini, 'is more disgusted than I am with the ambition, the avarice and the profligacy of priests. For one thing, they are unbecoming in those who claim to have special relations with God; for another, the vices are so opposed to each other that they can only co-exist in very strange natures.'

'You oppose them, then?' asked Russell.

Machiavelli laughed and Guicciardini raised his eyebrows at so ingenuous a question.

'How could I?' he said. 'As a servant of the Pope, I am forced to further the greatness of ecclesiastics for my own interest. But if it were not so, I should love Luther like a brother.'

Machiavelli, who was extremely devout, said: 'You would not turn Lutheran?'

'Not in his beliefs,' Guicciardini reassured him, 'but we are at one—and you, too, I dare swear, in your heart—in wanting this swarm of scoundrels[2] put in their place so that they may be forced to live either without their vices or without their power.'

No one disagreed with him and as the talk drifted, by way of a discussion on power, to the underlying principles of politics, Cromwell found his attention riveted.

Both Machiavelli and Guicciardini were not only men of wide practical experience, concerned with the actualities of war and government; they were great historians who had construed events and constructed philosophies in the light of empirical needs and thus brought a new dimension to European thought.

Guicciardini, fourteen years younger than Machiavelli, was in a sense both his pupil and his critic. The older man—he was now fifty-eight, though his great work, *The Prince*, had been written in his forties—had erected a science of statecraft on the basis of general principles which were to be rigidly applied. The younger considered that in politics no general rule held good but that each situation must be treated as a special case. But they were at one in their underlying assumption that the essence of government was the manipulation of the foolish many to serve the ruler's interest without any reference to accepted morality. The ruler should, indeed, take care to appear good and wise and generous, for by such a reputation his power would be increased, but, in the circumstances of the world, actually to be so was not only unnecessary; it was foolish and it might be fatal.

Cromwell listened spell-bound. Here was his own instinctive philosophy, presented with a rational cogency of which he was not capable. Indeed, to do him justice, he had never, even in his most conscienceless moments, imagined that the indecencies of his own struggle for survival could be elevated into maxims of the highest political wisdom.

His enthusiasm was so unbounded that, when at last he and Russell took their leave, Guicciardini said to Machiavelli: 'If

[2] The actual words Guicciardini used were 'questa caterva di scellerati'.

you have a copy to spare, here surely is a worthy recipient of your book.'

Though *The Prince* had been written fourteen years earlier, it was still unpublished; but Machiavelli, in accordance with the usual practice, had had made several manuscript copies, which he distributed to his friends and any who were likely to benefit by his instruction. He had now only one left and he had not been disposed to part with it; but Cromwell's fascinated interest suggested that it could not be better placed. Ill and ageing, Machiavelli had found at last the perfect disciple.[3]

Cromwell received the manuscript with thanks which would have seemed too flattering and profuse had they not been so patently honest. He handled it as he had been accustomed to handle some rare and expensive fabric which he had bought for an exclusive customer in the days when he was in the cloth trade or some rarely-wrought ornament he had reserved for himself from the spoliation of a monastery.

He said: 'I shall account this one of the greatest of my treasures.' And he meant it.

It was after midnight when they left Guicciardini's *palazzo* and, as the English Embassy was not more than ten minutes away, and the spring night was moonlit, they decided to walk. They had just crossed the Piazza Maggiore when from the shadows cast by the huge, still unfinished church of San Petronio, Cromwell noticed a man whom, by his cringing walk, he took to be one of the beggars who lay about in the arcades. He assumed he was coming to ask for alms. Since he was overtaking them on the right hand, Russell with his blind eye did not notice him, but Cromwell saw him suddenly straighten himself and detected—or thought he detected—the glint of moonlight on a dagger. There was no time for speech. He pushed Russell violently ahead, so that he himself was level with the man, and plunged his own dagger into his heart.

[3] Machiavelli died six weeks later.

As he fell, Cromwell put the precious manuscript, which he was carrying under his left arm, into Russell's hands with: 'Guard this for me, Sir John' and looked round to see if there were any other assailants. There were none. He decided that the man was probably a beggar after all and that it had been an error. It was not, however, without its compensation. Cromwell had forgotten how good was the feeling of the warm stickiness of blood. He bent down and wiped his hand on the dead man's hair, while Russell thanked him for saving his life.

The Imperial army had moved at last. It arrived before Rome, which was practically undefended, on May 5. The Pope was persuaded to take refuge in the Castel St. Angelo, which he reached only a few moments before, on the following day, the invaders swarmed into Rome. They were, if possible, the more undisciplined because Bourbon himself was killed on a scaling ladder as he led the assault (a death for which Benvenuto Cellini falsely claimed the credit) so that they had no leader to whom even to pretend obedience.

The Eternal City was given over to a terror worse than any that had been inflicted on it even by Alaric the Goth or Geneseric the Vandal. 'Hell,' wrote the Venetian envoy, 'is nothing to compare with the present state of Rome.'

The invaders' method was first to take from the houses and palaces all objects of value and then set a price of ransom on all the inmates—men, women and children. Those who could not pay were tortured and killed. Those who found the money discovered that the payment was merely a prelude to further demands which, if not met, resulted in similar death. Usually, once a house was stripped of its contents, it was set on fire.

Women were raped and murdered before the eyes of their husbands and fathers. Nuns were paraded half-naked through the streets and delivered to the brothel-keepers or sold for a ducat a piece in the market. The Spaniards from long practice were the most ingenious in inventing tortures and thus discovering treasure, though the renegade Italians, especially the Neapolitans, were a worthy second. The Germans were, on the whole, content with a simpler vandalism and paraded the streets, dressed in the richest clothes they had plundered, with gold ornaments round their necks and precious stones twisted through their beards, intent on uncomplicated rape and murder.

As Lutherans, they added a touch of religious controversy to the scene. One of the captains, dressed up as the Pope, ordered his companions, arrayed as Cardinals, to kiss his feet and accompany him to the Vatican where, with the sound of trumpets and fifes, Luther was proclaimed Pope. An ass was clothed in episcopal vestments, led into the church where a priest was ordered to cense it and offer it a consecrated Host. On his refusal, he was hacked to pieces.

The carnage was indescribable. The streets were covered with dead bodies, including those of children who had been flung out of windows by the soldiers. In the Trastavere alone, two thousand corpses were thrown into the Tiber and nine thousand eight hundred were buried. For a week the murder and robbery continued unchecked and an order, issued on the third day, that plundering was to stop was totally disregarded. The thirst for gold continued when the thirst for blood was slaked and even the sewers were searched and the tombs broken open.

Thomas Cromwell who, by expeditious travel, had managed to arrive in Rome three days ahead of the Imperial army but had not been able, despite careful bribery, to get a private audience of the Pope, watched from a distance Clement's flight to the Castel St. Angelo. The approaches to the fortress were obstructed by a crowd of merchants, priests, Jews and women all striving for the same safety. But as the Pope with the non-Imperialist cardinals and the higher dignitaries of his household pressed across the bridge, his guard drove back the fugitives of lesser importance and they, compelled to make way, were crushed to death or forced over the bridge into the Tiber, where they drowned.

46

At last the Pope's party managed to make the castle and as Cromwell saw the rusty portcullis lowered and the rest, terror-struck, abandoned to the fury of the oncoming mob, he realised that there was nothing more to be done. With the Pope in fact —whatever diplomatic language might be used to cover it— the Emperor's prisoner, the face of European politics had changed once more.

The news of the sack of Rome, outdistancing Cromwell, arrived in London towards the end of the month and was only with difficulty believed. Wolsey immediately ordered prayers in every parish church and a three-day fast for the deliverance of the Pope.

It was an unfortunate coincidence that a week before the full extent of the disaster was known the 'collusive suit' was abandoned as being too theologically intricate; and the matter of the King of England putting away his wife, the Emperor's favourite aunt, was referred to Pope Clement VII.

4

Reginald Pole comes home

Henry and Catherine remained scrupulously polite to each other, even after Henry had informed her that they had been living in sin for eighteen years and that they must now separate. Catherine had burst into tears, which, being so rare and uncharacteristic an action, had non-plussed Henry completely and made him, fumblingly apologetic, hasten to comfort her. He withdrew his suggestion that she should choose a residence of her own, protested his continuing affection for her and promised that 'all shall be done for the best'. He also begged her not to speak of the matter to anyone as it was, at the moment, most secret and confidential. In saying this, he had no intention to deceive her. He had no idea that it was being widely discussed. The Emperor's Ambassador in London had written to Charles: 'The Cardinal, to crown his iniquities, is working to separate the King and Queen. The plot is so far advanced that a number of bishops and lawyers have gathered secretly to declare the marriage null. Not that the people of England are ignorant of the King's intentions, for the affair is as notorious as if it had been proclaimed by the town-crier.'

Wolsey, on his side, with the failure of the secret conference, decided that he would act as Vice-Pope, summon the College of Cardinals to Avignon to discuss the freeing of the Pope and, almost incidentally, bring up the nullity matter which, in the Pope's name, he would ratify. Unfortunately for him, this scheme was wrecked by the unco-operative attitude of the other cardinals and the refusal of the Pope, even though in the circumstances he particularly wanted English friendship, to name him Vice-Pope.

Catherine then quietly cut through the complicated matter of the dispensation by pointing out that, as her marriage to Prince Arthur had never been consummated, the dispensation was quite unnecessary. She was a virgin when she married Henry and he was, within the meaning of the term, her only husband. To her confessor, she gave a detailed account of her marital experiences with Arthur and gave him permission so far to break the seal of confession as to report them to the Pope.

The key to the situation, however, as both husband and wife realised, lay with the Emperor. Henry was both willing and able to intercept ambassadorial dispatches and Catherine, in her increasing isolation, needed the assurance that her nephew, knowing the facts, would support her cause. She would send Francisco Felipez, who had once been her page and had served her faithfully for twenty-seven years, to Madrid to lay everything before Charles. The only difficulty was to get him out of the country. To accomplish this, she brought to bear all her diplomatic ability which Henry, who was content to leave everything to Wolsey, tended to under-rate.

Felipez applied to the King for a passport to go to Spain, so that he might receive a blessing from his dying mother. Henry immediately went to consult Catherine who said that she did not believe that Felipez had a dying mother and that his story was only an excuse to leave her because she had incurred the King's displeasure. Henry deplored Catherine's lack of charity and, giving Felipez the benefit of the doubt, provided him with a special safe-conduct through France.

The King then told Wolsey to regard it as a matter of priority that the French authorities should arrest Felipez somewhere along the route. He could be killed if necessary, as long as the 'accident' was attributable to neither government. The essential thing was that he should never cross the border to Spain. Wolsey made haste to ensure this.

Felipez, going by sea in a Spanish merchantman, was immediately received by the Emperor who, as a result of his report, sent a terse note to Henry, appointed the General of the Franciscans, the ablest Spanish canonist, to represent Catherine in Rome and delicately reminded the Pope of the realities of his position, which he did nothing to alleviate.

It then occurred to Henry that, even if he won his case, the circumstances of it might still not be conducive to the fulfilment of his real object, marriage with Anne Boleyn. Dynastic reasons played their part in dispensations and Wolsey was assuming that, once free, the King would marry into France. Henry therefore decided to negotiate secretly on his own. He sent his Secretary, Dr. William Knight, to ask the Pope for additional documents. One was a licence to commit bigamy and, in emulation of the Old Testament patriarchs, to have a young and fertile wife without actually discarding an old and barren one. Another was a dispensation to marry again in the same prohibited degree of affinity as that which made his first marriage invalid. He was a good enough theologian to realise that, as far as canon law was concerned, there was no difference between uniting himself with his mistress's sister and marrying his brother's wife. Unfortunately, he was not a good enough logician to see that his plea for the one neutralised his plea against the other.

Wolsey, when he discovered the King's duplicity (as he inevitably did), was apprehensive that Henry should act independently of him, was alarmed at his matrimonial intentions but, above all, was angry at his stupidity.

In such an atmosphere, it was imperative that Henry and Catherine should observe the *convenances*. The King still visited his wife's apartments and often spent the night with her. They received together, danced together, went hunting together. The only visible difference in public was that Catherine was gayer than usual and Henry more morose, though both these masks were at times suddenly discarded. A 'King's Party' and a 'Queen's Party'—as they might have been called—were gradually forming at court though their existence was ignored by the principals and the older and wiser courtiers remained, for the moment, neutral. In some cases, this was no more than a prudent refusal to commit themselves before the consequences were clearer and the issue more sharply defined; but as far as the Countess of Salisbury was concerned it sprang from affection for both Henry and Catherine and a determination to do nothing which might in the least degree harm the Princess, for whom she felt increasingly responsible.

When she informed them that she had heard that her son, Reginald, was at last on his way back from his eight years' stay in Italy, both the King and the Queen were delighted at the news. Here was someone for whom each had a genuine regard who, outside the constricting circle, might be able to bring to the matter a fresh vision.

For Henry it was the return of a brilliant young cousin whom he had educated and to whom he had made possible training in a diplomatic career and a knowledge of Europe. To Catherine, it was the return of the son of her greatest friend whom she would have chosen as the husband of her only daughter. For Margaret Pole, it was the answer to many prayers and the return, however belatedly, of her best loved child.

Reginald Pole travelled home slowly and with reluctance. It was only his mother's letters, each more insistent than the last, which had forced the decision. When two years earlier his return had been suggested, he had written to Wolsey and pointed out that, as 1525 was a Jubilee Year, it was fitting that, during it, he should make a visit to Rome.

The result of his permitted journey had surprised him. On the way down from Padua, although he had travelled as inconspicuously as possible with a few of his household, he was officially welcomed and presented with gifts in Florence and the other towns through which he had passed. This, as was his wont, he was quick to explain, tactfully but inaccurately, was not a personal mark of esteem but because he was 'the King of England's cousin'.

When he reached Rome he immediately fulfilled the conditions of the Holy Year of Jubilee—confession, Holy Communion and visits to the four great basilicas of St. Peter's, St. John Lateran, St. Peter and Paul without the Walls and St. Mary Major—but he did not, as he had intended, go to see the Pope. So extreme was his revulsion from Medicean Rome that, in the words of one of his household, 'after three or four days, having seen the abominations of the Cardinals, bishops and their officers, with the detestable vices of the city, he could in no wise tarry any longer' and went back to Padua.

Padua, 'the Athens of Europe' as Erasmus called it, had been Pole's home since, at the age of eighteen, he had been sent by the King to study at its great university, renowned both for its legal and its medical schools, but above all for the teaching of the classics. These Pole had studied under the famous Leonico, the first Professor to lecture on Plato and Aristotle from the Greek text; and he had been so brilliant a pupil that his tutor wrote of him: 'Pole is worthy of all praise. He makes such progress that few are to be found his equal and none his superior.' Leonico went further. He dedicated his own published dialogues to Reginald and, in the dedication, mentioned that his pupil had read all the works of Plato and Aristotle, as well as commentaries on them.

Pole's achievement in Greek was soon eclipsed by his brilliance in Latin. Latin had, of course, ever since his Oxford days, been his second language, but he had paid little attention to it, except as a conventional convenience, until, in Padua, he met Christophe de Longueil, a French lawyer, twelve years his senior. In his passion for all things Roman, de Longueil preferred to be known as Longolius and promised Cardinal Bembo, in whose rarefied circle he moved, never to read any books for five years except Cicero's and never to use any words which could not be found in Cicero's works.

Between Pole and Longolius there was an immediate mutual attraction. Longolius went to live with him and it was in his house, during Reginald's absence in Venice on a semi-official visit, that he died. He dictated a last letter to his friend, recalling their deep and inseparable friendship, which would, he believed, last beyond the grave, and, as the only gift he had to give, bequeathed to him his library.

On receiving the letter, Pole rushed back to Padua, but arrived too late to see him alive. To his friend's memory, he now dedicated all his time until he had prepared and published[1] a collection of his writings, prefaced by a memoir written in the most faultless Ciceronian Latin which had appeared—or, indeed, was ever to appear—since Cicero.

The death of Longolius was Pole's first real sorrow. The elegant, artificial life of the fashionable young humanists, revolving round Bembo's fabulous villa at Padua, lost its savour. The fashion of Ciceronianism began to appear not a little ridiculous even before Erasmus, a year or two later, took it upon himself to administer the *coup de grâce*. It was indeed fitting that Pole should have paid the last tribute to his friend in the way he had, yet he knew that his interests, had he lived, would have been in quite other fields; for, just before his death, Longolius had started to compose a detailed refutation of the whole system of Lutheranism. The Frenchman had seen that it was the German challenge which could destroy not only the new Rome but the old, and fashion a civilisation divorced from the ancient and accepted sanctities. Slowly Pole realised that what his friend had bequeathed to him, with his library, was not the defence of Cicero but of the Catholic Faith.

---

[1] It was published in 1524, the year before Pole's visit to Rome.

For this, he realised only too clearly he was not equipped. He must desert philosophy for theology. To his protesting circle he explained that in ancient times, when Plato, Aristotle and Cicero were formulating their teachings, a knowledge of philosophy might properly have been considered the highest aim of education. But it was not so today. In the light of the Christian revelation, philosophy must yield place to theology— the ocean into which all other streams of knowledge should flow.

His new preoccupation absorbed him. He found that theology 'does not easily admit the company of other interests'. His classical achievement now appeared to him nothing but the 'mastery of disciplines fit only for schoolboys'. The eloquence of Cicero and the poetry of Homer paled into insignificance beside the grandeur of Isaiah and the passionate utterance of St. Paul.

'Pole is studying divinity,' one of his friends reported to another. 'He now despises things merely human and terrestrial. What a transformation!'

It was in this mood that Reginald had gone to Rome—and fled from it. The shock of its corruption reinforced and also in a sense transformed his thought. He saw vividly that the greatest argument for Lutheranism was the actual state of the Church at its centre and that the first necessity was its reform.

He was back in Padua when news came of the sack of Rome, which his humanist friends bewailed as the tragedy of tragedies. But he interpreted it as an evidence of God's apocalyptic judgment.

And now he must set out for England. He would leave after attending for the last time the celebration of Corpus Christi in Venice, which, in that year, fell on June 20. On that feast-day the Doge, clad in cloth of gold and with a satin mantle and ducal cap of crimson, attended Mass in state at St. Mark's and afterwards took part in the great procession which followed the Blessed Sacrament. In this, each year, Pole had taken his official place, walking just behind the English Ambassador.

The present ambassador, Dr. Richard Pace, Dean of St. Paul's, a humanist and a correspondent of Erasmus, now in his early forties, had become one of Pole's personal friends. He too had been educated at Padua and he shared the younger man's view of Rome—'plainly monstrous', he adjudged it, 'full of all shameful vice, devoid of all faith, honesty and religion'. Pole had been staying with him in Venice when Longolius died; and he had been instructed by him in the tortuous ways of diplomacy during his earlier 'Ciceronian' phase. Now Pace gave him various messages for Wolsey and, for himself counselled him to return as soon as he could to Venice.[2]

Pole needed no persuasion. He had every intention of returning immediately he had fulfilled the obligations of courtesy to his family; and memories of the sun and splendour of the unmatched Republic that had become his home haunted his slow journey towards the greyness of his native land.

Nothing, however, was lacking in splendour and affection in the welcome he received in London. The French Ambassadors were still at court and the King took the opportunity to give an extra banquet for his young kinsman's reception. Henry was delighted at the change in him. Pole had left England a shy, uncertain student, just down from Oxford. He had come back an accomplished man of twenty-seven, moving among the courtiers and ambassadors with complete assurance and his Plantagenet charm.

His face was now adorned with a small, fair beard which he had grown on the journey. Henry rallied him on it.

'I am about to follow your example, Reginald,' he said. 'Though mine will be redder.'

'Barbarossa set that as a fashion for kings,' said Pole. 'It will become you greatly.'

[2] Venice was only twenty miles from Padua which, as the university town of the Venetian Republic, has been described as its *quartier Latin*.

55

'By which you mean to say that I am getting fat,' said the King.

'To one as thin as I am,' replied Pole without hesitation, 'all great men appear fat.'

'Yet I would wager,' Henry added, 'my wits are still as nimble as yours.'

'Nimbler,' said Pole, pleased that he could compliment his cousin honestly. 'Though your bounty has allowed me to sharpen mine as far as their material allows. And, such as they are, they are at your service.'

'I shall call on them soon enough,' said the King and clapped him affectionately on the shoulder.

Next day Pole waited on Wolsey at his palace of York Place[3] to pay his official respects and to deliver Pace's messages. It so happened that when he arrived the Cardinal was still engaged with the Bishop of Tarbes over some details in the draft of the French treaty and Reginald had to spend some time in the library into which Wolsey, not wishing to relegate him to the general anteroom, had had him shown.

Pole was looking at some copies of Greek manuscripts from the library of Cardinal Grimani in Venice which Wolsey had had made for presentation to Cardinal's College when Thomas Cromwell entered the room and introduced himself. In his own interests Cromwell thought it wise, as Pole was so obviously *persona grata* at court, to make his acquaintance as soon as possible.

Beneath the formal courtesy of their greeting, as the two men bowed to each other, there was an immediate and instinctive mutual antipathy.

They spoke of Italy, which both had so recently left, only to find that the conversation accentuated their difference. What points of contact there were served to emphasise that they had not moved in the same circles.

[3] Later the Palace of Whitehall.

Cromwell quickly shifted his ground.

'I should value your opinion,' he said, 'on the duties of those who are called to the councils of princes.'

'The first thing,' Pole replied, 'is for him to have his sovereign's honour at heart and to advise whatever conduces to that honour.'

Cromwell stifled a smile.

'Such an answer,' he said, 'sounds proper enough and would win you praise if you made it in one of your academic disputations. It would well become the pulpit. But it is of no use in statecraft. There, if it were not rejected, it would lead to ruin. You would not be applauded, but blamed. And rightly so.'

'Will it please you to expound?'

'Willingly. Considerations of honour rarely reflect the prince's real will. And the only duty of a royal counsellor is to discover that will and to carry it out.'

'Whether or not it is honourable?'

'Honour is not in question.' Then, quickly answering the objection only too obvious in Pole's expression: 'Of course princes must use the names of religion, equity and all other virtues, even though their designs are not regulated by them. True ability lies in managing affairs in such a way that rulers may obtain their ends and yet allow no open failure in religion and probity to be observed. Thus the work of a statesman is to find out the real will of his master, which is often hidden under a contrary pretence, and help him to achieve it without public loss of reputation. This requires much experience and high prudence and is not taught at universities.'

'I would agree with you in that,' said Pole. 'It is not.'

Privately he thought that, if Cromwell really believed this and had been Nero's counsellor at the time that Emperor murdered his mother, he would not have been at a loss to justify matricide. Aloud, however, he said that he assumed that Cromwell was merely speaking for the sake of argument and not expressing his true sentiments.

57

'Plato's philosopher-kings,' he continued, only to be interrupted explosively by Cromwell.

'Plato! What value have his dreams today? If you must draw your knowledge from books, at least you should read those which allow more to experience than to speculation. A short discourse by an experienced person is more to the purpose than a library of philosophers. It happens that I have a book written by a very acute modern who has laid down maxims and observations which are confirmed by daily experience. If you will allow me and will promise to read the book I will lend it to you.'

'May I know the name of the author?'

'You may have heard it. Niccolo Machiavelli, the Florentine.'

'I have heard his name and know something of his ideas,' said Pole.

He did, indeed, know them. They had been discussed in Padua and Venice. Pole's own verdict on them was that Machiavelli was an enemy of the human race and that—as he had put it in a letter to one of his friends—'if Satan himself were to leave a successor, I do not well see by what other maxims he would direct him to reign.'

He did not think it prudent, however, to admit so much to Cromwell. He was at least experienced enough to realise the advantage he had over his would-be instructor, who had now revealed himself completely. He would certainly not give confidence for confidence and he managed to control both his voice and his expression as he thanked Cromwell for his offer and promised to read the book.

'It is a precious manuscript,' said Cromwell.

'You may trust me with it,' replied Pole. 'At least the university has taught me how to care for precious manuscripts.'

'I have a great regard for you,' said Cromwell. 'You must not mistake my strictures; but I can foresee that you will be exposed to great difficulties here at court if you let yourself be carried away by notions of men unacquainted with the world, however learned they are in other matters.'

'I am grateful for your concern,' said Pole.

They parted with a renewed exchange of civilities; but Cromwell, after some consideration in which he regretted his frankness, decided not to lend Pole the book.

Pole's conversation with Wolsey was gratifying enough. The Cardinal commended him for his grasp of diplomacy, cross-examined him shrewdly on Venetian affairs particularly in relation to the Republic's real attitude to the Holy League and finally appointed him Dean of Exeter so that he should have a sufficient income to live comfortably until the King had made up his mind in which sphere to use his talents.

Not until his official interviews were over did Reginald feel free to visit his family though, as he was staying at his mother's town mansion by Dowgate Hill, he saw something of her when she was not at court. Now he left London to spend a short time first with his elder brother, Montagu, at Bisham, and then with his younger at Lordington, not far from Chichester, which Geoffrey had recently acquired by marriage. As Lordington was only a few miles from his mother's favourite residence, Warblington Castle, he persuaded her to get leave of absence from court and meet him there. He had decisions to make and he wanted her wisdom and affection to guide him. His brothers had had only one topic of conversation—the state of affairs existing between the King and Queen. This, though now delicately referred to as 'the King's great matter', was, for those not directly involved in it, so much a matter of contradictory rumours, wild conjectures and unfounded scandals, that he had wearied of hearing about it and had made a firm determination at all costs to hold himself aloof from it, if he could.

His intention was to continue his theological studies untroubled by interference from the outside world. He had paid a courtesy visit to the Carthusian monastery where he had received his early education—then 'House of Jesus of Bethlehem at Sheen'—and the Prior had suggested to him that he might care to occupy the house in the grounds which the great Dean of St. Paul's, John Colet, had started to build during the last year of Reginald's schooldays there—'a nest for my retreat with the Carthusians where I may remain dead to the world', as Colet had described it in a letter to his friend, Erasmus.

It had been in this very house that Pole, before he had left England for Italy, had taken his farewell of Colet, who, as one familiar with Italy and as one of his lecturers at Oxford, had given him advice for the future and commendation for the past. Before Pole arrived in Padua, Colet was dead—'a death so bitter to me', said Erasmus, 'that the loss of no one for the last thirty years has affected me more': a death, said Sir Thomas More, which took from England the most holy and learned man she had produced for two generations. Since then his 'nest' had stood empty, being used only from time to time for Carthusian hospitality to eminent guests. Now Pole might have it, if he so wished. There was no one, the Prior assured him, whom Colet would have approved of more. On his part, Pole was certain that there was no place in England which he would have preferred.

When he informed his mother of this, Margaret's first question was whether he intended to take Holy Orders.

'Madame my mother,' he replied, 'I never forget that when I was a child you dedicated me to God's service. It may be that one day I shall be worthy of the priesthood; but that time has not yet come.'[4]

He started to tell her something of his disillusion in Italy and, in particular, in Rome.

'I think this may be known,' he said, 'as the age of the apostates.'

'But surely, Reginald, you have not found it so here?'

'The little I have seen gives no ground for hope. Most priests can do nothing but patter up their matins and mass, mumbling

[4] Pole did not in fact become a priest till twenty-eight years later. He, like Becket, was priested only the day before he was made Archbishop of Canterbury.

what they do not understand. The monks are in the main idle abbey-lubbers, apt for nothing but eating and drinking—'

'But you,' Margaret interrupted, 'are to make your home among them.'

'With the Carthusians,' he replied. 'They are holy men of strict life who keep their vows. So are the Bridgettines. And the Franciscan Observants. I visited them when I was at Greenwich. But as for the rest, above all the Benedictines, they are so set on comfort that, if they were made to stand to their vows, their monasteries would be empty.'

'Son, son, this is a harsh judgment.'

'You asked for my thoughts, mother. And I do not sit in judgment. I only say that I will not add one more to the number of the unworthy. That surely would be your wish for me?'

'My wish for you, Reginald, is what it has been always— that you should faithfully serve God and King. But you must find your own way. Go to Sheen, if you wish; but do not forget how much gratitude you owe Henry, should he need your service.'

'In his suit against the Queen?'

It was a shrewd retort, but Margaret outfaced it serenely. 'That is not our business; let us pray Our Lady to make it Hers and so avert it.'

'Amen to that,' said her son; 'but if our prayers are not answered?'

'Then we must follow our consciences, but I do not think they will divide us from each other.'

'I am certain of it.' He kissed her and added: 'I shall be able to see the clearer at Sheen.'

Before the envoys whom the King and Wolsey had sent to the Pope arrived at the Castel St. Angelo, Clement VII had managed to escape from it.

On the evening of December 9, 1527, disguised as one of his own servants, he walked unchallenged through the gates, wearing a long false beard and a large tattered hat, a basket on his arm and an empty bag over his shoulder. With a single peasant for his companion, he procured a cart and drove to his summer residence at Orvieto.

Once more the pattern of politics had changed.

5

The defiance of Queen Catherine

Hardly was the Pope settled in Orvieto before two more English envoys arrived to pester him about the nullity suit. This time Wolsey had chosen two of his own secretaries, Cambridge lawyer-academics with their way to make—the thirty-two year old Edward Foxe, Provost of King's, and the forty-five year old Stephen Gardiner, Master of Trinity Hall. They might succeed where the older, more conventional diplomats had failed.

Their consultations were held in Clement's bedroom, of which they gave an unflattering description: 'Ere we come to his privy bedchamber, we pass three chambers, all naked and unhanged, the roofs fallen down and, as we can guess, thirty persons, riff raff and other, standing in the chambers for a garnishment. And as for the Pope's bedchamber, all the apparel in it is not worth twenty nobles, bed and all.'

In these surroundings of almost apostolic poverty the Medici Pontiff, on a plain bench against a bare white wall, discussed the matter with Foxe and Gardiner, seated on peasants' stools. The argument continued for weeks. Eventually the Pope agreed to set up a legatine court in England to try the case. Wolsey, of course, was to be one of the judges. The other was Cardinal Campeggio.

Lorenzo Campeggio, who was now fifty-five—three years older than Wolsey—was one of the great legal celebrities of the day. He had been professor of Canon Law at Bologna but, more to the point, he had been Legate to England before Wolsey and still held the see of Salisbury. He was also Cardinal-Protector of England.

Clement privately informed him that he was on no account to hurry. As Campeggio suffered agonies from gout, he was unable to, even had he wished it. He arrived in London eight months later.

That summer, as Campeggio was making his way slowly and painfully across Europe, England was in the grip of the worst epidemic of the 'sweating sickness' that had been known for forty years—since the King's father, Henry VII, had had to postpone his coronation because of it.

No visitation was more dreaded. 'One has a little pain in the head and the heart,' wrote one observer. 'Suddenly a sweat breaks out and a physician is useless. In four hours, sometimes in two or three, you are dead.'[1] And no one was more terrified of it than the King. At the first rumour of it, he rushed away from Greenwich, shifting his dwelling every few days, each time further from London, each time with a smaller number of courtiers. He kept his physician and his confessor in perpetual attendance, spending his time between prayers and medicinal experiments, confessing daily, communicating often. He made his will thirty-nine times.

One of Anne Boleyn's maids died of the sickness. Henry, at Waltham, wrote to Anne, at Hever: 'I should have had no rest had I not ascertained that you have felt nothing. I trust and am indeed well assured that it will cease where you are, as I trust it is doing here. It may comfort you that, in truth, as they say, few women or none have this malady and none of our court have died of it. Wherefore I implore you, my entirely

[1] Eighteen persons died within four hours at Lambeth Palace on this occasion and Wolsey's household at Hampton Court was decimated.

beloved, to have no fear at all, nor to let our absence vex you too much, for wherever I am I am yours.'

Anne did in fact fall ill, though not of 'the English sweat'. Henry, still in flight from it, wrote again: 'News has come suddenly to me tonight, the most unpleasant that could be brought, which I lament for three reasons. First, to hear of the illness of my mistress, whom I esteem more than all the world, whose health I desire as much as my own and half of whose malady I would willingly bear to have you healed of it. Secondly, for the fear I have to be yet again longer oppressed by absence, my enemy, which up to the present has given me all possible annoyance and as far as I can judge is determined to do worse, though I pray God to rid me of such an importunate rebel. Thirdly, because the physician in whom I have most trust is absent at the very time when he could please me most, for by him and his assistance I should hope to obtain one of my chief joys in this world, which is, to have my mistress healed. Nevertheless, for lack of him I send you the second, who alone remains, praying God that he may soon restore your health. I trust soon to see you again, which to me will be more sovereign remedy than all the precious stones in the world. Written by that secretary who is and always will be

Your loyal and most assured servant,

H (AB) R.

Whether or not it was due to Dr. Butts's ministrations, Anne speedily recovered, though she still remained away from court. Now that Campeggio was on the way and it was, as she reckoned it, a mere matter of months before she became Queen of England, she was willing to become *maîtresse en titre* in name if not in fact and asked Henry to provide her with suitable apartments, once the summer Progress (or flight) was over and the court had settled down to its accustomed autumn routine.

'Darling,' Henry was able to assure her, 'as touching a lodging for you, we have gotten one by the Lord Cardinal's means, the like of which could not have been found hereabouts, as this bearer shall show you. As touching our other affairs, I assure you that no more can be done or more diligence used or all manner of dangers better provided for.'

Anne was willing to accept that her 'lodging' was to be at Greenwich rather than at Westminster, but she chafed at the continued delay of the Cardinal-Protector of England; and the moment reliable news arrived that Campeggio had left Paris on the last stage of his journey, Henry wrote with relief: 'I trust by next Monday to hear of his arrival at Calais; and then I trust to enjoy that which I have so longed for. No more at present, mine own darling, but that I would you were in my arms, for it seems long since I kissed you.'

When Campeggio arrived—greeted on his way from Canterbury to London by a crowd of two thousand women calling: 'No Nan Boleyn for us!'—he was too ill to enter the capital in state and had instead to take to his bed. Henry, grateful that Anne made at least some attempt at controlling her temper, wrote 'to inform you what joy it is to me to know of your conformity to reason and of your suppressing your useless and vain thoughts and fantasies with the bridle of reason. Good sweetheart, continue the same, not only in this but in all your doings hereafter. The unfeigned sickness of the well-willing legate somewhat retards his access to your presence; but I trust that, when God sends him health again, he will with diligence recompense his demur.'

Campeggio as soon as he was able to get about immediately grasped the situation in terms that had hitherto been hidden from him and wrote to the Pope: 'This passion of the King is a most extraordinary thing. He sees nothing, he thinks of nothing but Anne; he cannot do without her for an hour and it moves one to pity to see how the King's life, the stability and downfall of the whole country hang upon this one question.'

Meanwhile the French Ambassador reported to his master that 'Mademoiselle Boleyn' had arrived in London and that 'the King has lodged her in a very fine lodging which he has furnished very near his own. Greater court is paid to her every day than has been for a long time paid to the Queen.'

It was the Queen, however, as Campeggio now saw clearly, who held the key to the situation, for the King's mind was irrevocably made up. 'He told me briefly and in the plainest possible terms that he wanted nothing but a declaration whether his marriage was valid or not, he himself presupposing always its invalidity; and I believe if an angel were to descend from Heaven he would not be able to persuade him to the contrary.'

'We then discussed,' the Legate added, 'the proposal to persuade the Queen to agree to enter some religious house. And this solution was extremely pleasing to him.'

It was not however pleasing to Catherine. Campeggio pointed out to her that, if she would become a nun, 'she would preserve her dowry, her jewels, the guardianship of her daughter, her own rank as Princess, everything, in short, that she wished to demand from the King, without offending either God or her own conscience'.

Catherine retorted that she had no intention of violating the sacrament of matrimony; that she had come to Henry a virgin and was his legal wife; and that if she were to be torn limb from limb for saying so and then to rise from the dead, she would die a second time in defence of that truth.

If Henry was certain that the Legatine Court would find for him, Catherine was even surer that the Pope would find for her. She both told Campeggio and wrote to her nephew the Emperor: 'For the Pope to undo what his predecessors have done, would reflect on his conscience and honour and bring grave discredit on the Apostolic See which should stand firmly on the Rock which is Christ. Were the Pope to waver now, in this case, many might be led astray into thinking that right and justice are not with him.'

Campeggio, seeing nothing but disaster ahead, privately advised the Pope to advoke the case to Rome. Publicly, he set Christmas for the sitting of the court.

Before Christmas arrived, however, Catherine found her case immeasurably strengthened and Henry his thrown into confusion by the discovery in Spain of a document both of them had overlooked.

When Pope Julius II had originally issued the Bull dispensing the first degree of affinity and so allowing Henry to marry his brother's widow, he had given as a reason for the new marriage the importance of the friendship of Spain and England and the necessity of preventing war at that time. He had also left open the question of the consummation of the earlier marriage by the use of the word 'perhaps' (*forsan*).

It was on these grounds that Henry's lawyers were attacking the Bull. They could show that the alleged political reasons were nonsense and that, as Catherine had slept with Arthur seven times, they had only her word for it that she had emerged from the experience *virgo intacta*. Their case, in fact, seemed overwhelming enough to justify the King's certainty that he must win it.

But on the same day that Julius had issued the Bull, he had sent a Brief (which had the same binding effect in law) to Catherine's dying mother which differed from the Bull in two vital particulars. 'Perhaps' was omitted and 'and for other reasons' was added to the political reasons.

The Emperor had now found this Brief in the archives in Madrid and had sent a copy to his aunt. She produced it and the whole of her husband's case collapsed: the validity of the dispensation could not now be attacked on either of the grounds he had prepared. In fact, the validity of the dispensation could not be successfully attacked on any grounds whatever. In addition, there was another delay, which the Pope welcomed, while the new evidence was examined.

Henry, after failing in his attempts, first by fraud and secondly by intimidation, to get Catherine to ask her nephew to send the original Brief to England so that it might be 'examined', despatched another embassy to Rome to try to persuade the Pope to pronounce it a forgery. This time he chose an even tougher couple than Foxe and Gardiner. They were Sir Francis Bryan and Peter Vannes.

Bryan (who, like Sir John Russell, had lost an eye in French wars) was one of the King's intimate circle, whom Henry had nicknamed his 'Vicar of Hell'. The appellation had no particular theological significance, but referred to his habitual high-spirited conduct, such as was shown on the occasion when he nearly provoked a riot in Paris by throwing to the crowd, which was expecting English largesse, 'eggs, stones and other foolish trifles'. To his presumed ability to intimidate the Pope, he added the qualification of being Anne Boleyn's cousin.

Peter Vannes, an Italian, was an amoral and infidel cleric, a sophisticated man of the world, the first of the professional diplomatists, who was not likely to be influenced even by such scruples as might have intimidated Foxe and Gardiner.

The choice of Bryan, at least, had one advantage. He was not afraid of Henry and he saw no point in not telling him the truth. After doing his best with Clement, who, though he occasionally burst into tears, remained surprisingly firm, he wrote: 'Plainly the Pope will do nothing for your Grace. If I wrote otherwise I should put you in a hope of recovery where none is to be had. We have assayed him both by fair means and foul, but nothing will serve. There is no man living sorrier to write this news to you than I am; but if I should not write it, I should not be doing my duty.' Then he added: 'Sir, I am writing a letter to my cousin Anne, but I dare not write to her the truth of this, because I do not know whether Your Grace will wish her to know it so shortly or not.'

As Anne's patience had now reached snapping-point, Henry thought it was well that she should not know it 'so shortly' and

69

assured her that all would be well in the Legatine Court which Campeggio had now summoned for June.

Londoners left little doubt where their sympathies lay. The briefest appearance of Catherine was enough to raise a cheer; Wolsey was booed. When Campeggio arrived, the rumour that he had been sent to put the Queen in a nunnery led to uncomplimentary scrawls on the walls and demonstrations in the streets.

The Spanish Ambassador was, indeed, exaggerating and thinking wishfully when he informed the Emperor that 'if six or seven thousand men were to land on the coast of Cornwall, prepared to espouse the Queen's cause, they would be joined by 40,000 Englishmen'. The French Ambassador, more realistic, reported the increasingly frequent appearances of Anne at court: 'I see they mean to accustom the people by degrees to endure her, so that when the great event comes off it may not be thought strange. However, the people remain quite hardened and I think they would do more if they had more power.'

The King and Wolsey were much of the same opinion. They ordered a search for arms to be made throughout the city and all weapons found to be confiscated, 'so that no worse weapon remains than their tongues'. As a more positive attempt to gain popular support Henry decided to unburden himself to the city magnates. He summoned the Lord Mayor, the aldermen, the burgesses, the lawyers of the Inns of Court and as many other citizens as could crowd themselves into the Great Hall of Bridewell Palace and told them that, for the sake of them and their children, he was concerned that, when he died, there should not be a disputed succession which might lead to another civil war, like that between York and Lancaster. To avoid this catastrophe, he must set at rest all doubts about the validity of his marriage. Having consulted 'the greatest clerks in Christendom' to know whether he was living in lawful matrimony or in wicked adultery, he had now sent for a legate from Rome to decide. Cardinal Campeggio had come 'for this only cause I protest before God and on the word of a Prince'.

'And as touching the Queen,' he continued, 'if it be adjudged by law of God that she is my lawful wife, there was never anything more pleasant and more acceptable to me in my life. She is a woman of most gentleness, of most humility and buxomness and of all good qualities appertaining to nobility without comparison, as I, this twenty years, have had experience. If I were to marry again I would, provided the marriage was lawful, certainly choose her above all other women.'

He was not widely believed; but, as in all attempts to mould popular opinion, though the knowledgeable are aware that the only reliable confirmation of the truth of a rumour is its official denial, there are always a few innocents who are deceived by it. Yet even most of them had, by this time, heard of Anne Boleyn. The result was that the booing of the cardinals and the cheering for the Queen increased rather than lessened and Henry, increasingly furious, sent a deputation of Privy Councillors to call on Catherine.

The message they were charged to deliver was that the King was grieved at her conduct at a time when she should be—as he was—overborne by grief at the sin they had committed. Instead of manifesting a proper contrition, she was gaily showing herself in public even more than usual and smiling and nodding and beckoning to the ignorant populace quite beyond her usual custom. This was very near to sedition and she was now 'to keep herself in seclusion and to beware of stirring up the commons'.

She obeyed, of course. She had always obeyed Henry. But there were lawful occasions on which she had to go out; and the only result of the order was that the people thronged in greater numbers round the palace gates, watching for her rare appearances, and cheered the louder when she made them.

At the outbreak of the epidemic of sweating sickness, Margaret Pole and Princess Mary had returned to Ludlow, where they remained throughout the year, making the official summer

71

progress, which was shorter and smaller than usual because of the reduced budget on which for pressing reasons of economy Wolsey had insisted.

Rumours of 'the King's great matter' inevitably filtered through to the West and though, privately, Margaret tended to believe them, openly she was careful to discount them for the sake of Mary. She saw no reason why the girl, now in her thirteenth year, should have her youth overcast by apprehensions which might never be realised.

But at Sheen Reginald Pole, despite his intended isolation and his determined attempts to concern himself only with theology, found that the world bore in on him. He was near enough the centre of things to learn, willy-nilly, the truth about them. The theories of dispensation were coupled with the fact of Anne Boleyn. The demeanour of the King as a conscience-stricken suppliant to an ecclesiastical court had to be set against his obviously growing inclination to play the political tyrant. In observing this, Reginald was surprised at his own dislike of monarchy and the extent to which he had unconsciously imbibed the republicanism of Venice.

He put down his impressions of England while he was still sufficiently a stranger to see them clearly. Noting them thus, he would have a guide as to how others might see them. The two most obvious evils which he noticed after his eight year absence were a decline in the population and a high degree of poverty. What wealth there was was badly distributed—'some have too much, some too little, some never a whit'. The nobles had too many idle hangers on; the church was over-provided with lazy monks and priests, and among the merchants there were too many who 'busy themselves in making and procuring things for the vain pastime and pleasure of others'. The rich not only neglect their Christian duties to the poor but are obsessed with 'the receiving of rents and revenues of their lands, with great study of enhancing thereof, to the further maintaining of their pompous state'.

At the root of all ills was the greatest of political evils, the possibility of royal tyranny. Pole thought that the monarchy should be not hereditary but elective and that the authority of the people in Parliament should be vested in a council consisting of four peers, the Archbishop of Canterbury and the Bishop of London, four of the chief judges and four leading citizens of London, which should have power to depose the King, if necessary.

Reginald's interest in these things in reality sprang, as, by examining himself, he came to realise, from his intense revulsion from Machiavelli. In retrospect, that brief, unexpected conversation with Thomas Cromwell began to loom so large that it dwarfed things of greater importance. It seemed like the death-knell of the civilised and Christian world, and Pole could do nothing else until he had set down—not as a publishable polemic but for his own private satisfaction—the outlines of an answer.

He drew together the Christian teaching that 'we are all members one of another' and the Hellenic ideals of proportion and beauty in the body politic. He admitted, (for observation left him no alternative) that most men, under pretence of serving the public good, really pursued 'the private and the singular weal'. So much he must concede to Machiavelli. But whereas the Italian made the acceptance of this the basis for action, Pole made the rejection of it the first essential of a healthy state, whose strength and endurance might depend on all members doing their duty, each in his own station, for the good of the whole 'with brotherly love'. Moreover, the State must have that beauty which results from due proportion in all its parts 'so that one part ever be agreeable to another in form and fashion, quantity and number'.

It was almost impossible to imagine a greater contrast to the existing state of England.

On Friday, June 18, 1529, in the Great Hall of Blackfriars, the Legatine Court at last opened. On chairs of cloth of gold, before a table covered with a rich tapestry, sat the two Cardinals, a vivid and formidable splash of scarlet. Above them, to the right, was a royal canopy under which was a seat, covered with cushions of gold tissue, for the King. Below them, on their left, was a chair, also cushioned but less opulently, for the Queen.

The King was not present, but was represented by two proctors. It was assumed that the Queen would similarly absent herself and there was no little consternation when she appeared, a self-possessed, dumpy but regal figure, to inform the court that her presence must not be taken to mean that she acknowledged its competence and that she had come only to challenge it on three grounds—that it was hostile, that it was prejudiced and that it was, because the Pope was engaged in examining the Brief, unnecessary.

Wolsey said that she should be answered on Monday.

On Monday the King took care to be present to hear the Legates inform his wife that the court was regularly constituted under the authority of the Pope and was thus competent to proceed.

Catherine immediately rose in her place and, in silence, made her way to the King's daïs and knelt at his feet. Courteously he tried to raise her, but she resisted and continued kneeling to make her plea to him: 'Sire, for all the love that has been between us, and for the love of God, let me have right and justice. Show me some pity and compassion, for I am a stranger, born out of your dominions. I come to you as in the fount of justice within your realm.

'I take God and all the world to witness that I have been to you a true, humble and obedient wife, loving those whom you loved only for your sake, whether I myself had cause or not and whether they were my friends or my enemies. These twenty years I have been your true wife and by me you have had several children, although it has pleased God to call them out of the world, for which I cannot be blamed.

'And when you first had me, I take God to be my judge,

74

I was a true maid, without touch of man. Whether or not this is true I put to your conscience.'

The King, uneasily silent, did not look at her.

She continued: 'I most humbly require you, in the way of charity and for the love of God, Who is our last Judge, that you spare me the extremity of this new court. And if you will not, then do your pleasure and I will commit my cause to God.'

She rose, made a profound curtsy to her husband and without looking at the Legates, left the hall. Though called, she refused to return. 'This is no court of justice for me,' she said. 'I will not tarry.'

Next day, in her absence, she was declared contumacious and the trial proceeded without her.

But, before any conclusion was reached, the Pope quashed the proceedings and advoked the case to Rome.

6

Thomas Cranmer makes a suggestion

Henry, summoned to appear with Catherine before the Curia in Rome, retorted by issuing writs for a new parliament at Westminster. The object of this unexceptionable constitutional action —there had been no parliament for six years—was quite well understood. The French Ambassador reported: 'It is intended to hold a parliament here this winter and then bring about the divorce by their own absolute power.' Henry concluded a heated argument with Catherine by telling her that if the Pope failed to declare their marriage null and void he 'would denounce the Pope as a heretic and marry whom he pleased'. And to the new Ambassador from the Emperor, a hard-headed lawyer of forty, Eustache Chapuys, he said bluntly that the only power any ecclesiastic had over the laity was that of absolving them from their sins.

On the August day on which Henry gave the order for the issuing of the Parliamentary writs he was at Waltham. Another epidemic, though a milder one than the sweating sickness, was afflicting London and the eastern counties. In attendance on him were Stephen Gardiner and Edward Foxe, who, as the guest rooms of the Abbey where the King was lodged were uncomfortably crowded, had found beds at the house of a gentleman named

Cressy. In this house they met an old Cambridge acquaintance, Dr. Thomas Cranmer of Jesus College, who was tutor to Cressy's two sons and with them had fled from the infection of the epidemic in Cambridge.

By comparison with Gardiner, who was the King's Secretary, and Foxe, who was now a trusted ambassador, Cranmer was —and was very conscious that he was—a person of little importance. Even academically, as a Fellow of Jesus and a Lecturer in Divinity (even though he had refused an offer from Wolsey to join the staff at the new Cardinal's College at Oxford) he was hardly of the same mettle as the Provost of King's and the Master of Trinity Hall. When supper began, he said very little and confined his few and deferential remarks to University anecdotage.

Thomas Cranmer, though he was now forty, had, more than most men, never recovered from his school-days. His father had 'set him to school with a marvellous severe and cruel schoolmaster who appalled, dulled and daunted the wits of his scholars'. That, at least, was how Cranmer himself described him and added that, as a result, he 'lost much of the benefit of memory and audacity in his youth' which he was never able to retrieve. When, at fifteen, he arrived at Cambridge, he found a tutor of a different, if not vastly superior, kind—one who, 'when he came to any hard chapter that he did not well understand would skip over to another chapter in which he had better skill'.

Between them his mentors produced a timid, diffident young man who had to work very hard indeed to get his degree. His reading was not helped by his poor sight or his career by his marriage to a girl in the *Dolphin*, who, however, released him by dying in childbirth when he was twenty-one.

Since then, he had never left Cambridge nor wished to. He took Holy Orders, worked for his doctorate, watched, without envy, the greater academic triumphs of his contemporaries and turned into the unworldly, self-effacing, kindly man, with a gift for words and a compelling voice which made them sound even better than they were, who now, by a stroke of chance, was allowed to discuss 'the King's great matter' with the great.

He had however one advantage over them. They were legists; he was a theologian. When they asked him his opinion, he modestly insisted that he had not studied it as they had but that it seemed to him that perhaps they were going the wrong way to work. Legal processes, especially now that they had shifted to Rome, were interminable. What was more, the matter was one which concerned theologians: 'Had or had not the Pope power to dispense regulations laid down in Holy Writ?' Might it not possibly, therefore, be a good idea to canvass the opinions of the Doctors of Divinity in all the Universities of Europe and, supposing, as was most probable, that they found in favour of the King in this matter, for 'His Highness, his conscience quieted, to determine with himself that which shall seem good before God' and act accordingly without waiting for the 'frustatory delays' of the Papal Court?

Foxe and Gardiner thought the idea good enough to report it to Henry. Henry said: 'Mother of God! That man has the right sow by the ear' and demanded to see him.

Reginald Pole, who with his elder brother and his mother, had been present at Blackfriars on the day of Catherine's plea, had now determined to leave England again at the first opportunity. For one thing he was afraid of a dissension in the family. Montagu had been in attendance on the King, the Countess on the Queen and, though in each case it was a matter of official duty, their opposite sides indicated their sympathies. The Countess, because of her intimate personal friendship with Catherine, was naturally the more determined; but Montagu, though deploring Anne Boleyn, was prepared to argue with his mother by putting Henry's side of the question more vehemently than he actually felt.

Reginald's greater fear, however, was that he himself would

78

get involved in the argument not in the privacy of the family circle but on the public stage. As the battle of wits continued, more and more people were called for consultation and he was in danger of being summoned either by the King or by the Queen. For this he was not ready. He knew that he did not know enough. And he was certainly not prepared privately to anticipate the judgment of the Curia. His only safety, as he saw it, lay in flight. He petitioned the King that he might be allowed to go to Paris to continue his studies at the University there.

In the ordinary course of events, the King was not likely to have allowed it and Pole was in fact surprised at the alacrity with which Henry gave his consent. And not only his consent but his blessing and the same annual pension as he had allowed him in Italy.

Less than two months after the dissolution of the Legatine Court, the French Ambassador wrote to his master: 'The King is now sending his relative, Pole, one of the most learned men known, to visit France and continue his studies. He will pay his respects to your Majesty according to instructions. He and his relations, who are great lords, have asked me to recommend him to you.' And at the beginning of October Pole himself, with a few friends and some personal servants, duly embarked, with two mattresses of white fustian, five chestful of belongings, two hogsheads full of books, his virginals and a canvas mattress for his servant Jack to lie on on deck in the crossing to Dieppe.

He had no idea of the purpose for which Henry intended to use him in Paris.

The interview between the King and Dr. Thomas Cranmer was eminently satisfactory on both sides. Henry immediately recognised a potential servant who would obey without question anything he was ordered to do. Cranmer welcomed an incredible opportunity and pondered the text: 'The first shall be last and the last first.'

'Mr. Doctor,' said Henry, 'I pray you—and, nevertheless,

because you are my subject, I command you—to set all your other business on one side and write down for me your opinions on this case in a form that can be presented to the universities.'

To make it the easier for him, Henry ordered Anne Boleyn's father, (whom he had just created Earl of Wiltshire to pacify her increasing impatience), to entertain him at Hever while he performed his set task. The result, speedily and efficiently done, was approved to such an extent that the King decided to send Cranmer, as chaplain, with the Earl of Wiltshire and the new Bishop-elect of London, Dr. John Stokesley, to make a last assault on the Pope.

As if the sending of a mission headed by Anne Boleyn's father were not tactless enough, the envoys arrived in Italy at a singularly unpropitious moment. The Emperor had determined to visit the Pope in Bologna to be solemnly crowned by him with the old iron crown of Lombardy and so to become *Imperator Romanorum*. The ceremony itself was to be postponed until the February of the following year on Charles's thirtieth birthday, but when the Emperor arrived in Bologna in December, he took up his residence near the Pope and spent hours every day in friendly conversation with him.

Charles's suspicions of Clement's real intentions, Clement's anger at Charles's holding him a prisoner in the Castel St. Angelo, were alike forgotten. The *amende honorable* was made publicly enough when 'the Emperor's entry into Bologna was done with a pomp and majesty worthy of his lordship and with no less splendour the Pope awaited him, in full pontifical attire with the Triple Crown on his head'. The Emperor knelt and kissed the Pope's foot; the Pope immediately raised the Emperor and kissed him on both cheeks. When, subsequently, they went out together they shared the same canopy. 'Under one baldachino the two great luminaries of the world shone out like sun and moon.' An eye-witness, Bishop Jovius, described the effect Charles had on Clement: 'He gazed at him for a long time and found him manly and full of majesty; for he had been described to him as rough and wild in appearance, looking like a Goth, as coarse as his own soldiers; and now he saw the opposite and detected in him no trace of cruelty and haughtiness but found him (as he later said) worthy of the great *imperium*.'

This was hardly the moment for an English embassy—that recurring phenomenon of which in any case Clement was heartily sick—to induce the Pope to take steps against Charles's aunt. Sadly Cranmer wrote to the King: 'As for our successes here, they be very little; nor dare we attempt to know any man's mind because of the Pope; nor is he content with what you have done; and as for any favour in the Curia I look for none, with the Pope and all his cardinals against us.'

Nevertheless Clement and Cranmer liked each other personally. They were, essentially, two of a kind. Both had been bullied and both had, partly in consequence, become past-masters in the art of using words ambiguously. It was unfortunate that their masters demanded of them mutually exclusive actions which no form of words could reconcile. As a private mark of esteem, however, Clement created Cranmer Penitentiary for all the dominions of King Henry VIII.

Reginald Pole had hardly arrived in Paris when he received a letter from the King asking him to undertake the task of sounding and directing into the right channels the University's opinions on the dispensation. This unexpected blow to his happiness—so he wrote in later years, remembering it—'for some time robbed me not only of speech but of the faculty of thinking'. As soon as he had recovered his equanimity, he wrote to the King, pleading that he was entirely unfitted for such a task. The sounding of university opinion needed special gifts which he did not possess.

This, Henry realised, was true. Reynold had never been in a position where he needed to use bribery and, in consequence, he was not practised in the art. A beginner might make serious mistakes. On the lowest level it was easy enough, but lesser personages than a royal kinsman were already touring the university cities of Europe to provide 'needy rabbis fished out of ghettoes to opine on Deuteronomy at ten crowns a head'. When it came to offering generous expenses to famous Doctors of Divinity in Paris, tact, finesse and, above all, knowledge were needed. Even Gardiner had had a difficult time at Cambridge. The first meeting had ended in uproar and the last, when the ultimate of bribery, intimidation and careful selection had been used, had merely affirmed that by divine and natural law a man might not marry his brother's widow, but had refused to mention the Pope's dispensing power in the matter. If this could happen at home among his own subjects when the matter was proposed by his own Secretary, Henry realised that he could not be too careful abroad. He sent Edward Foxe to act as Pole's Co-Adjutor accompanied by Sir Francis Bryan, as an expert on Paris.

Pole received them with a courtesy increased, if possible, by relief. Foxe became his guest but 'the Vicar of Hell' preferred to make his own arrangements. Thereafter Reginald acted only in cases where his official confirmation was required or where his name was deemed necessary and left the work of persuasion to Foxe and Bryan.

He had himself, however, to see the French king.

Francis I was now thirty-six and, though his defeat at Pavia and his imprisonment in Madrid had left their marks on him, he was still the gay, witty, volatile, amorous *roi politque* whom his fellow monarchs found so unpredictable. He retained the impish energy of his youth and, some would say, had fulfilled his predecessor, Louis XII's, judgment on him: 'That great baby will ruin everything.' On the other hand, he was capable of a political subtlety greater than that of either Charles V or Henry VIII. He might try to combine contradictory policies to deceive others but he never deceived himself as to what, at any moment, was his dominant need. What he needed now was enough money to redeem his sons whom the Emperor still held as hostages, and he was presuming that Henry VIII—who, after all, was the prospective father-in-law either of himself or of one of those sons—would provide it.

Pole put him at his ease on that score immediately. He explained that he had been sent by his royal cousin to assure Francis that, in pursuance of the new treaty between their two countries, all reasonable assistance would willingly be given.

Francis, looking down his long nose, asked if there were not some slight return which he, impoverished as he was, could make.

Pole replied that it would be ample recompense if the King could suggest who would best promote Henry's cause in the University debate.

Without hesitation, Francis answered: 'Nicholas Dorigni, President of the Chamber of Requests.' He was totally venal.

The official business having been thus satisfactorily concluded, Francis brought all his charm to bear to make Pole unbend and discuss English matters in general. Unfortunately, he chose Anne Boleyn as his first topic and repeated his *mot* about her sister being '*my* mare'.

Reginald was not amused and the French King, dismissing him mentally as a prig, dismissed him in actuality as soon as he deemed it polite.

As soon as Henry had received Dorigni's name, he wrote to him explaining that 'by his beloved cousin, Reynold Pole's letter' he understood that Dorigni would promote his cause in Paris; he asked him to be diligent and 'to receive the directions of Reynold Pole'. To Pole himself, he wrote that 'to your dexterity and faithfulness we ascribe the furtherance of our cause', thanked him 'for acting so stoutly on our behalf' and enclosed a gift of £70.[1]

Reginald found himself troubled in conscience. It was obvious that Henry assumed that he was a partisan of his. His scrupulous neutrality had apparently made no impression. All he had done was to show his gratitude for Henry's life-long kindnesses to him by acting in a diplomatic capacity in a matter which he was not competent to judge. He was no Doctor of Divinity; and what Doctors of Divinity decided was, at the moment, irrelevant to his own convictions. When he had studied more deeply, he hoped he would be able to make up his own mind. He was thankful when, on July 2, 1530, the faculty of Paris, after a series of debates, several of which ended in blows, found for the King by 53 votes to 44 and he was able to return to London and take refuge once more in his 'nest' among the Carthusians of Sheen.

[1] It is almost impossible to equate Tudor money with that in the 1960s. Pole's yearly allowance, on which he had maintained himself and his household at Padua, was only £100. It would certainly run into several thousands, in today's values.

7

The end of Cardinal Wolsey

The house at Sheen, during Pole's absence from it, had had another occupant. On Ash Wednesday in that year 1530 Cardinal Wolsey had taken up his residence there and had remained for five weeks until Passiontide[1] when, on an order from the King, he had set out to travel northward to his see of York.

During his sojourn with the Carthusians he had availed himself of the penitential season to the utmost. He had attended the monastic Offices; he had made a scrupulous examination of his conscience and confessed often; he had fasted; and, as a token of his purposed amendment of life, he had begun to wear a hair shirt next to his skin.

He had fallen from power.

As soon as the King's suit had been advoked to Rome, Wolsey knew in his heart that his doom was sealed. He had failed Henry in the one thing he wanted and for this there would be no forgiveness. And with the King's favour gone, he would be defenceless before his multitude of enemies.

His disgrace had come with dramatic suddenness. On October 9, 1529, the opening of the Michaelmas Term—just

[1] Passion Sunday fell that year on April 3.

after Pole had embarked for France—Wolsey, as Lord Chancellor, went to Westminster Hall in his accustomed state. The same day he was himself indicted in the King's Bench of *praemunire*[2] under a 137-year-old statute passed in the reign of King Richard II. The original object of the twin Statutes of Praemunire and Provisors was to limit the effects of a universal Church on a national state (during the Hundred Years' War with France, for instance, the Pope had installed a Frenchman in an English benefice). It was made illegal to connive at the interference of the Pope in the disposal of English benefices without the King's approval or to allow any cause to be referred to the Curia in Rome which manifestly should have been dealt with by the King's courts in Westminster. The penalty was the surrender of all the offender's property, and his person, to the King.

Wolsey was now enmeshed in *praemunire* on the grounds of his legatine powers. The charge was absurd, because he had applied for them at Henry's express command and used them only to carry out Henry's wishes. He had, in fact, locked away in one of his coffers, the King's authorisation to prove it. But, if he were to save his life, the Cardinal knew he dared not plead this. He, of all people, was aware how things could be manipulated against those destined for destruction. He promptly threw himself on Henry's mercy. He acknowledged that 'on authority of bulls from the court of Rome by which he was made legate and which he published in England contrary to the Statute, he had incurred the penalties of *praemunire*, by which also he deserved to suffer perpetual impri-

[2] The statute takes its name from the first words of the writ directed to the officer, bidding him warn the offender when and where he is to appear to answer charges brought against him: '*Praemunire facias* Thomas Wolsey etc—Cause Thomas Wolsey to be forewarned.' This neutral word had, as one historian has put it, 'acquired the sound of treason through two hundred years of unpleasant history. Indictment carried tacit judgment and condemnation'. (The Statute of Richard II confirmed and strengthened an earlier one.)

sonment at the King's pleasure and to forfeit all his lands, offices and goods'. He prayed his 'most gracious and merciful sovereign lord', as a partial recompense for his offences, 'to take into his hands all his temporal possessions, all debts due to him and all arrears of pensions'.

Henry accepted with alacrity. He would take Hampton Court and York House at once. Two days later, the King, accompanied by Anne Boleyn and her mother, went to inspect York House which he had promised to give Anne as her own residence, to be renamed The White Hall. Here they found that, by Wolsey's instructions, all his treasures had been laid out for them to see.

In the words of his faithful gentleman usher, George Cavendish, who helped to superintend the operation, 'in his gallery were set divers tables upon which were laid great store of rich stuffs, whole pieces of silks of all colours, velvets, satins, damasks, taffetas, grograms, sarsnets and other rich commodities. Also there were a thousand pieces of fine Holland and the hangings of the gallery were cloth of gold and cloth of silver and rich cloth of baudkin[3] of divers colours. On one side of the gallery hung the rich copes which were made for his colleges; they were the richest that ever I saw in all my life. Then he had two chambers adjoining the gallery, the one called the Gilt Chamber and the other the Council Chamber, wherein were set two broad and long tables, whereupon were set such abundance of plate of all sorts, as was almost incredible to be believed, a great part being all of pure gold; and upon every table and cupboard where the plate was set were books importing every kind of plate and every piece, with the contents and weight thereof.' Both Henry and Anne were delighted. Henry ordered a great banquet to celebrate his gift to her of this new palace and, at it, so that there should be no mistake about his ultimate intentions, he gave her precedence of her aunt, the Duchess of Norfolk, and kissed her before the

[3] Cloth of gold and silk.

87

assembled company. But, as long as the Cardinal lived, Anne would not be satisfied.

Anne, in her attitude to Wolsey, was not quite sane. At the root of everything lay the hatred engendered by his breaking off her love-match with Henry Percy. She had, of course, realised long ago that he was only acting on the instructions of a jealous king, but this had led to no mitigation of her hate. Had she loved the King, it might have been otherwise; but she did not, and never would, love Henry Tudor; the deepest emotion she had known was her passion for Henry Percy. The way of ambition had its compensations and she luxuriated in them; but her gaiety, though it might deceive others, did not deceive herself. She knew what she had lost.

But Wolsey now was blocking even her ambition. She blamed him for the failure of the Legatine Court and did it with so little attempt at concealment that the Imperial Ambassador could report: 'The Lady who is the cause of all this disorder, finding her marriage delayed that she felt so secure of, suspects that the Cardinal put impediments in her way from a belief that, if she were Queen, his power would decline.'

As long as Wolsey lived, she would not be appeased. Dining alone with the King, she said that, if others had done 'the things that he hath wrought in the realm to your great slander and dishonour' they would have been impeached and executed. When Henry attempted to defend the man who had been his friend for twenty years and had taught him kingship, she raged out of the room.

'The Lady,' wrote the Imperial Ambassador again, 'does not cease to weep and regret her lost time and her honour, threatening the King that she will leave him, in such sort that the King has much trouble to appease her.' In desperation, her besotted lover promised her that he would, at least, never see the Cardinal again. It was a triumph of a sort. The French Ambassador evaluated it: 'I have visited the Cardinal in his troubles, but I have been able to do little. The worst of his trouble is that Mlle. de Boleyn has made her friend promise that he will never give him a hearing, for she thinks he could not help having pity upon him.'

Anne even turned on her uncle, the Duke of Norfolk, who had hated Wolsey longer than she had, because 'he had not done against the Cardinal as much as he might'.

But Norfolk had always done against the Cardinal everything that was in his power. As the premier Duke and leader of the nobility, he despised Wolsey as an upstart; as a soldier—he had been Lord Admiral, had led the vanguard at Flodden, had devastated alike the Scottish border and the French coast—he had the natural contempt of the born fighter for the soft churchman; as the hereditary adviser of the Crown and president of the Privy Council, he resented Wolsey's statesmanship—the more bitterly as he himself was so illiterate that he could not be used on an embassy, even when Wolsey wanted it, because his French was so bad. His spare, almost skeletal, body; his flat cheeks and long chin; his hard, insolent eyes might have been constructed as the very antithesis of Wolsey's ingratiating rotundity. But even Wolsey at his worst did not match him in cringing subservience to the King, in ambition, and, when diplomacy seemed to demand it, in lack of honour and consistency.

And now, at last, at fifty-seven, he had the game in his hand. He persuaded the King to deprive Wolsey of the Lord Chancellorship and himself hurried to him to demand the Great Seal.

'Where is your commission?' asked Wolsey.

'The King gave it by word of mouth.'

'That is not sufficient for me,' retorted Wolsey; 'not without written commandment of the King's pleasure. The King himself delivered me the Great Seal of England to hold for my lifetime, with the ministration of the office and high room of the Chancellorship. I can show you the King's letters patent.'

There was an argument and some recriminations, but the

Cardinal held his ground and the Duke returned to the King without the Great Seal.

It was a small enough victory—a mere twenty-four hour's postponement. Norfolk returned, not only with the written authorisation, but with the order that Wolsey was to withdraw himself beyond a ten-mile limit from London and to take up his residence at Esher, a small, plain house, which had belonged to the see of Winchester and which the Cardinal had occasionally used as a retreat from his magnificent palace of Hampton Court.

When, with his shrunken household, Wolsey arrived at that new abode 'in the moist and corrupt air of Esher' (which he knew, from experience, was bad for his health) he discovered that it was—as Cavendish reported—'without either beds, sheets, table-cloths or dishes to eat meat in or money wherewith to buy any; but there was a good store of all kinds of victuals, and of beer and wine plenty'. He made the best of it and sent some of his servants to borrow the necessities from the Bishop of Carlisle's London house.

That morning of All Saint's Day Cavendish noticed something which made him doubt his eyes. Standing by the great window of the hall, gazing out across the desolate park, stood Thomas Cromwell, a prayer-book in his hand and tears streaming down his cheeks, saying the *Little Office of Our Lady*.

Cavendish, who himself was genuinely fond of Wolsey, had never suspected Cromwell of such depth of concern. He assumed that things must be even worse than they seemed. Crossing to Cromwell, he asked: 'Why, Mr. Cromwell, what does this mean? Is our master in any new danger that you are weeping for him?'

Cromwell, who saw no reason for pretence with such a simple soul as Cavendish, retorted: 'My tears are for myself. I am likely to lose everything I have worked for for the whole of my life simply because I have served my master faithfully.'

'Why sir,' said Cavendish, 'you are far too wise a man to do anything on the Cardinal's instructions that you would not do of your own will.'

'That may be,' Cromwell replied, 'but what is quite clear is that I am disdained because of our master's disgrace and an evil name once gotten will not lightly be put away.'

'We who have had the good,' said the loyal Cavendish, 'must stomach the bad as best we may.'

'I never had any promotion from him,' said Cromwell, 'nor any increase of my living.'

'What do you intend to do?'

'This much I will tell you. As soon as the Cardinal has dined, I am going to ride to London and the court, and I will either make myself or mar myself before I come here again.'

'I wish you good luck,' said Cavendish.

Cromwell was, in fact, caught in a situation which might have taxed the ingenuity of Machiavelli himself. On the one hand, it was obviously necessary to desert Wolsey; on the other hand, it was equally necessary not to be seen too openly to do so, for fear of incurring general contempt. Sleeplessly, he had battered his brain to find a solution and, when he was almost at the point of despair, it had suddenly come to him, superb in its simplicity. On November 3, Parliament was to meet. He must become a Member of the Lower House. In such a capacity, he would escape into neutrality. It might even be that, without endangering himself, he would be able to appear to help his fallen master.

But how? The Duke of Norfolk had twenty or so seats in the Commons, scattered through various counties, to dispose of; but Norfolk was unlikely to sponsor anyone connected with Wolsey. Cromwell's one chance was through Sir John Gage, the King's Vice-Chamberlain, whom he had recently put under an obligation by successfully conducting a peculiarly shady business deal for him. He immediately sent his confidential clerk, Ralph Sadler, to see Gage and put the matter to him.

That All Saints' morning he had just received the reply: 'My Lord of Norfolk has spoken with the King and His Highness is very well contented that you should be a Burgess, as long as you will order yourself in the Commons' room according to whatever instructions the Duke of Norfolk shall give you from the King's Highness.'

The opening of Parliament was now but two days away. Cromwell must subject himself to Norfolk at once. He bowed to the necessity, which he had sought; but his vexation and tears were caused by the swiftness of it. He would have preferred much longer to reorientate himself.

Parliament, in which Thomas Cromwell duly sat as the burgess for Taunton, had, at least in Henry's intention, one overriding object. It was to be his weapon against the Pope, should Clement decide against him. One contemporary observer wrote of the 'great care taken that only those should be present who would favour the King's business'; another, (who later became a judge)[4] that the King 'chose for knights and burgesses such as he and his council were persuaded would malign the clergy, namely divers of his own councillors and household servants and their servants'; and Queen Catherine admitted to the Countess of Salisbury: 'My husband has played his cards so well that he is likely to get a majority of votes in his favour and may be tempted to get by this means what he has not been able to get in any other way.'

At the opening of the session, however, the matter of Wolsey overshadowed everything else. The new Lord Chancellor, Sir Thomas More, led the attack, praising the King for seeing through 'the rotten and faulty' man who 'so craftily, so scabbedly, so untruly, juggled with His Grace'. More put his name first in the signatures to the forty-four articles which impeached the Cardinal,—a farrago of the obvious, the ridiculous and the malicious.

[4] William Rastell, Sir Thomas More's nephew.

The document began by calling attention to Wolsey's 'high, orgollous and insatiable mind' which caused him to obtain 'the authority legatine' by which he 'hath spoiled and taken away from many houses of religion the substance of their goods. It accused him of making unauthorised decisions in foreign policy and of sending letters abroad beginning 'The King and I'. It informed the King that, 'Whereas Your Grace is our Sovereign Lord and Head, in whom standeth all the wealth and surety of the realm, the Lord Cardinal, knowing himself to have the foul and contagious disease of the great pox broken out upon him in divers places of his body, came daily to Your Grace, whispering in your ears and blowing upon your most noble grace with his perilous and infected breath, to the marvellous danger of Your Highness, if God in His infinite goodness had not protected Your Highness; and when he was once healed he made Your Grace to believe that his disease was a cold in his head and no other thing.'

So the catalogue continued from accusations that he had, by his complaint to the Pope 'shamefully slandered many good religious houses and good virtuous men dwelling in them' and that he had accused the clergy of sodomy 'which slander to your church of England shall for ever remain in the register at Rome against the clergy of this your realm' to accusations that he had bought 'corn and cattle, fish and all other victual at Your Grace's price, which is against the laws of your realm' and that 'of his pompous and presumptuous mind' he had 'imprinted the Cardinal's Hat under your royal arms in your coin of groats made in your city of York, which deed hath not been done by any subject within your realm before this time'.

'Finally,' ran the last article, 'the Lord Cardinal, by his outrageous pride hath for a long season greatly shadowed Your Grace's honour, which is most highly to be regarded, and by his insatiable avarice and ravenous appetite for riches and treasure hath so grievously oppressed your poor subjects by bribery and extortion that Your Grace's realm is thereby greatly decayed and impoverished; and also by his cruelty, iniquity, affection and partiality hath subverted Your Grace's laws to the undoing of a great number of your loving people.'

In the debate that followed, it was not difficult for Cromwell to appear as Wolsey's partisan merely by applying the corrective of truth and no risk was incurred since Henry took no notice of the petition and the matter was dropped.

The King, indeed, regretted the Cardinal. He sent secret messages to him assuring him of his continuing affection. He allowed him to leave Esher and take up his residence in Richmond Park, where his proximity to the palace alarmed his enemies. 'To reinstate him in the King's favour would not be difficult,' Eustache Chapuys wrote to Charles V, 'were it not for the Lady'. But the Lady was even more determined against him than ever, since Henry had raged at her uncle that affairs were not so well managed as they had been in the Cardinal's time, saying 'that the Cardinal was a better man than any of them and, repeating this twice, left them'. When Sir John Russell—recalled now from his Italian embassy and fulfilling his duties as Knight-Marshal of the Household—dared to speak in Wolsey's favour, Anne took it upon herself to berate him soundly in public and thereafter refused to speak to him.

Henry, unable eventually to resist domestic pressure, ordered Wolsey to take up residence in his see of York. The Cardinal saw this as tantamount to a decree of exile and an indication that all chances of his restoration to court were at an end. It was then that he had voluntarily exchanged his house in Richmond Park for a retreat among the Carthusians. If he was to spend his last years in the exercise of those priestly functions he had so long neglected, he would prepare himself as best he could. He had intended to keep Easter in that atmosphere of holiness, but just before Passion Sunday, Norfolk sent him word by Thomas Cromwell that, if the Cardinal did not leave at once for the North, the Duke 'would tear the butcher's cur with his teeth'.

'Marry, Thomas,' said Wolsey, 'then it is time to be going.'

By Maundy Thursday he had reached Peterborough and in the Abbey there he solemnly washed and wiped and kissed the feet of fifty-nine poor men, one for each year of his age.

As he drew near Cawood Castle, his official residence about seven miles from York, he found his progress halted at St. Oswald's Abbey by a great crowd of parents and children who had come from miles around. He 'confirmed children' Cavendish reported 'from the hour of eight till twelve of the clock at noon; and, making a short dinner, resorted to the church again soon after one of the clock; and, for weariness, at the last was constrained to call for a chair and confirmed more children until the hour of six of the clock. And the next morning he prepared to depart towards Cawood and before he went, confirmed almost a hundred children more, and then rode his way from thence. And on the way, at a plain green a little beyond Ferrybridge there were assembled, at a great cross made of stone, more children, accounted by estimation to be about the number of five hundred; and from thence he never removed until he had fully confirmed them every one. And then he took his mule and rode on to Cawood, where he stayed long after with much honour and love in the countryside, both of the worshipful and the simple, doing good deeds of charity'.

Reginald Pole, once more in Colet's house in the Charterhouse of Sheen, was informed of the Cardinal's residence there and his so-greatly-changed way of life. Admiration for it fitted the mood of his return, which was one of bitter disillusion. Not only had the University of Paris found for the King, but also Bourges, Toulouse, Orleans and Angers; and in Italy Bologna, Ferrara and his beloved Padua, where the majority was eleven, obtained, according to the Spanish Ambassador in Rome, 'from as many friars for ten ducats apiece, most of them illiterate and men of bad lives'.

Fortified by this expert opinion—even though the Spanish

universities were, as expected, unanimous for Catherine—Henry procured the signature of eighty-three of his notables to a letter to the Pope, citing the strength of European theological judgment on behalf of 'his Royal Majesty our head and so the soul of us all' and threatening that, if His Holiness did not act accordingly and pronounce the nullity, 'we shall certainly interpret it that our case is remitted to ourselves, so that we may seek remedies elsewhere'.

Clement replied that, as men of experience, the signatories could hardly expect him to ignore the reasoned protests of Catherine and her supporters, 'the clamour of which fills all Christendom', and, by not hearing the case properly argued by both sides, falsify the King's conscience as well as his own.

After Pole had made his report to the King, in which he warned Henry that, as far as he could see, France—whatever the Universities might have done—was not to be trusted because 'they never keep league with us except for their own advantage', he washed his hands of the whole affair, retired to Sheen and, as far as he could, emulated the piety that Wolsey had shown there.

Wolsey had chosen November 7, 1530 the Monday after All Saints' Day, as appropriate for his installation as Archbishop of York. He had also issued a call for a Convocation to meet at York on the same day. Unfortunately he had neglected to obtain the Royal mandate which was technically necessary. It was enough. Anne and her uncle Norfolk persuaded Henry that this was a deliberate act of disobedience which betokened that the Cardinal was consolidating power in the North to use, if necessary, against the Crown.

On All Saints' Day, while the Cardinal was at dinner, the Earl of Northumberland arrived at Cawood with a body of attendants and, almost trembling with fright, laid his hand on Wolsey's arm, saying 'in a faint and soft voice': 'My Lord, I arrest you for high treason.' The Earl of Northumberland was young Henry

Percy who had recently succeeded to the title on his father's death.

The progress south to the Tower started on the Sunday, the day before that set for the installation. Before it had gone very far, Wolsey remembered that he had left an important red buckram bag in his bedroom, sealed with his seal. He obtained permission for it to be fetched. Cavendish was sent for it and arrived with it that night, while the Cardinal was resting at Pontefract. It contained three hair shirts.

At Sheffield, Sir William Kingston, Constable of the Tower of London, arrived with twenty-four Yeomen of the Guard to take charge of the prisoner. The twenty-four were all Wolsey's old servants and had, Kingston said, been specially sent by the King 'to defend you against your unknown enemies so that you may come with safety to His Grace'. He further assured the Cardinal: 'He has commanded me to tell you at once that he bears you as much good-will as ever he did and he bids you to be of good cheer.'

But it was neither the malice of unknown enemies nor the possible continuance of his greatest friendship that was uppermost in Wolsey's thought. It was death. His stomach had suddenly started to trouble him; and nothing that his doctors could do could alleviate it. On one day he had fifty stools.[5] He was so weak and ill that 'he was likely several times to have fallen from his mule' and the Yeomen showed their concern and affection for their old master in unrestrained tears.

At the Abbey of St. Mary of the Meadow, just north of Leicester, not far from the Grey Friars where the broken, despoiled body of King Richard III had been buried after Bosworth, Wolsey could go no further. The Abbot, coming to welcome him at the gate, was greeted with: 'Father Abbot, I am come hither to leave my bones among you.' The Cardinal was too

[5] It is possible that, as many believed at the time and some historians have believed since, he was poisoned by Anne Boleyn's order and Henry Percy's connivance.

97

weak to walk unaided the distance from the gate to the Abbey.

He died on St. Andrew's Day. Before he died, he said to Kingston: 'If I had served God as diligently as I have done the King, He would not have given me over in my grey hairs. Nevertheless this is a just reward for the worldly diligence I have had to do the King service only to satisfy his vain pleasure, not regarding my godly duty.'

The King, when the news of the Cardinal's death reached him, cross-questioned the messenger as to what had happened to the fifteen hundred pounds which Wolsey was supposed to have been carrying with him, and Anne Boleyn had a farce written for the amusement of the court entitled: 'Of the going to Hell of Cardinal Wolsey'.

A few days later Henry sent the Duke of Norfolk to Sheen to offer Pole the vacant Archbishopric of York.

8

Henry loses Pole and gains Cromwell

Pole refused the Archbishopric out of hand as soon as he realised that acceptance would imply support for Henry's cause. The terms in which he couched his refusal, given on the spur of the moment to Norfolk, represented exactly his feelings both then and for many years afterwards.

'I cannot sufficiently thank the King for his goodness,' he said.

'It is, indeed, a very great honour,' said Norfolk, reflecting that Reginald was only thirty.

'I esteem it a very great honour to serve him in any position, however lowly, provided only that I am allowed to safeguard his true interests,' replied Pole. 'But I must refuse to accept any position, however exalted, in which this is not possible.'

Norfolk, to whom such considerations were incomprehensible and approached *lése majesté*, asked in surprise: 'Surely you will not refuse this great mark of His Highness's favour?'

'I do not account it a favour if I cannot protect his honour.'

Norfolk was even more shocked when, having reported this to the King, Henry merely sent him back to Pole with the request that he would take at least a month to consider the matter before he gave an irrevocable answer. It might be that some way could be found by which he could support the King without violating his conscience.

For in the strange, false, self-interested tide that swirled round the Throne, Henry recognised his cousin's uniqueness. He endorsed the French envoy's description of him as one 'of honourable life and admirable learning with whom no one could compare for the indifference with which he regarded those things which most move the ambitions of men'. To some Reynold might appear the prig that Francis I had thought him; to others, the impractical idealist dreaming of the past whom Cromwell despised: but to Henry, whatever the tensions between them, he remained the young kinsman the genuineness of whose devotion was matched only by the soundness of his judgment and the disinterestedness of his advice.

Pole promised that he would spend the next month trying to devise some means by which he could serve the King without violating his conscience.

His brothers descended on him at Sheen, clamouring for him to accept. Montagu even allowed himself to show some anger. He had signed the letter of protest to the Pope, not out of accommodation but from conviction. Did Reynold blame him for that? Reginald said he did not. Then why, asked Montagu, was he boggling at the Archbisopric? Because that, retorted his brother, concerned *his* conscience, not Montagu's.

Geoffrey Pole was a little too obviously alarmed at the possible repercussions of Reginald's refusal on the family. He had four small children. Reginald tried to put him at ease by explaining that Henry was unlikely to take vengeance on anyone, certainly not on children.

'The matter rests between the King and me. I believe that he understands I cannot change my direction.'

'When I was small,' said Geoffrey, 'and we were in our mother's garden at Warblington, watching boats in the harbour, you explained to me how a good helmsman could trim his sails and seem to keep a contrary course yet bring his ship safe into port.'

'I promise you, Geoffrey, as I have promised the King, that I will use all my skill. I care not where I seem to face, but you must allow me to gauge the strength of the wind.'

The person whose advice Reginald most valued was his mother and she seemed to refuse to give him any.

'In this matter, Reynold,' said Margaret, 'and at this time, I am swayed by my affection. Mary and I are with the Queen and I see things through their eyes. For you to see them so might unbalance your judgment.'

'I do not think it, but leave it so if you wish. Tell me only one thing. Would it please you if I were Archbishop of York?'

'You know, son,' said Margaret, 'that I dedicated you to God in your cradle.'

'That is no answer, mother.'

'If you were as the Cardinal in his ending,' she answered, 'yes.'

He realised that she had narrowed the matter to the priesthood, which he was still fiercely refusing, and, so, had made him probe deeply into his motives. Was this, after all, the true grounds of his refusal?

As if she had read his thoughts, she said: 'If you mistrust your own judgment, why do you not consult Thomas More?'

The new Lord Chancellor, who was now fifty-two, had known and admired Pole and his family ever since Reginald had been an undergraduate at Oxford. They shared the same concern for the reform of the clergy and More's satire *Utopia* was one of Reynold's favourite books, which he had endeavoured to popularise in Italy. Both were friends of the formidable Erasmus; and both, even more pertinently, were friends of King Henry. What Pole needed at this juncture, as his mother had realised, was contact with More's cold, legalistic mind.

When Reginald put his problem to him, More epitomised it

for him immediately with: 'Do you think it is more possible for me to accept the Lord Chancellorship than for you to accept the Archbishopric of York? If I can succeed the Cardinal in the one, why should you not succeed him in the other?'

'The King will expect me to support his cause.'

'Has he said so?'

'My lord of Norfolk made it plain enough.'

'That is natural. He is the Lady's uncle. But have you anything from the King in person?'

'No.'

'Reynold, you must learn not to build on hear-say, even if it comes to you on the highest authority.'

'But there can be no doubt that the King will expect me to be his partisan.'

'He does not expect it from me,' said More. Answering Pole's look of surprise, he continued: 'He had many whose consciences allowed them to support him in his "great matter" but, knowing that mine did not, he never asked it of me but used me in his other business. He has never wished to put any man to ruffle or trouble his conscience and I settle my mind in quiet to serve him in other things.'

'And you would say I should do the same?'

'By my office I am Keeper of the King's Conscience, but not even by courtesy of yours. I can but tell you what I have found. Your decision must be your own.'

While Pole was agonising, Cromwell was acting. He had extricated himself from any untoward circumstances which might have affected him in Wolsey's fall; he was slowly making his mark in the House of Commons; but he had not the ear of the King; and it was this that he had determined to get. Without it he would, at least in his own estimation, remain 'marred'. Also, for his purpose it was necessary to see the King alone. To speak to the King in company with Norfolk or with some of his fellow Members of Parliament or even with Sir John Gage would have presented little difficulty—and would have been as little effective. Carefully Cromwell played the card he had been saving for just such an occasion.

Sir John Russell was in high favour with the King and Sir John Russell, ever since that night in Bologna when, as he thought, Cromwell had saved his life, had promised, if ever he was in a position to do so, to show his gratitude in tangible form. Now, when Cromwell asked him, he agreed to arrange a private meeting with the King as soon as possible.

Face to face with his sovereign, Cromwell decided that, since he was risking everything on this chance, directness was best. It was no secret that Henry had two passions—money and Anne—and as (so Cromwell from his knowledge of men estimated) the former was likely to be more enduring than the latter, Cromwell would shoot first at that mark. When the King asked him why he had sought the interview, he said: 'Because I had a great matter to propose to Your Highness. I humbly crave that you will allow me to make Your Highness the richest king in Christendom.'

'If you can indeed do so, Master Cromwell,' said Henry, laughing, 'they have kept you from me too long. Expound!'

Cromwell, claiming quite truly that he was the only person who knew the intricacies of Wolsey's financial dealings, offered to unravel them.

The mention of Wolsey made the King pensive. 'I would not have lost the Cardinal for twenty thousand pounds,' he said.

'His Grace was a very great man and my benefactor,' said Cromwell. 'May he rest in peace!' They both crossed themselves. Having paid the necessary tribute to sentiment, Cromwell recalled the King to practicalities. 'But I can assure Your Highness that, being dead, he will yield Your Highness more than twenty thousand pounds.'

'So much? I had thought there was but fifteen hundred to be accounted for.'

'He was secret in his investments,' said Cromwell, 'but you

may have my head if I do not find twenty thousand for you.'

'Give me half that and I will keep your head for my own service. Yet even the full sum would not make me the richest King in Christendom.'

'Sire,' said Cromwell, satisfied that he now had the King, 'the Cardinal was guilty of *praemunire*.'

'Unfortunately,' said Henry, who could not see why this, now Wolsey was dead, should be brought into the conversation.

'But if he was guilty in issuing the Pope's bulls without the necessary permission of Your Highness, as Sovereign of this realm, then all the clergy are equally guilty in obeying them.'

The King stared at Cromwell in unconcealed admiration. 'Mother of God,' he exclaimed. He was going to say 'why did I not realise that myself?' but deciding it would be injudicious to reveal himself to so new an acquaintance, he changed it to; 'we cannot imprison all the clergy.'

'Most assuredly not, sire. Yet, if they knew that Your Highness had power to do so, might they not show their gratitude for your clemency by a gift in Convocation?'

'Proceed, Master Cromwell,' said the King.

Sure now of his ground, Cromwell unfolded his whole plan. The basis of *praemunire* was that the King of England was the temporal head of the Church in England and that there were matters ecclesiastical in which the Pope's writ did not run. This had never been disputed but neither had it been sufficiently emphasised. Let Convocation now declare that the King was in fact the Supreme Head and Protector of the Church in England and many difficulties would vanish. For one thing, it would then be no longer necessary for him to wait for the Pope's consent to the nullity suit. Fortified by the opinions of the theologians, not only in England but in France and Italy, the Church in England might properly make the judgment which had, improperly, been referred to the Curia.

Henry, fascinated, saw only one objection. Might this not be considered Lutheranism?

104

How could it be, said Cromwell in a shocked voice, when all the world knew the King as the Defender of the Faith against Luther? At the moment Lutheran books were being sought out and confiscated and their peddlars punished. Had there not been that year two burnings for heresy in London?

'I will see to it, if Your Highness will allow me, that the style and title of "Supreme Head and Protector" shall first be used to describe Your Highness's work against heresy, so that none shall be mistaken.'

'It matters not how you put it as long as none can think I am parted from my wits and claim to be Head of the mystical body of Christ.'

'None could be so absurd, sire; but to guard against such an error perhaps Your Highness would be so gracious as to draft the words when the time comes.'

Henry assented, thanked Cromwell and dismissed him with the promise that they must often speak together. Next day, he made him a Privy Councillor.

Reginald Pole, in his quest for advice, called on John Fisher, Bishop of Rochester. Fisher, now sixty-one, was the recognised leader of those churchmen who still took Catherine's side. His reputation was so great that, at the beginning of the nullity affair, while it was still relatively secret, Wolsey had thought it worth while to make a special journey to lie to him in confidence that it was Catherine, not Henry, who wanted the nullity. When Fisher discovered the truth, he offered himself to lead Catherine's cause at the Blackfriars' trial.

There, when the Archbishop of Canterbury, old accommodating William Warham, nearing eighty, asking nothing but a quiet life and prone to reiterate: 'A king's displeasure is death,' was droning through the list of bishops who had endorsed the King's cause and had come to 'Rochester', suddenly the ascetic, hollow-eyed, lantern-jawed Fisher rose in his place and thundered: 'That is not my hand or seal.'

'My lord,' said Warham, 'we spoke of the matter together, and—'

'And I said to you that though you and many other lords had asked it of me, I would never consent to such an act.'

'True,' said Warham, 'but at the last you were persuaded that you would allow me to sign for you and to put a seal to it myself.'

'Under your correction, my lord,' said Fisher bitingly, 'nothing is more untrue.'

Campeggio had been impressed enough to write that evening to the Pope: 'This affair of Rochester was unexpected and unforeseen. You know what sort of man he is and may imagine what is likely to happen.'

The Boleyns, too, knew what sort of man he was and Anne started her own proceedings to get rid of him. As her father's town mansion was near Fisher's London palace, it was easy enough for one of her trusted servants to become friendly with one of his kitchen staff and to persuade him, for a jest, to put some powder she gave him into the food. It was quite harmless, she said, except that it produced diarrhoea.

It so happened that the Bishop did not taste the dish, but, of those who did, all were violently ill and seven died.

Shortly afterwards, as a chronicler recorded, 'a gun was shot through the top of the Bishop's house not far from his study where he accustomably used to sit; which made such a terrible noise over his head and bruised the tiles and rafters of the house so sore, that both he and divers of his servants were suddenly amazed thereat. Wherefore speedy search was made whence this shot should come and what it meant. Which at last was found to come out of the Earl of Wiltshire's house who was father to the Lady Anne. Then he perceived that great malice was meant towards him and calling speedily unto him certain of his servants, said "Let us truss up our gear and begone from hence, for here is no place for us to tarry any longer." '

Reginald Pole found him at Rochester in his library where

he had spent so much time with his friends, Erasmus and Thomas More, and of which Erasmus had complained that it was so cold and draughty that he could not be there for more than three hours without feeling ill. Additionally, as Erasmus had noted, 'the near approach of the tide, as well as the mud which is left at every ebb of the water, makes the whole place unhealthy'. Pole, that raw winter's day, wondered how even Fisher's extreme asceticism could endure it. The Bishop, he thought, looked so frail that he was unlikely in the course of nature to live much more than a year.

'I trust,' said Fisher, after welcoming him affectionately, 'that you have come to tell me that we are to have an Archbishop of York who is worthy of trust.'

His question anticipated, Pole could only reveal his misgivings: 'I fear I am unworthy of the priesthood.'

'All men are; but that you should think so makes you the less unworthy.'

The Bishop continued to speak quietly, citing examples from his own long experience, of the meaning of the Sacrament of Orders and the responsibilities of a bishop. He made so profound an impression on his hearer that Pole was then immediately certain of what he was later to tell the King—'were you to send through all the nations of Christendom, you would not easily find a bishop who has such love of his flock'.

After such spirituality, the politico-legal question seemed irrelevant. Yet it had to be asked: 'And where does my duty lie in the complication before the courts?'

'It is a simple enough matter,' said Fisher, 'and made to appear otherwise only because certain men wish it so. Christ said: "Whom God hath joined together, let no man put asunder." There is no doubt that the King and Queen are truly married and that the Vicar of Christ must find it so.'

'And if the King refuses to obey?'

'Then you must stand against the King. And you will have better standing as Archbishop of York than as Dean of Exeter.

But the King may not refuse. Sufficient unto the day . . .'

When Pole got back to Sheen, he wrote to Henry saying that he was prepared to accept the great honour which the King proposed to bestow on him.

Henry, delighted, received him alone in his private gallery in the White Hall, which Pole had not visited since it had been York House and he had seen Wolsey there and had been lectured by Thomas Cromwell. It may have been this circumstance which unconsciously affected him (he was now accustomed to think of Cromwell as 'Satan's Legate') and accounted for his inexplicable conduct; though he was never able satisfactorily to explain it, even to himself.

'When the King came towards me,' he recorded, 'full of expectation, as he told me himself, and I, prepared to fulfil that expectation, attempted to speak, I found that my tongue was hampered, my lips refused to move and when at last, recovering myself, I began to speak, I uttered every argument most opposed to the theory I had come to defend.'

Henry changed colour, almost strangled with rage, and pulled out his dagger. He would have killed Reynold, so he told Norfolk later, had it not been that the innocent honesty of his face made it quite clear that he was only concerned, as he said he was, with the King's honour. When Pole began an apology for having so displeased him, he snapped: 'I will consider your opinion and will then reply to it,' turned on his heel and went out banging the door as loudly as he could, leaving his cousin in tears.

The King remained alone for an hour. Pole, after suffering another extremity of anger from his brothers, went back to Sheen and began carefully to write out his argument for the King. In quietness, the King might read it.

He urged Henry to abide by the Pope's judgment, whatever it might be. He pointed out that any other judgment would be suspect. The Universities could, as he knew, be persuaded either way. In any case, their favourable judgment meant, in practical terms, that Henry had been living in incest for twenty years. This was not likely to endear him to his subjects or to increase the respect of his fellow-monarchs. Also in practical terms, the existence of the children of two wives might lead to the same conditions as had brought about the civil war of Lancaster and York, whose wounds Henry had done so much to heal; and the putting away of Catherine—even should the Pope rule it possible—would permanently estrange her nephew the Emperor, who was now the unquestioned master of Europe and who could crush England instantly should he decide to declare war. Indeed, 'he may injure us without drawing a sword by merely forbidding traffic in Flanders and Spain'. Finally, and above all, there was Henry's honour. 'You stand on the brink of the water,' he concluded, 'and may yet save all; take but one step further and all honour is drowned.'

Having sent the letter by the hand of Sir John Russell who promised, as Pole was the writer, that he would deliver it 'happen whatever please God', Reynold asked Montagu to seek an interview with the King to discover what effect it had had. Montagu grasped the opportunity, not to help Reynold, with whom he was now hardly on speaking terms, but to have a chance of apologising for him and so, he hoped, averting the Royal wrath from the family.

He was surprised to hear Henry say: 'I have read the letter and your brother has spoken the truth. I cannot feel any anger against him, because, although it is very much against my will, it is written in sincerity and shows his love for me. I only wish he could change his opinions so that I might prove my love for him.'

The King passed the letter to Dr. Cranmer, whom he had now put in charge of his propaganda, and asked his opinion on it.

'Though it is contrary to your royal purpose,' said Cranmer, 'it is written with such wit and eloquence that if it were set forth and known to the common people, it would not be possible to persuade them to the contrary.'

Henry thought so, too. It almost persuaded him.

Unfortunately at that moment the Pope sent him an injunction, forbidding him to remarry until the case was heard at Rome and declaring that, if he did, the offspring would be at once declared illegitimate. Clement also forbade anyone in England, ecclesiastical or secular, who was concerned with the universities, Parliament or courts of law, to make any decision on a case reserved for the Holy See. The penalty for disobedience was excommunication.

There were also troubles with Anne. Enraged at the slowness with which things were progressing, she 'had words' with Henry and followed them up by refusing to see him. Eventually he went to her father and her uncle, 'with tears in his eyes', and implored them to make his peace with her.

In the circumstances, his honour seemed an academic concept and he spent much time with Thomas Cromwell and Thomas Cranmer.

When Convocation assembled in the middle of January, 1531, Pole took his place as Dean of Exeter and listened to the agitated debate of a clergy which knew that a writ of *praemunire* was pending against them in the King's Bench. They hurriedly voted a free gift of £40,000 and described it as a recognition of the great benefits conferred on the Church by the King, especially by his defence of the Faith against heresy. News of this being conveyed to the palace, a strong hint was returned that this was nothing like enough and three days later, the bribe was raised to £100,044. 8s 8d. After keeping them waiting a fortnight—for Cromwell knew to a nicety the effects of suspense—the King declared himself willing to accept it provided the clergy admitted the true reason for their generosity. They were to acknowledge that they offered the money in consideration of the Royal pardon for their breaches of penal laws and they were to describe the King as 'Protector and Supreme Head of the English Church and Clergy'. The message was brought to the Chapter

House by Anne Boleyn's brother, George, Viscount Rochford.

There were four days of debate, but before the end Pole had ceased to attend. The spectacle it afforded nauseated him and convinced him, as nothing else had, of the poor quality of the English clergy and the venality of the bishops. The King's intention was unequivocally clear yet they either would not or could not see it. Their deplorable speeches were those of the 'simple smatterers of divinity' that they were. Eventually they proposed that the words 'after God' should be inserted which, in the context, meant nothing; then they discussed 'as far as Canon Law allows' which, indeed, nullified the new title but which they withdrew as soon as the King—again through George Boleyn—objected to it. When Henry sent, one by one, for the clerics who seemed likely to make a stand, and assured them in audience, on the solemn word of a king, that he meant no innovation, they came back flattered and satisfied to reproach any doubters for showing 'great mistrustfulness in His Highness, seeing that he had made so solemn and high an oath'.

Pole was, perhaps, unjust in his contempt for them. In their ignorance and simplicity they could not be expected to see affairs as he, in his privileged position, saw them. But at least they might have listened to Fisher.

'Take good heed,' the Bishop of Rochester cried, 'of the mischief you will bring on the Church if you grant this unreasonable and unseemly title which has never even be asked by any other temporal ruler. If you grant the King's request in this matter, it seems to me that you will bring the Church into great and imminent danger. What if he should shortly change his mind and exercise indeed the supremacy over the Church in this realm? What if he should die and his successor claim the continuance of the same?'

He was greeted by shouts of anger 'saying that whoever would refuse the King's demand was not worthy to be accounted a true and loving subject', and threatening 'that he should be thrown into the river'.

Unruffled 'my Lord of Rochester, perceiving they would make this grant only from fear and not upon any just ground, rebuked them for their pusillanimity and advised the Convocation that, seeing that the King had faithfully promised and solemnly sworn that his meaning was to require no further than is allowed by the law of God, those conditional words "as far as the law of God allows" shall be expressed in the grant'.

For very shame, Warham put this proposition to the assembly. No one spoke. The Archbishop interpreted the silence as one which gave consent.

The King, as the addition really meant no more than the vague 'after God' and could, in any case, be omitted when necessary, was graciously pleased to accept it.

Before he retired again to Sheen to immerse himself in theology, Reginald paid another visit to his mother who was with the Queen and Princess Mary at Greenwich. Margaret was overjoyed to see him. She had heard of his recent actions mainly from Montagu and in such terms that she felt it necessary to reproach her eldest son for the bitterness of his report. When he had admitted that he found the King's attitude incomprehensible, she said sharply: 'Henry understands Reynold better than you do.' Yet she was disturbed and anxious to hear from Reginald himself the reasons for his action.

When she discovered that he himself was perplexed, she did her best to reassure him. To his: 'But why, mother, could I not speak? Why did I refuse what I had gone there to accept?' she replied: 'It may have been God's grace, my son. He may need you for other tasks.' But in her heart, she was by no means convinced of this. She knew well enough that his temperament was one which inclined rather to refusal than to acceptance. The fears she had once had that he was succumbing to a dilettante life of elegant idleness in Italy returned and were not allayed by his conversational remark that he corresponded regularly with

Bembo or by his announcement that he was going to ask the King for permission to return to Padua as soon as possible.

'You will not stay here and help us in these difficult times?' she asked. 'This was not what I had hoped.'

'Yet believe me,' he replied, 'if I could be of any help, I would stay. But what is there I could do? The King is ruled by the Boleyns and Satan's Legate—'

'Who?'

'Cromwell. My name for him.'

'Secretly, I hope. Even a whisper is dangerous here,' she warned him and reflected that Reynold was sometimes liable to curious indiscretions.

'Most secretly, mother,' he reassured her. 'But fear him as you would his master.'

'I have never feared Henry,' she said.

'I do not mean Henry and Henry, I would wager you, will not long remain master, if he is so still.'

'Then should you not stay here and fight him?'

'That battle is lost. Already he is more powerful than ever the Cardinal was. But from Italy I might be able to do a little. At the very least I could advise His Holiness and see the Emperor.'

Margaret was satisfied.[1]

The Countess was the only one who knew her son's motives. To others, it appeared that he was going into exile because he had opposed the King. Even his cousin, Henry Courtenay, Marquis of Exeter, so far mistook the situation as to write: 'Lord Cousin Pole, your departure from the realm shows in what a miserable state we find ourselves. It is to the universal shame of all us nobles, who allow you to absent yourself when we ought most to avail ourselves of your presence, but being unable to

---

[1] Since, in general histories, Pole is seldom given his due place, it may be well to quote here (from Philip Hughes's *The Reformation in England*: vol. I): 'It was between Cromwell and Reginald Pole that Henry had to make his choice; and only by the narrowest of chances did the King opt for Cromwell. In that moment the long duel began between these two subjects of the king that was never, thenceforward, to cease.'

find any other remedy for this, we pray God to find it himself.'

But, for many months, Henry refused to let Pole go; and Pole was still at Sheen in October, when his mother and Princess Mary came, on Henry's orders, to take up residence, with a depleted household in Richmond Palace. The King had determined to try to break the Queen's spirit by assaulting her affections. While he was on a hunting expedition with Anne, he sent word to Catherine that he never wished to see her again and that she was to leave Windsor and take residence at The More in Hertfordshire before he got back. Mary was to leave her mother and go to Richmond. That was the blow.

So it came about that, during her son's last days in England, Margaret had at least the consolation of seeing him more frequently than had been possible for many years. No week passed but at least once, and usually oftener, Reynold, who loved walking in the country, took his exercise by going across to the Palace; and his mother would join him in the Privy Garden where they could talk without being overheard in the quiet autumn sunshine. They grew closer in understanding. From his Oxford days, he had always had a tendency to try to instruct her in academic matters—then, it had been the superiority of Greek over Latin—and, realising that, merely by listening, she was answering his need, she had usually allowed her thoughts to take their own course. But now she concentrated her attention and it was his thoughts she followed. She was surprised how, wide-ranging at the start, they narrowed to a simple conclusion: the Pope, as Vicar of Christ, was the one necessary, unchallengeable and unique power in the world.

Both deplored that Clement VII should hold the office and agreed that the ways of the Holy Ghost were past man's comprehension; for it was Clement now who, by procrastinating for over a year in the hope that Catherine would die and so extricate him from his difficulties, was, by delaying the case, supporting in fact, if not in intention, the King's side. But the man must not be confused with the office. That mistake reduced everything to foolishness.

'Henry is bent on making himself Pope in England,' said Reynold.

'But,' answered Margaret, 'only as far as the law of God allows.'

'The law of God does not allow it at all,' retorted her son. 'And Henry knows it. How he must despise us in Convocation!'

'And how will you fight it in Padua?'

She was about to congratulate herself on a shrewd thrust when, to her surprise, Reynold answered: 'It was in Padua that the evil started. Because we debated it in Padua, I can smell it here.'

He explained to her how, in his middle years at Padua—in 1522—there had been printed for the first time a treatise written two centuries earlier by a learned doctor of that university named Marsiglio, in which it was argued that all religion should be wholly dependent on the State because the Church, as a society, does not exist, but is merely the name given to the mass of believers. The only reality is, therefore, the State, of which the Church is the religious aspect. Thus, in the Church, it is the ruler of the State who is supreme and the clergy are merely the functionaries who officiate at religious ceremonies, believing and acting as the ruler directs.

The printed version of *Defensor Pacis*, as it was titled, had caused a great stir in the university, coming as it did at a time only eight years ago when even devout Christians were not averse to using it, in argument at least, as a stick to beat the clergy and the Papacy.

'You took part in the arguments?' Margaret asked.

'Many times; but always against it,' said Reynold. 'If Henry should read it, he has everything to his hand.'

'And in Padua you would learn to counter it?'

'I think I can counter it well enough now; but there I shall be able to see better how it has grown.'

'But should it so happen,' said Margaret, 'that Henry will not give you leave to go, you will attend the new Convocation after Christmas?'

'I promise you, mother, that I shall be in my place.'

At the year's end, the Imperial Ambassador wrote to the Emperor: 'The son of the Princess's Governess, who refused the Archbishopric of York because he would not adopt the King's opinion, could not obtain a licence to study abroad till the other day. He told the King that, if he remained here, he must attend Convocation; and if the nullity suit were discussed, he must speak according to his conscience. On this, the King immediately gave him leave to go, and promised to continue his income and to allow him to retain his benefices.'

On the same boat as Pole was, unknown to him, one of Cromwell's agents, also bound for Padua, with instructions to bring back copies of Marsiglio's *Defensor Pacis*, which Cromwell intended to have translated and printed at the Government's expense and distributed throughout the country.

9

The Lady pays a visit to France

Eustache Chapuys, the hard-headed, cynical Savoyard lawyer
whom Charles V had chosen as his ambassador to England in
preference to an aristocratic Spaniard precisely because he was
less likely to be over involved in sympathy for Catherine of
Aragon, had in fact become the Queen's most ardent champion.
He devoted himself to acting as her adviser and she, accepting
his ability and recognising his honesty, was accustomed to
address him as 'My especial friend'. His partisanship did not
affect his judgment of English affairs; he never mistook wishes
for facts; but he did allow himself the occasional luxury of
annoying Henry whenever he safely could.

Shortly after Pole had left England, Chapuys was visiting the
King to make a commercial report and was surprised to be
greeted by a volley of irrelevant and unexpected abuse of the
Emperor shouted at the top of Henry's not inconsiderable voice.
He tried to turn the conversation to deal with the subject he
had come to discuss, but Henry insisted on continuing his
tirade. Shifting his position slightly, Chapuys noticed at a little
window opening on the Great Gallery the listening head of
Anne Boleyn. Maliciously he then pretended to take offence
at what Henry was saying, with the result that the King grasped
his arm and marched him down the Gallery, dropping his voice

and changing his insults to apologies, but, as Anne could see even if she could no longer hear, maintaining for her benefit his emphatic gestures.

Anne's frustration at the interminable delays was, in fact, making her such a virago that even her uncle Norfolk had become disgusted with her and would, observers thought, have changed sides and opposed the nullity suit had he not been 'one of those men who will do anything to cling to power'. He was, additionally, becoming frightened at the increasing strength of the popular outcries against Anne which culminated in an episode described by the Venetian Ambassador: 'Anne Boleyn was supping alone at a villa on the Thames when a mob of 7,000 or 8,000 women of London, and of men disguised as women, attempted to seize her and she would have fallen a victim to their anger had she not escaped by crossing the river.'

Carlo Capello, the Ambassador, added for the information of the Doge: 'My lady Anne is not the most beautiful in the world; her form is irregular and flat; her flesh has a swarthy tinge; her neck is long and her mouth large; it is generally reported that she has borne a son to the King, who died soon after its birth.'

The information was false, but it was a rumour that might have been expected and, in her desperation, Anne was on the point of succumbing to the King, partly as the only way of holding him, partly as a defence against her own thwarted sexuality.

She was surrounded by her brother George's set—Francis Weston and William Bryerton, who had both been the King's pages and were now, in their early twenties, Gentlemen of the Privy Chamber; Harry Norreys, Keeper of the Privy Purse and one of Henry's favourite courtiers; and Thomas Wyatt, the poet, who was the first to introduce the sonnet into English verse and who, more pertinently, made no secret that he was in love with Anne. In, of course, a platonic manner and recognising the claims of royalty:

> Graven with diamonds, in letters plain
> There is written, her fair neck about
> '*Noli me tangere*, for Caesar's I am
> And wild for to hold, though I seem tame'.

So he had ended one of his sonnets. It was permitted courtliness. Even Henry approved. But there was something more than courtliness in another poem:

> Since that so oft you have made me to wake
>   In plaint and tears, and in right piteous case,
> Displease you not if force do now me make
>   To break your sleep, crying 'Alas! Alas!'
>
> It is the last trouble that you shall have
>   Of me, Madame, to hear my last complaint;
> Pity at last your poor unhappy slave,
>   For in despair, alas, I faint, I faint.

And some of the courtiers wondered who was the real subject of the stanza in Wyatt's poem, *Remembrance*:

> Thanked by Fortune it hath been otherwise
>   Twenty times better; but once, in special,
> In thin array, after a pleasant guise,
>   When her loose gown from her shoulders did fall,
>   And she caught me in her arms, long and small,
> Therewith all sweetly did me kiss
> And softly said, 'Dear heart, how like you this?'

Anne was not, in fact, attracted by Wyatt, whose wooing of her had started in the days when she first gave her heart to Henry Percy, and Henry Tudor had not yet come upon the scene. But she was flattered by him and enjoyed his company; as she enjoyed Francis Weston's and his skill at cards. Francis was usually her partner at *PopeJoan* and they won money regularly from Henry—£9 6s. 8d. on one April day this year,

£20 the next day and £18 13s. 4d. the next. (On the fourth day the King decided to play Anne a single-handed game and lost £11 13s. 4d.) As she enjoyed Harry Norreys' rivalry at bowls (she lost £12 7s. 6d. to him, but she got the King to pay it). As she enjoyed . . .

She recognised that, in her mannered flirtation with the young men, in which she indulged to keep Henry's jealousy at a suitable pitch as much as for any other reason, there was some slight element of danger. But in the case of Mark Smeaton, the danger was intense.

Mark Smeaton was her dancing-man and musician. His father was a carpenter, his mother a seamstress, but the beauty of his face and the elegance of his carriage suggested that he was not meant for a life of manual toil and would make his way better at court. He had soon become a general favourite and during the last three years as many as forty grants had been made to him of shirts, hose, shoes, buskins, boots and money.

When the King and Anne were on their latest hunting expedition, in the New Forest, they lay the night at Winchester, Anne in apartments above the King's. She excused herself from the hunt next day and when Henry had departed she, still in bed, sent for Smeaton, explaining that she wanted him to play while her ladies danced. By the glance that passed between them, he knew exactly what she wanted; but, even had he been willing, there was no opportunity.

Back in London, there was even less, yet she realised that it was only circumstances which prevented it. Mark Smeaton began to fill all her thoughts. It was to him that she would have used Tom Wyatt's words: 'Dear heart, how like you this?' Mark's obvious misery, increased by being 'a low-born servant' among the young nobility who surrounded her, told her that he reciprocated her feelings. She knew that despite all dangers she would be driven to find a way to him unless someone could satisfy her.

So she capitulated to 'Caesar'.

Henry celebrated the occasion by creating her the first female peer that England had known, the Lady Marquis of Pembroke —the title of his great-uncle, Jasper Tudor—and prepared to take her to France with him on an official visit.

She was satisfied that the marriage would take place immediately on their return. Warham had at last died and Henry, at Anne's suggestion, had appointed as his successor as Archbishop of Canterbury Dr. Thomas Cranmer who was at the moment at Mantua. He had been summoned home to be consecrated and, as his first action, to marry Henry to Anne, whatever the Pope might decide. There would be no failure this time. The one thing that could be relied on in all circumstances was that Dr. Cranmer would do whatever the King ordered.

The Queen had retired to Ampthill, a quiet manor in Bedfordshire, and, on Chapuy's suggestion, decided to write herself to her nephew, Charles. The Emperor was in Vienna, leading the Christian defence against the Turks under the Sultan Suleiman the Great, who had announced that he would turn the spire of St. Stephen's Cathedral in Vienna into the most lovely minaret in all Islam and have the faith of Mohammed proclaimed from the top of it.

'Though I know that you are engaged in grave and important Turkish affairs,' she wrote, 'I cannot cease to importune you about my own, in which almost equal offence is being offered to God. I see no difference between what these people are attempting here and what the enemy of our Faith aims at where you are. There are many signs of wickedness being meditated here. New books are being printed daily full of lies and blasphemies against our Holy Faith. These people will stop at nothing, now, to have the suit determined in England. The prospective interview between the kings, the companion the King now takes everywhere with him and the authority and place he allows her have caused great scandal and widespread fear of impending calamity. Knowing the fears of my people,

I am compelled by my conscience to resist, trusting in God and Your Majesty, and begging you to urge the Pope to pronounce sentence at once.'

She was still writing the letter when the Duke of Norfolk arrived with a message from the King. His Highness required her to lend him her jewels. For what reason? So that the Lady Marquis of Pembroke could wear them in France.

'Have you a written order?' asked the Queen.

Norfolk admitted that he had not.

'Then you must procure one. I find it difficult to believe that my husband has so far taken leave of his senses. It is, too, against my conscience to lend my jewels to adorn a person who is the scandal of Christendom and a disgrace to the King who dares to take her to such a meeting. However, if you return with my husband's written request, I will obey him in this, as I do in all things.'

Norfolk returned with it and she gave him all the jewels she had. But in the interim between his leaving and coming again she added to her letter to the Emperor a last sentence: 'What goes on here is so ugly and touches so nearly the honour of my lord, the King, that I cannot bear to write it.'

Though Princess Mary was forbidden to visit her mother, Margaret Pole saw no reason why she herself should refrain from going to Ampthill if the Queen needed her. She went quite openly and was prepared to argue with Henry should he question it. On this occasion she went uninvited by Catherine merely to offer her consolation. The affair of the jewels had scandalised even the King's partisans at court and Margaret thought it might hearten the Queen to know it.

They discussed the impending French journey, on which Montagu was in attendance in his capacity as a peer of the realm.

'I wish,' said Catherine, 'he could let us know what is afoot there.'

'That is impossible, but we have made arrangements that you shall know what can be found out.'

'How?'

'Geoffrey will go, too, disguised as one of his brother's servants and he will send news back to me.'

It had been Geoffrey's idea and Montagu had allowed it rather as the indulgence of a somewhat childish prank than as a serious contribution to policy. The twelve years which separated him from his brother had always had the effect of making him regard Geoffrey as a boy to be advised and protected rather than as a responsible adult, especially as he was prone to devise improbabilities. On this occasion, both brothers felt a slight sense of guilt about Reynold. Now that he was in Italy they could allow themselves to think how useful he could be if he were in England. He had, of course, been far too uncompromising. On the other hand, as things seemed to be shaping, a choice would be forced on everyone before long. In the meantime, it was advisable to serve both sides as far as it was possible.

When the expedition arrived in Calais after a smooth October crossing, Geoffrey remained in Montagu's apartment all day and, after dark, stole out, disguised by a false beard and a patch over his left eye, to collect what gossip he could.

Most of the gossip concerned Anne and whether she would or would not go to Boulogne. The plan of the visit was that Henry should first be entertained by Francis in Boulogne and then the hospitality returned by Henry in Calais. But there was an immediate hitch. What lady was to receive the Lady Marquis of Pembroke? The Queen of France obviously could not. She was Francis's second wife, whom he had just married, and as she was the Emperor's sister, Francis could explain her non-appearance as a consideration of his guest. He was sure that the mere sight of a Spanish dress, especially when worn by Catherine's niece, would be as unwelcome as the devil to Henry. Instead of his queen, his hostess would be his sister, Marguerite of Navarre. Would Henry approve of this?

Henry would, but the formidable Margot—poet, romanticist, humanist, patroness of the late Renaissance and one of the great women of Christendom—would not. She told her brother that she had little inclination to meet the King of England and none at all to meet his whore, and refused to leave Paris.

In desperation, Francis then suggested the Duchess of Vendôme whose reputation was such that even Anne considered it an insult and declined to visit Boulogne at all. The absence of women facilitated the business between the men, and Francis, who had arranged for his son, Henry, to marry the Pope's niece, Catherine de' Medici, promised, when he saw Clement at the betrothal ceremony in a week or two, to use all his influence to persuade the Pope to take the King of England's side in the still unsettled nullity suit.

The lack of junketings at Boulogne was more than made up for when Francis and his suite came to Calais. Here, according to an onlooker, the Banqueting Hall 'was hung with tissue raised with silver and framed with cloth of silver raised with gold. The seams of the same were covered with broad wreaths of goldsmiths' work, full of stones and pearls. In this chamber was a cupboard of seven stages high, all plate of gold. Besides that, there hung ten branches of silver-gilt and ten branches all-white silver, every branch hanging by a long chain of the same sort, bearing two lights of wax. The French King was served three courses, dressed after the French fashion; and the King of England had like courses after the English fashion. The first course of every kind was forty dishes, the second sixty, the third eighty, which were costly and pleasant.

'After supper on the Sunday evening came in the Lady Marquis of Pembroke, with seven ladies in masquing apparel of strange fashion, made of cloth of gold slashed with crimson tinsel satin, puffed with cloth of silver and knit with laces of gold. These ladies were led into the state chamber by four damsels dressed in crimson satin, with tabards of fine cypress. Then the Lady Marquis took the French King and every lady took a lord. In dancing, King Henry removed the ladies' visors so that their beauties were shown.'

When the dancers unmasked, Francis discovered to his admirably pretended surprise that he had been dancing with one he had known as Maid of Honour to his first queen. Next morning he sent her a jewel worth 15,000 crowns to memorialise the occasion.

On the last day of October, the two kings rode through the gate of Calais to French ground where they dismounted, joined hands, swore eternal friendship, kissed each other and so parted. But the weather was so tempestuous and the Channel crossing so dangerous that the English party could not leave for a fortnight, which Henry and Anne treated as a rehearsal for their honeymoon.

They landed at Dover on November 14 and, as soon as possible, were secretly married.[1]

---

[1] The time and place of the marriage are still a matter of speculation. It was probably in the December of 1532, though it may have been as late as January 25, 1533. Anne's child was born on September 7, 1533.

10

The Beginning of the Terror

Cromwell had well pondered that section of Machiavelli's book which discussed 'whether it is better to be loved than feared'. His own experiences in his various fields of action made him agree wholeheartedly that 'it is much safer to be feared than loved; for it may be said of men in general that they are ungrateful, volatile, dissemblers, anxious to avoid danger, and covetous of gain. They have less scruple in offending one who makes himself loved than one who makes himself feared; for love is held by a chain of obligation which, men being selfish, is broken whenever it serves their purpose; but fear is maintained by a dread of punishment which never fails.'

As a first step, Cromwell had already started to create a system of espionage such as the country had never known. In every place were planted his agents, carefully selected from his servants and their acquaintances; from the human flotsam he had encountered in his business of usury; from the weaker clients he had met in his legal practice; from malicious or apostate monks who came his way during his work on Wolsey's dissolved monasteries; from ambitious or extravagant servants in great men's houses; from young men anxious for his favour and old men frightened of his power.

He sat spider-like at the centre of the web and at a twitch

knew that in a Worcestershire village an old man of eighty, trudging home from the market in the rain, had asserted that there had never been good weather since the 'King's business' started; that in a Sussex churchyard after Mass the vicar had remarked to one of his parishioners that the King's counsellors made him drunk before asking his signature for the Acts of Parliament; that a spinster in Suffolk had said that the King ought not to marry one of his subjects and that her friend had called Anne Boleyn 'a goggle-eyed whore'. Simple countryfolk were everywhere hauled before the local magistrates so that the terror was ubiquitous. No one knew who Cromwell's spies were or against whom the next accusation would be made.

One of his agents was Gervaise Tyndale, who was master of the free school at Grantham. He was an earnest follower of his more famous kinsman, William Tyndale, and when, on All Souls' Day, a visiting preacher, in a sermon on Purgatory, suggested that the fire of Purgatory was to earthly fire as a man was to a painting of a man, and made the usual pleas for the congregation to aid their dead relatives to escape it by contributing liberally to the collection, Gervase Tyndale rose in his place in church and contradicted him on his theology.

The argument was the classic one which, fifteen years earlier, Luther had had with Tetzel[1] and the preacher was undoubtedly in the wrong in not following the Church's correction of Tetzel's errors. Possibly he did not know it; certainly the congregation did not and they rallied round the preacher, who called Tyndale a Saxon heretic, and urged them to take their children away from the free school lest their master should infect them with his opinions.

The young of Grantham were sent instead to the Franciscans and Tyndale, his occupation gone, had to write to Cromwell for money, some of which he intended to spend in discovering whether the friars were practising necromancy.

Cromwell's greater interest at the moment, however, was in

[1] See 'The Marriage made in Blood' p. 200 et seq.

Gervaise's kinsman. William, who was somewhere on the Continent and whom three separate letters, sent to three different places, had so far failed to find. Cromwell was urgent that he should come home to England.

William Tyndale, after a scholastic career at both Oxford (where he just overlapped Reginald Pole) and Cambridge, had been ordained and spent the early 1520s as a parish priest in the neighbourhood of Bristol. While at Cambridge, he had become one of the 'White Horse set'—the left-wing theological group who met at the White Horse Inn and discussed the new Lutheran and Zwinglian doctrines now in Germany—and in his preaching he so far propagated the new ideas that he was delated to the Bishop of Worcester on the charge of heresy. He received, however, no censure from the ecclesiastical enquiry and was allowed to leave it without giving any undertaking to refrain from expounding his views.

Nevertheless the experience embittered him and as an antidote to what he considered the corruption of the clergy he decided to produce an annotated New Testament in English.

The existence of a vernacular version of the Bible, accessible to everyone, was the pivot of his doctrine, which was that whatever a man's study of the Bible taught him was in fact God's message to his soul. Nothing else mattered. Whoever 'believed' was 'saved'. Emotion was an unfailing guide. 'Where is the Spirit, there is feeling; the Spirit maketh us feel all things.' Salvation was by 'faith' alone.

Thus there was no need for the hierarchical system or for the Sacraments. The Pope was 'that great idol, the whore of Babylon, antichrist of Rome': the Mass was a matter of 'nodding, becking, mewing, as it were apes' play'. Those who still believed the traditional faith and practice were 'beasts, without the seal of the Spirit of God; but sealed with the Mark of the Beast and cankered consciences'.

In order that the simple reader of his New Testament, in

search of salvation, should not be misled, Tyndale had to make mistranslation after mistranslation. Thus he rendered the word that should have been 'priest' as 'elder' and 'church' as 'congregation' and noted: 'By a priest, then, in the New Testament, understand nothing but an elder to teach the younger' and explained that the two sacraments which Christ ordained, baptism and holy communion, were 'nothing but the preaching of Christ's promises'.

He prefaced the Beatitudes with a warning note, lest any reader should suppose that good works availed anything: 'All these deeds here rehearsed, as to nourish peace, to show mercy, to suffer persecution and so forth, make not a man happy and blessed, neither deserve reward of heaven; but declare and testify that we are happy and blessed and certify us in our hearts that the Holy Ghost is in us.'

On the verse: 'How shall I curse whom God curseth not?,' he noted: 'The Pope can tell how!': to 'Neither bring the hire of a whore nor the price of a dog into the house of the Lord thy God', he added the explanation: 'The Pope will take tribute of them yet and bishops and abbots desire no better tenants'; he defined a formal blessing: 'To bless a man's neighbour is to pray for him and wish him good, not to wag two fingers over him'. The 'blind guides' were the heathen priesthood 'and of these priests of idols did our compassing ivytrees learn to creep up little by little and to compass the great trees of the world with hypocrisy and to thrust the roots of idolatrous superstition into them and to suck the juice out of them'. The great corpus of theological learning which St. Thomas Aquinas had given to the Church by his revival of Aristotelianism was 'false glosses to confirm Aristotle's false learning'.

It was not altogether surprising that when Tyndale's annotated translation was discovered in Cologne—where he had settled to finish it after a visit to Luther at Wittenberg—the Catholic authorities denounced him as a heretic and warned Wolsey and Warham to beware of the 6,000 copies on their way to England.

Warham bought up as many as he could and burnt them before they arrived and the King, as Defender of the Faith, strove to arrest the heresy at its source—the printing-presses of the Low Countries—by diplomatic requests to the Emperor to take measures against the printers and to arrest Tyndale. The translator, however, fled to Marburg and the protection of Philip, the twenty-two year old Landgrave of Hesse, who was living bigamously by permission of the Pope-free Luther and 'had gone reforming like a Turk or a Tartar' and given the inhabitants of his territory the choice 'either to confess Christ or to emigrate'.

Henry, having denounced Tyndale as 'a perverter of God's word', entrusted the task of replying to him to Sir Thomas More whose *Dialogue concerning Heresies* and *Confutation of Tyndale* stated, though somewhat overlengthily, the Church's case. To have more time to defend the Faith satisfactorily, More resigned the Lord Chancellorship. As he himself put it, 'having tasted plentifully of this world's pursuits, the thing which he had wished for from a boy that he might enjoy some of his last years free and have leisure to meditate on his future immortality, that thing at last, by the incomparable kindness of his most indulgent King, having resigned his honours, he hath obtained'.

To Cromwell, who had no interest in theology and no understanding of religion, the controversy was of peripheral interest. Distinctions between one creed and another affected him only in so far as they were politically useful. He would conform to expected usage but he was not touched by either Catholicism or Lutheranism. They were merely pieces in his great game. This indifference led him to make one of his few mistakes. He assumed that because Tyndale was against the Pope and because Henry was also, for the moment, against the Pope, the two protesters could be yoked in double harness.

After his edition of the New Testament, Tyndale had written *The Obedience of a Christian Man and how Christian Rulers ought to Govern* which, even better than Marsiglio, provided a popular apologia for the Supremacy of the King.

The book was constructed on the basic thought that the greatest scandal in Christendom was that kings should be, in certain respects, subject to prelates. Nothing had so lowered royal prestige in the eyes of subjects as the general knowledge that kings, too, are subject to the Church. This was 'a shame above all shames and a monstrous thing'. Churchmen, by God's plan as revealed in the New Testament (or, as More described it, ' "Tyndale's Testament", for so had Tyndale changed the New Testament from the good and wholesome doctrine of Christ'), were as completely subject to the King as were the laity. Therefore 'let Kings rule their realms themselves with the help of lay men'; and let the King's first care be to repudiate the oaths he has sworn to protect the liberties of the Church. Separate ecclesiastical jurisdiction must be abolished. 'One King, one law in the realm; no class of men exempt from the temporal sword, no law except the law of the land, is God's ordinance in every realm.'

This was exactly what Cromwell needed for carrying through the Royal Supremacy, as a small pamphlet by one of Tyndales disciples calling on the King to confiscate the monasteries and to flog the monks at the cart's tail as vagabonds unless they found honest work exactly suited the policy by which he intended as soon as possible to implement his promise to make Henry the richest king in Christendom.

In these circumstances Cromwell decided that Tyndale ought to return to England to be at hand as adviser and propagandist. Efforts at finding him were at last successful and Tyndale wrote to Henry, enclosing a manuscript of his new book against Sir Thomas More, called *The Answer*.

The result was not what Cromwell had hoped. Henry, in a towering rage, said that *The Answer* was 'filled with seditious, slanderous lies and fantastical opinions, shewing neither learning nor truth'. He said that Tyndale 'lacked grace, learning, virtue, discretion and every other good quality' and wondered how Cromwell could think of 'favouring the evil doctrine of so malicious and evil a person' or could suggest that he should come to England 'to seduce, deceive and disquiet the people of this realm and sow sedition among them'. Henry continued, in a torrent which Cromwell was at least wise enough to make no attempt to stem, that, 'seeing the malicious, perverse, uncharitable and obdurate mind and disposition of Tyndale, he rejoiced that he was out of the country' and, should he be temerarious enough to return, he would be dealt with as he deserved.

Cromwell had seriously underestimated the King's real interest in theology and his knowledge and use of it which had gained for him the Papal title of *Defender of the Faith*. Nor had Cromwell allowed for Henry's present attitude to the Church. The King then, and to the end of his life, thought of himself as a devout and pious Catholic and, apart from the matter of the Papal supremacy—which he regarded as political and constitutional, rather than religious—he was in fact so. As Lutheranism grew stronger in his realm, so did his horror of it. His practical grievance against the Pope was largely justified by Clement's shifty, weak-willed procrastination. His perception that the Church was in urgent need of reform was shared, among others, by Erasmus, More and Pole. He was, comprehensibly, myopic about Anne Boleyn's relevance to the larger issues; but he was keen-sighted enough immediately to recognise the role of Tyndale. And, in terms which could not be misunderstood, he left Cromwell in no doubt about his feelings.

Cromwell bowed to the storm and wrote hurriedly to his agent in the Low Countries who had found Tyndale for him: 'For the love of God, not only utterly forsake, leave and withdraw your affection from Tyndale and all his sect, but as far as you can, persuade his followers to change their erroneous opinions. In doing this you will not only highly please Almighty God, but will also deserve the high thanks of the King's Royal Majesty, who will not forget your labours on that behalf.'

In so far as his mistake had a little lessened his influence with the King, Cromwell considered it of some importance to take steps to decrease also, if possible, the standing of the Catholic and aristocratic opposition to him, as represented by the Bishop of Rochester, Sir Thomas More, the Marquis and Marchioness of Exeter and the Countess of Salisbury. For this purpose he thought that an investigation into the activities of the 'Nun of Kent' might prove fruitful.

Elizabeth Barton, who was now twenty-six, had been a maid-servant in the parish of Aldington in Romney Marsh—a parish of which Erasmus was the absentee incumbent and was paid a yearly pension of £20 by the acting parish priest, Richard Masters. When she was nineteen, Elizabeth Barton had a serious illness which lasted for some months. During it she started to have trances and make prophecies, uttering warnings against sin and vice. She had a vision of Our Lady who foretold her cure. When she was well again, the visions, trances and prophecies continued and her master and her neighbours were at a loss to know whether she was inspired by God or an instrument of Satan. Father Masters, watching her carefully and noting both the content of her utterances and the notable piety of her life, had inclined to the opinion that it was God, but suggested that the whole matter should be investigated by a more competent authority than himself. The Archbishop of Canterbury, Warham, had appointed two monks of Canterbury, one of whom, Dr. Edward Bocking, was a scholar and an administrator, to examine Elizabeth. Their conclusion was favourable and the young woman took up residence with the Benedictine nuns at St. Sepulchre's in Canterbury, with Dr. Bocking as her confessor and spiritual director.

Her fame spread, not only throughout Kent but further afield. Her visions were widely discussed and she was thronged with visitors asking her advice. She visited the Brigittines at Syon and the Carthusians at Sheen—it was there that Reginald

Pole and his mother had seen her, though neither was particularly impressed by her—and she travelled abroad as far as Calais, where she was during the visit of the King and Anne.

When, on that November 14, 1532, the weather at last allowed Henry and Anne to return to England, they found the Nun of Kent—as Elizabeth Barton was now generally called, except by her more fanatical adherents who preferred 'The Holy Maid of Kent' and likened her to Joan of Arc obeying her Voices—already at Canterbury, demanding to see the King when the royal company arrived there for the night.

She told Henry that an angel had commanded her to speak to him and bid him amend his life. If he married Anne Boleyn, the vengeance of God would plague him and he 'should not longer be king of this realm' but 'should die a villain's death' within six or seven months after the marriage. She had—though she did not tell him this—actually seen in a vision the particular place in Hell prepared for him.

Henry took no notice of the warning but was interested in the effect the Nun was having on the common people of the countryside and agreed with Cromwell that, whatever might have been the validity of her earlier spiritual visions, her present excursion into politics was worth rigid investigation, more particularly since her confessor was known to be a supporter of the Queen. If Cromwell could somehow implicate Catherine in the Nun's treasonable ravings, it would be a triumph indeed.

It would be as well, however, to get Henry's marriage with Anne and her coronation over before taking any definite steps.

Anne, having endured an additional and inescapable fortnight with Henry in Calais, found herself more in love with Mark Smeaton than ever. Fortunately, there was now one risk the less in indulging it. As Smeaton refused to make the first move, she took into her confidence an old waiting-woman named Margaret, who lay at night in the antechamber of her room, between it and the gallery where, within hearing, the rest of Anne's ladies slept.

In this antechamber there was a cupboard where sweetmeats, candied fruits and preserves were kept. Here, one night, Margaret concealed Smeaton. When all was quiet Anne called out: 'Margaret, bring me a little marmalade' and the waiting-woman, leading Smeaton by the hand, said: 'Here is the marmalade, my lady.' Then Anne, so that the ladies in the gallery could hear as they had heard the rest of the exchange, called out: 'Go along now: go to bed!'

At the end of the following February, the court was treated to a delicious tit-bit of scandal. As the courtiers were waiting in the gallery outside Anne's apartments, she suddenly appeared, looked round and, seeing Sir Thomas Wyatt there, went over to him and almost hysterically told him 'that for the last three days she had had such an incredible fierce desire to eat apples as she had never felt before, and that the King had said to her that it was a sign that she was with child'.

Wyatt, embarrassed, merely stared at her, which provoked her to loud laughter and the remark: 'But it is not so at all; it is not so!'

There was an uncomfortable silence and, with another burst of wild laughter, she went back into her room, leaving the courtiers 'abashed and uneasy'.

No one quite knew what to make of it. Wyatt affected to believe that it was her way of telling him that he must hence-forth change his attitude of courtly gallantry to her and he wrote his last poem to her:

Forget not, oh! forget not this,
How long ago hath been and is
The love that never meant amiss.
Forget not yet!

No one believed Anne's denial of her pregnancy, though all

thought it a strange way to announce it. The King was not pleased.

The over-riding consideration was now speed. It was essential that the child should be born in legitimate wedlock. This involved not only a public marriage but the freeing of Henry from Catherine. Cranmer, as the properly consecrated Archbishop of Canterbury sanctioned by the Pope, was the indispensable agent in the matter. On March 30, Passion Sunday, he was so consecrated and avoided the difficulty which might arise from his oath of spiritual obedience to the Pope (which was a necessity if he was to obtain the pallium) by swearing the day before, before witnesses, that his public oath at his consecration would be a matter of form only and therefore invalid. 'Other perjurers,' as Reginald Pole was to tell him later, 'are accustomed to break their oath after they have sworn. You broke yours before.'

On Easter Eve, Cranmer openly married Henry and Anne. She went to the ceremony as Queen and a fortnight later letters were sent out summoning all the notables to her coronation on June 1.

In the meantime, Henry must be released from Catherine. 'It was thought convenient by the King,' Cranmer reported in a letter to a friend, 'that I should repair unto Dunstable, which is within four miles from Ampthill, where the Lady Catherine keepeth her house, there to call her before me to hear the final sentence in the matter. Notwithstanding, she would not at all obey thereunto.'

With considerable relief that the Queen ignored his summons —for her appearance would have prolonged the proceedings far beyond the acceptable limit—Cranmer pronounced her contumacious and in her absence declared her marriage to Henry null and void from the beginning on the grounds that her marriage to Arthur had been consummated and that, therefore, no Pope could dispense an impediment which was imposed by the law of God. Four days later the Archbishop made another announcement. He declared that he had fully investigated the situation as it affected the marriage of the King and the Lady Marquis of Pembroke and had found it good and valid. He was only just in time. It was May 28.

Anne's coronation, on June 1, was, in spite of the enormous expenditure to make it as splendid as possible, in some ways a disappointment to her. For one thing, her six-months' pregnancy was a drawback. For another, Henry's attempt to give her special public honour by ordering the City authorities to set everywhere among the decorations the letters HA was unkindly distorted by the London crowd into 'Ha! Ha! Ha!' When Henry asked her how she had enjoyed the procession, she told him: 'I liked the city well enough, but I saw a great many caps on heads and heard but few tongues.' The majority of ordinary people, even if they were not all bold enough to shout as one or two did: 'God save Queen Catherine, our own righteous Queen', remained stolidly silent and refused to uncover as Anne passed and she became exasperated enough to order her jester to shout at them: 'You must have the scurvy, that you are so afraid to show your heads.' There could be no doubt that on the whole they agreed with the man who remarked to his neighbour (who, unfortunately for him, was one of Cromwell's spies): 'I am not such a fool, nor such a sinner neither, as ever to take that whore Nan Bullen to be Queen.'

The greatest insult, however, as Anne saw it, was that the late Lord Chancellor, Sir Thomas More, refused, for good reasons of his own, to attend the coronation and spent the day quietly in his old clothes in his garden at Chelsea.

In Rome, Clement moved with unaccustomed—and un-expected—celerity. Within a month of Anne's coronation, he quashed the Dunstable decree and excommunicated Cranmer for having given it; he ordered Henry to leave Anne and return to Catherine and threatened that if he had not done so by the beginning of September, before the child was born, the King would be excommunicated also. The Pope also broke off normal diplomatic relations by withdrawing the Nuncio.

Cromwell decided that the time for action had arrived. The day after the arrival of the Pope's letters he ordered the arrest of the Nun of Kent and her closest associates and ordered trained and pitiless inquisitors to subject them to the most thorough examinations. Cranmer was put in official charge of the investigation and was left under no illusion as to what was required—the implication of any great personages who had consulted the Nun.

The Archbishop handled it in his own way. He asked the Prioress of St. Sepulchre's 'to repair to me at my manor of Otteford and bring with you your Nun'. When they arrived, he was at his most charming and sympathetic and allowed the Nun to go where she wished for a week in order that a new trance might throw light upon matters which the last had left uncertain. But, as Cromwell's agent noted: 'My lord doth but dally with her, as if he did believe her every word.'

Cromwell himself took a quicker and more direct way. Of two of the Friars Observant which his spies had arrested at Greenwich, he wrote to the King: 'It is undoubted that they would confess some great matter if they might be examined as they ought to be, that is to say, by torture.'

The terror had begun.

II

The Persecution of Princess Mary

The Princess Mary was now seventeen-and-a-half. With her father's reddish hair and her mother's hazel eyes, a fresh complexion and full red lips, she was considered to be more than moderately pretty, even when the usual flattery due to princesses was allowed for. She was indeed small and thin and, despite all Margaret Pole's training, tended to rush about rather than to move elegantly. But her urgent gait no more detracted from regality than did her mother's bustling movement. She had inherited Catherine's delicate constitution and Henry's loud, deep voice and laugh. Devoutly religious and an inveterate gambler; an intellectual prodigy with a passion for fine clothes and jewels; a brilliant musician with an excessive addiction to horse-riding, she exhibited rather than reconciled opposites. And, once she had attained the age of puberty, the ordinary comfort of life was dominated by what she was to come to call her 'old guest'—menstrual irregularity, accompanied by great pain.

She was still officially affianced to Francis I's son, though there was not great insistence on it. She still had her own household, consisting of 162 persons, headed by the Countess of Salisbury as Governess and the septuagenarian Lord Hussey, who had once been Comptroller of the Household of her grandfather, Henry VII, as her Chamberlain. Her seat was at

Newhall, one of the Royal residences, in Essex. But it was clear to everyone—and particularly to Margaret Pole—that this state of affairs would not be allowed to continue long after Anne Boleyn's coronation. For one thing, Anne had transferred to Mary that exclusive and hysterical hatred which once she had directed against Wolsey.

When Mary asked permission to visit the King, Chapuys noted that 'it has been refused to gratify the Lady, who hates her more than she hates the Queen. When the King praised her, the Lady was very angry and began to vituperate the Princess very strangely'. The last time the King had seen his daughter was just before the visit to France when, in his hunting, he happened to meet her walking in the country. Standing to talk among the stubble of a reaped field, he had just time to ask her how she was and to say that he would soon see her more often, when he noticed two of Anne Boleyn's servants approaching rapidly to within earshot and had ridden quickly away, leaving Mary disconsolate in the pale sunshine.

By circumstances forced more and more on the side of the mother whom she was now forbidden to see, Mary still loved her father and her one prayed-for ambition was, even at this last hour, to reconcile them. But when she talked of this to her Governess, Margaret had little comfort for her. Matters had gone too far.

The situation was made clear enough when, six weeks after Anne's coronation, the King sent to demand Mary's jewels. Lord Hussey denied ever having seen any jewels except those which the Princess wore.

The Countess of Salisbury was asked for an inventory. No inventory could be found.

'The most that I could get my Lady to do,' wrote Hussey to Cromwell, 'was to bring forth the jewels and set her hand to the inventory of them I then had made.'

'Will you not now, my Lady,' asked Hussey, 'surrender them to the King's messenger?'

'Neither now nor at any time,' retorted Margaret, 'until I have the King's own request under his hand and seal.'

The King's order duly arrived and was obeyed, only to be followed by another demanding the surrender of the Princess's plate. On this, the Countess was prepared to make a stand. She could postpone the return of the jewels for as long as possible, but, because the Queen had already obeyed the King in a similar demand, she could not ultimately refuse them. The plate, however, was another matter. She referred the royal messenger to the Clerk of the Princess's Jewel House. He denied ever having seen any plate. The Countess then explained, with a brusqueness which admitted of no argument, that because of the Princess's illnesses all the plate was always in use and that, if the King elected to demand its return, he would have to supply an equal amount to replace it. The matter was dropped.

One other demand was made which, though it was addressed to the Queen, was aimed at the Princess. The 'triumphal cloth' which Catherine had brought with her when she came as a bride from Spain and in which she had wrapped all her children at baptism—the cloth in which Margaret Pole had carried Princess Mary to the font—was required for Anne Boleyn's child, now shortly to be born. Catherine's reply was short and decisive: 'It is not pleasing to God that I should be so ill-advised as to grant any favour so horrible and abominable.'

Catherine, at Ampthill, continued to maintain her position. When, that same July, the King sent a deputation reluctantly headed by her old friend and Chamberlain, Lord Mountjoy, to explain that she was now 'Princess Dowager', she retorted that she was, and that she intended to be addressed as, Queen and added: 'The King may do in his realm by his royal power what he will, but my matter depends not on the universities nor on the realm, but in the court of Rome, before the Pope, whom I account God's Vicar and judge on earth.'

When, at last, the Pope pronounced in her favour and

threatened Henry with excommunication, she announced that many souls now in danger of perdition would be saved and that her daughter's rights would be established. But she was in no doubt of the possible cost to herself. 'I am told,' she said, 'that the next parliament is to decide whether I am to suffer martyrdom. If it is to be so, I hope it may be a meritorious act. I am not afraid, for there is no punishment from God except for neglected duty.'

Cromwell, in reluctant admiration, commented: 'Nature wronged the Queen in not making her a man; but for her sex she would have surpassed all the heroes of history.' And Henry was under no illusions as to what might happen if his wife should decide to implement the excommunication and endeavour to depose him in favour of Princess Mary: 'The lady Catherine is a proud, stubborn woman of very high courage,' he told the Council. 'If she took it into her head to take her daughter's part, she could quite easily take the field, muster a great array and wage against me a war as fierce as any her mother Isabella ever waged in Spain.'

In the circumstances, he thought it wise to remove Catherine to another house. She was ordered to leave Ampthill and take up her residence at Buckden, in the sparsely inhabited country on the edge of the great fens, where the east winds and the marsh mists might contribute to the decline of her spirit if not of her life. As she travelled northward, she found the entire way lined with people of every kind and class shouting encouragement and proclaiming that they were ready to live and die in her service. It was a spontaneous demonstration of loyalty which moved Catherine to tears and her gaolers to considerable unease. When it was reported to the King, he decided that, as soon as convenient, she must be moved again and began to consider the possibilities of a lonely, decaying house, notably malarial, in the midst of the Cambridge fens, which, surrounded by marshes and ponds, was accessible only by a single road which, in parts, was a mere causeway.

At the moment, however, there were more important things to consider. Anne Boleyn was lying-in at Greenwich.

One of the richest beds in the royal treasury, literally worth a king's ransom, had been placed in the Chamber of the Virgins at Greenwich, so called because it was hung with tapestries illustrating the parable of the wise and the foolish virgins. Here the heir of England was to be born. No one doubted that it would be a boy and its name, Edward, had been chosen in advance. Doctors and astrologers agreed on the masculinity and in the letters prepared to announce the nativity the word 'prince' was used.

Unfortunately, it had to be altered to 'princess'. The child to whom Anne gave birth after long and dangerous travail on the afternoon of September 7—the eve of the Nativity of Our Lady—was a girl. Anne tried to make light of it by saying that the room at last deserved its name 'for a virgin is now born in it on the vigil of that auspicious day when the Church commemorates the nativity of the Virgin Mary'.

But she knew her danger. Unless she could bear a son, her position was perilous. She had indeed taken the precaution of arranging for Richmond to marry her cousin, Mary Howard, Norfolk's daughter, so that, if the King should decide to legitimise his only son and name him his heir, the family connection would be unimpaired; but this hardly safeguarded her own position. Henry was already tired of her and was considering the charms of one of her ladies-in-waiting, the twenty-four-year-old Jane Seymour. When Anne, who knew every move of that particular game, protested, the King told her sharply that she must learn to close her eyes as her betters had done before her. For several days he pointedly refused to speak to her.

Mary, who had been ordered by the King to attend the birth at Greenwich, found herself faced with a new problem. 'She was present,' reported the Venetian Ambassador, 'with the relatives and friends of Anne Boleyn in the lying-in chamber when Lisabetta was born; and there she heard, among the ladies and persons of the court, such scandals relative to the conduct of the mother, as made her declare that she "was sure the infant was not her sister".' What she was sure of, more precisely, was that Elizabeth's father was not King Henry VIII but Mark Smeaton.

The shock of the knowledge was never to leave her. As Elizabeth grew up her resemblance to Smeaton became marked, as Mary was to point out to her friend, Jane Dormer. The Princess would, for the sake of the *convenances*, call the child 'sister', just as she called Richmond 'brother', though Richmond was indeed her half-brother whereas Elizabeth 'was neither her sister nor the daughter of King Henry, but born of an infamous woman who had so greatly outraged the Queen, her mother'. Mary always refused to acknowledge any relationship in blood and twenty-four years later, when she was herself Queen, she was to give her evidence to a specially appointed tribunal about 'that which my conscience holds, as it has held these twenty-four years'—evidence which satisfied the enquirers.[1]

This secret knowledge made even more bitter the open and official insults to which Mary was now subjected. A week after Elizabeth's birth the royal heralds proclaimed in the City to a sullen and silent crowd of Londoners that Elizabeth and not Mary was now Princess of Wales; and when Mary arrived back in Newhall she discovered that her servants' liveries showed patches where her own device had been cut off to be replaced by the King's. Her servants were to be henceforth not her own. Meanwhile Anne was publicly announcing that she intended to make Mary her serving-maid. She added amusedly that 'she might perhaps give her too much dinner on some occasion'. At this threat of poison, the Imperial Ambassador wrote to

[1] For a fuller treatment of the subject see *The Parentage of Queen Elizabeth I* in *Enigmas of History* (1957).

144

Charles V and implored him to take some action to safeguard his aunt and his cousin. The Emperor's protest to Henry was answered by a terse: 'Our daughter, the Lady Mary, we do order and entertain as we think expedient. We think it not meet that any person should prescribe to us how we should order our own daughter, we being her natural father.'

Henry's ordering was to send Lord Hussey to inform Mary that she was no longer Princess of Wales, that her household was to be reduced and that she was to leave Newhall which he required for Anne's brother, George Lord Rochford.

Mary demanded to see the letter and, having read it and found herself described as 'the Lady Mary, the King's daughter' instead of 'the Princess of Wales', she went to her room and wrote to her father: 'I verily trust that Your Grace was not privy to the letter as concerning the leaving out of the title of Princess, as I do not doubt that Your Grace takes me for your lawful daughter, born in true matrimony. If I were to admit the contrary, I should in my conscience run into the displeasure of God, which I hope assuredly that Your Grace would not wish that I should do. In all other things Your Grace shall have me, always, as humble and obedient daughter and handmaid as ever child was to father.'

But Henry was in no mind to allow a seventeen-year-old girl to wreck his elaborate edifice. The implication of 'the Lady Mary, the King's daughter' was, as all Europe knew, that she was illegitimate because Henry's marriage with Catherine was no marriage. The implication of Mary's title as 'Princess of Wales' was that Elizabeth was illegitimate, because Henry's marriage with Anne was no marriage. The entire struggle was epitomised in the terminology.

The King immediately sent a deputation consisting of three earls and a dean to explain to Mary that by her letter 'she had worthily deserved the King's high displeasure and punishment by law, but that, on her conforming to his will, he might incline, of his fatherly pity, to promote her welfare'.

Mary would not conform. She was as insistent that she was 'Princess of Wales', not 'the Lady Mary, the King's daughter' as her mother, isolated at Buckden, was insistent that she was 'the Queen' and not 'the Princess Dowager'.

Both women knew the risk they ran, though it was clearer to Catherine and when she learnt that Cromwell's plans included presenting Henry with a legal excuse for the execution of both herself and Mary, she wrote to her daughter.

'I heard such tidings today, that I perceive, if it be true, that the time is come that Almighty God will prove you. I beseech you to agree to His pleasure with a merry heart. I pray you, good daughter, to offer yourself to Him. Shrive yourself; take heed of His commandments and keep them as near as He will give you grace to do so; for then you are sure armed.'

Regarding Mary's attitude to the King's orders, Catherine counselled her: 'Answer with few words, obeying the King, your father, in everything, saving only that you will not offend God and lose your own soul; and go no farther with learning and disputation in the matter. And, wheresoever and in whatsoever company you shall come, observe the King's commandments. Speak few words and meddle nothing.'

Meanwhile there was the daily round of life. 'I will send you two books in Latin; one shall be *De Vita Christi*[2] with a declaration of the Gospels, and the other the Epistles of St. Jerome that he did write to Paula and Eustochium and in them I trust you shall see good things. And sometimes for your recreation use your virginals and lute, if you have any.'

Catherine had heard that Mary was to be bribed to accept her new title by the promise that, if she did, she would be at once married to the French prince to whom she was affianced. 'But one thing especially I desire you,' the letter continued, 'for the love you owe to God and to me to keep your heart with a chaste mind and your body from all ill and wanton company, not thinking or desiring any husband; neither determine your-

[2] Possibly Thomas à Kempis's *Imitation of Christ*.

146

self to any manner of living till this troublesome time be past.'

As it was Mary's title rather than her own which was now politically important, Catherine warned her that the beginning of the attack would be on her: 'And now you shall begin and by likelihood I shall follow. I set not a rush by it, for when they have done the uttermost they can, then I am sure of the amendment. I pray you recommend me unto my good lady of Salisbury, and pray her to have a good heart; for we never come to the Kingdom of Heaven but by troubles.'

And she signed it:

> 'Your loving mother,
> Catherine the Queen.'

The first blow fell with unexpected suddenness. On December 16 the three-month-old Elizabeth was carried in pomp through London on the way to Hatfield which was to be her residence as Princess of Wales. The next day the Duke of Norfolk waited on Mary with the instruction that she was to make ready at once to attend the Princess of Wales.

'That,' retorted Mary, 'is the title which belongs to me by right and to no one else.'

'I have come here, my lady, not to dispute with you but to see that the King, your father's, commands are obeyed.'

The Countess of Salisbury intervened with: 'It will take the Princess some time to prepare for the journey.'

'I can allow her only half-an-hour.'

'Even I shall take longer than that.'

'You, my lady,' said Norfolk, with relish, 'will not be accompanying her. No arrangements have been made for your entertainment at Hatfield.'

'Then I will go myself and provide the Princess with a household and servants at my own cost.'

'The Lady Mary will have no need of servants. She will be among many.'

'Then I will myself be her servant,' said Margaret.

'Unless you have taken leave of your senses, my lady, you know that the King would not by any means allow it.'

'It is not my senses that are awry in this court, my lord,' said Margaret, biting back a more bitter retort lest it should harm Mary.

To the Princess, as she was getting into the litter provided to take her to Hatfield, she said, speaking in Latin—which she knew Norfolk did not understand: 'Everything that can be done shall be done and God will give you strength.'

At Hatfield, Norfolk asked Mary, before she was shown to the room assigned to her—which was 'the worst in the house'—whether she did not wish he pay her respects to the Princess.

'I know of no other Princess in England but myself,' said Mary, 'the daughter of Madame of Pembroke certainly is none; though if the King chooses to acknowledge her as his daughter, I am willing to call her sister, as I call Richmond brother.'

'Have you at least a message for the King?'

'None,' she said, 'except that the Princess of Wales, his daughter, asks for his blessing.'

Norfolk stared at her. 'It is as much as my head is worth to take that message,' he said, and left her in the charge of his sister, Lady Shelton, who had been instructed by Anne Boleyn to give Mary 'a box on the ears now and then for the cursed bastard she is'.

So Mary, alone, ill and indomitable, passed into the more severe stage of her trials. The two maids she had been allowed to bring with her were dismissed before Christmas and she was given no one but a common chambermaid, specially engaged, who was pointedly ordered not to taste her food, so that she lived daily under the fear of poison.

Reginald Pole, in Italy, learning of these things from his mother's letter, wrote that, in the darkness that was England, Mary 'remained precisely like a feeble light, buffetted by raging winds for its utter extinction, but kept burning and defended by her innocence and lively faith'.

In Europe their names were linked. Chapuys wrote urgently to Charles V: 'The Queen knows of no one in the world whom she would like better to marry the Princess; and nothing is more certain than that, if Your Majesty assisted, the people could declare themselves, especially as there are innumerable good personages who hold that the true title to this Kingdom belongs to the family of the Duke of Clarence. The Lord Reynold's younger brother, Sir Geoffrey Pole, is often with me, and would be oftener, but that I have dissuaded him on account of the danger he might incur. I have said nothing to him about his brother, except that long ago I told him that he ought rather to go begging his bread than come back to this trouble.'

Early in the New Year, Reginald heard from Montagu that the continuous strain had told even on the unbending Countess: 'Mother is with me at Bisham and is very weak.'

12

Friends in Italy

A visitor to the great Benedictine Abbey of San Giorgio Maggiore in Venice, that spring of 1534, calling to enquire after the health of the Lord Abbot, recorded that 'tempted by the pleasant season and the early hour and by the beauty of the spot, I asked them to open the door of their most lovely garden; and one of the brothers having done so, while the singing of the birds filled the heavens, I perceived the Lord Reynold at the entrance of the little wood in earnest talk urging that virtue alone could conquer fortune and make man immortal'.

To Reginald Pole that garden, where every problem of the day was discussed by the greatest scholars in Italy, equalled, if it did not surpass, another Benedictine garden, fifty miles away in the hills, which he called his 'Paradise', not only on account of its beauty but 'by reason of the companions whose society I enjoy and hear nothing but the praise of God'.

Chief in this circle of friends was Gaspar Contarini, seventeen years older than Pole. He was the eldest son of a noble Venetian house who, at an early age, had been elected to the Senate and, by reason of his gifts of mind and character was, while still in his thirties, appointed Ambassador first to Charles V and later to the Pope.

Like Pole, Contarini had studied philosophy and the classics at the University of Padua and, whatever the pressure of public affairs, he continued throughout his life to devote three hours a day—no more, no less—to study. He began each session with exact repetition and proceeded relentlessly to the conclusion of every subject he selected. He eschewed subtleties, believing that 'nothing is more astute than falsehood'. Equally he was indifferent to the niceties of literary style, but strove to enunciate simple truths simply, once he had arrived at them and tested them. 'Nothing which the human mind can discover by its own powers of investigation was unknown to him'[1] it was said, 'and nothing wanting to him that the grace of God has imparted to the human soul'.

Contarini's dominant passion was the reform of the Church. While Luther was still unprotesting in his convent at Augsburg, Contarini had written a book on the duties of a bishop, in which he had pointed out that 'nothing is more unbecoming to a pastor of a Christian flock than such outward pomp as grand dinners, a huge crowd of servants, a large and exquisite collection of tapestries and silver vessels, not to mention the more disgraceful expenses'—sentiments which made him not altogether *persona grata* to Wolsey whom he met during a brief visit to England six years after his *Concerning the Office of a Bishop* had been published.

In later writings, he attacked the abuse of dispensations as trenchantly as did Luther and criticised unsparingly the up-holders of papal absolutism, accusing them of idolatry. 'The law of Christ,' he declared, 'is a law of freedom and forbids a servitude so abject that the Lutherans were entirely justified in comparing it with the Babylonish Captivity. All true dominion is a dominion of reason, whose aim is to lead all whom it governs to happiness. The authority of the Pope is equally with others a dominion of reason. God has conferred this rule on St. Peter and

---

[1] He was in Spain when the ship *Vittoria* returned from the circumnavigation of the globe and was the first to solve the problem of her entering port a day later than she should have done according to her log-book.

his successors that they might lead those entrusted to their care into everlasting blessedness. Not according to his own pleasure must a Pope command or forbid or dispense, but in obedience to the rule, the cult, to reason, to God's commands, and to the law of love, referring everything to God and doing all in consideration of the common good only.'

Contarini's three years as Ambassador to the Holy See convinced him, reluctantly, that no movement for reform was likely as long as Clement VII was Pope, but he remonstrated passionately with Clement about his obsession with politics.

'Your Holiness,' he said, 'should not suppose that the well-being of the Church of Christ is bound up with this little temporal state. Before ever such a state existed, there was the Church and, indeed, the Church was then in her best condition. The Church is the community of all Christians. The Papal state is merely the state of an Italian prince joined to the Church.'

To this Clement could only give the characteristically Medicean answer: 'Nowadays the world is in such a state that the astutest and craftiest man gains the greatest fame, while if one acts otherwise, one is considered merely a good-natured but worthless fellow.'

'If Your Holiness,' retorted Contarini, 'would consider the contents of Holy Scripture, you would see that nothing is stronger and more vigorous than truth, virtue, goodness and a right intention.'

Such arguments carried no weight with Clement and Contarini was relieved when his three-year spell of service in Rome was over and he was able to return to Venice.

During the first days of his ambassadorship, Clement's first minister was Gian Matteo Giberti, the illegitimate son of a Genoese admiral, who in obedience to his father but against his own inclinations (which were for the cloister) had, at the age of eighteen, become secretary to Clement while he was still the Cardinal Giulio de' Medici. Giberti had served his master faithfully and had remained with him in his imprisonment after the sack of Rome, and, among other benefices, Clement had bestowed on him the Bishopric of Verona.

Now, at the age of thirty-five Giberti decided that he had fulfilled his personal and political obligations to the Pope and when his friend Contarini returned to Venice, Giberti left Rome to retire to his diocese of Verona, a mere seventy miles distant from Venice. Here he would endeavour to put into practice the ideals which Contarini had enunciated in his book. The Reform should have at least one bishopric to which it could point.

Giberti began with his own household. He modelled it on a semi-monastic pattern, with stated times for divine service, for the giving of audiences, for meals, for study. He never allowed himself more than seven hours' sleep, rose early and devoted the beginning of the day to religious exercises. After his morning Mass, he gave audience, always receiving the poor first. During the day he occupied himself with the work of his diocese and with editing the works of the Fathers—he had collected many works of Chrysostom, Basil and Eusebius and had set up a printing-press in the episcopal palace—and books of devotion. He ended the day with the recitation of the penitential psalms with his household.

The Bishop made the most exhaustive visitation of his diocese, which was in a lamentable state. Non-resident clergy who left the cure of souls to immoral and ignorant curates, many so ignorant that Giberti had to order the rubrics of the Missal to be translated into Italian because they knew no Latin, most so immoral that the prisons were soon filled with *concubinarii* —priests living with women; preaching at a discount; the confessional lax; churches in such disrepair that they looked like stables; monasteries and convents whose evil repute was deserved—these the Bishop found everywhere and set himself with immense energy and pertinacity to set to rights until the diocese of Verona became a model for Christendom.

Giberti made provision for bodies as well as souls. He founded orphanages, hospitals—a special one for aliens—and homes for reformed prostitutes; he devised a poor law which differentiated between the sturdy beggar and a man willing but too old or weak to work; and as the centre and inspiration of all his social policy instituted his 'Fraternity of Charity' whose object was, as a contemporary described it 'that no man should suffer hunger, no man do injury to his neighbour, no man commit sin, no man be deprived of the necessities of life; finally, that enmity and all hatred and anger should be taken away, so that we, as men once did in the first and happiest days of the Church, should live with one heart and one soul in the fear and praise of God'.

The 'Fraternity of Charity' owed something to an earlier association, the 'Oratory of Divine Love', which Giberti had joined on its foundation in Rome when he was twenty. The members of the Oratory were clerics, mostly holding high positions in the Vatican, who, amid the debauchery and splendour of Medicean Rome, wished to renew their inward lives by prayer, meditation and works of charity undertaken in common. They met at the Church of St. Dorothy in the Trastevere near the place where, according to tradition, St. Peter had lived and presided over the first assemblies of Christians in Rome.

The most remarkable members of the Oratory were two noblemen, the thirty-five-year-old Gaetano di Tiene (better known in history as St. Cajetan), a Pronotary Apostolic at the Papal Court, and the forty-one-year-old Gianpietro Caraffa who had been Bishop of Chieti since he was eighteen, when his uncle, Cardinal Oliviero Caraffa, had resigned that see in his favour. As the Latin name for Chieti was Theate, the young Caraffa was thenceforward familiarly known as 'Theatinus'.

Few friends could have been more dissimilar than Cajetan and Caraffa,—Cajetan, a Venetian, small and elegant, speaking little, given to prolonged reveries and seeking a self-effacing anonymity which pointed the saying that he wished to reform the world without permitting it to be known that he was in the world; Caraffa, a Neapolitan, immensely tall and thin, with the burn-

154

ing eyes of a fanatic, tirelessly active with an interfering energy which surpassed even Giberti's and a torrential eloquence which ceased only on his death-bed.[2] But the mutual affection of such opposites was cemented by their passionate religious devotion and their common concern for the reform of the Church.

They soon found that, for the achievement of their purpose, they needed some organisation more strict and closer knit than the 'Oratory of Divine Love', which now included about sixty priests of varying views. On the Feast of the Finding of the Holy Cross, May, 1524, with two other companions from the Oratory, they founded a new Order, dedicated to the Cross, which they adopted as their emblem. At Cajetan's wish, 'Theatinus' became the first General of the Order which was named in consequence the Theatines. Giberti, though his position and duties at the Papal court prevented him from joining it, used his influence with Clement, who had just become Pope, to persuade him—reluctantly—to establish it, and, on the Feast of the Exaltation of the Holy Cross, September, in that same year, 1524, Cajetan, Caraffa and their two companions made their solemn profession before the High Altar of St. Peter's and took the three monastic vows of poverty, chastity and obedience. They were, however, not monks, but Clerks Regular—priests living in the world under strict discipline.

Both Cajetan and Caraffa stripped themselves of their wealth. Cajetan, giving back his patrimony to his family, said: 'I see Christ in poverty and I am rich. He is despised and I am honoured. I wish to draw one step nearer to him and therefore renounce all yet remaining to me of this world's goods.' Caraffa's renunciation of his two bishoprics (he was, as well as Bishop of Chieti, Archbishop of Brindisi) caused a sensation at the Vatican and when the Pope insisted on him remaining at least Bishop of Chieti, he replied by retaining the office but relinquishing the emoluments.

[2] He died, as Pope Paul IV, in 1559 at the age of eighty-four, having outlived all the reformers.

To the vow of poverty, the Theatines added a further refinement. The Franciscans, by their ceaseless cry for alms and their addiction to spurious miracles to wring contributions from the unwary, had brought Holy Poverty into such disrepute in Rome that the Theatines would not even beg their bread. They would await what alms might be brought to their dwelling.

In the three years between their foundation and the sack of Rome, their strictness was such that few were found sufficiently dedicated to join them and they never numbered more than twelve. They lived in a small house on the Pincian Hill which was at that time deserted.[3] Below them was spread out the Eternal City; but, at first, they did not visit it. They remained, in their self-imposed poverty, training themselves in spiritual exercises and studying the Gospels. Only when they were sufficiently mortified did they descend into the city to preach—Caraffa looking like some gaunt Desert Father with a defiantly large tonsure—to visit the sick and to comfort the dying.

After the sack of Rome, the Theatines decided to leave the capital for a season and attempt to establish themselves in other cities. So it was that Caraffa came to Venice[4] and joined Contarini's circle where he met and influenced Reginald Pole, who found 'Bishop Theatinus' twenty-five years his senior a 'most holy and learned man', but did not on that account feel called to join the new Order.

To his three great Italian friends, Contarini, Caraffa and Giberti (whom he had originally known while he was studying at Padua before his return to England), Pole soon added a fourth, a youth still in his teens who found in the Lord Reynold all that he wanted in the world. Alvise Priuli, the youngest son of a noble Venetian family—both his elder brothers became in due time Doge—was never to leave Pole. For the next twenty-

[3] The Villa Medici was not designed and built till twenty years later.
[4] Cajetan went to Naples.

four years he was to accompany him on all his journeys over Europe and it was in his arms in London that Reginald was to die.

Priuli more than filled the place of the dead Longolius and in his villa near Treviso he provided Pole with a perfect retreat from the world whenever he needed it. Priuli was not greatly concerned with either religion or politics; he cared only for personal things and interested himself in whatever affection demanded. In their mutual devotion, Reginald Pole and Alvise Priuli became one of the legendary friendships of history.

There were also the English friends of Pole's household. Chief among them was reckoned Father Thomas Starkey, Reginald's senior by a year and his contemporary at Oxford, where Starkey became a Fellow of Magdalen and remained for a short time as a lecturer in natural philosophy.

Starkey had acted as Pole's secretary during his visit to Paris on the nullity matter and on their return he had taken Holy Orders and been given a living in Kent by Archbishop Warham. He remained, however, with Pole, as chaplain-secretary in the retreat at Sheen and set out with him on his return to Italy. On the way he stayed at Avignon for a year to study civil law there and rejoined Pole at Padua in the summer of 1533 to continue his legal studies at the University.

For one who had been so close to him for so long, Pole had developed that curious blindness which so often comes from such familiarity. He assumed that Starkey, because of an apparent identity of attitudes, in reality shared his views. Reginald could not, because of his nature, see—what was obvious to everyone else—that Starkey, a poor but clever Cheshire nonentity with his way to make in the world, would use his undergraduate connection with the Lord Reynold precisely as long as it was profitable. Already the revolution taking place in England had made him ripe for desertion, on the highest principles.

In this he differed entirely from young Richard Moryson,

the latest acquisition to Pole's household. Personable, witty, studious, with considerable literary ability, Moryson was an indigent scholar at Padua who, by his own account, would 'have perished of misery if the kindness of Mr. Pole had not rescued him from hunger, cold and poverty'. Reginald, supposing it to be true, did not suspect that his protegé had been placed there deliberately as a spy by Cromwell, who, in view of the revival of the idea of marrying Reginald to the Princess Mary, thought it as well to have direct insight into Pole's manner of life. Cromwell's attention to detail was never better exemplified than in the manner he chose for Moryson's introduction. With none of the Poles could the appeal to charity ever fail.

Moryson succeeded in making himself popular in the household. He was cheerful and he never complained. George Lily, on the other hand, the son of the first headmaster of St. Paul's School, was always complaining. His chief grievance was that he had not sufficient time to study because in Padua he had, according to the prevailing etiquette, to accompany Pole whenever he went out. This not only took up time which the young man would have preferred to give to his books but, because of his master's energy, made him so tired that he was not fit for study when he returned. George preferred their visits to Venice where a hired gondoliere relieved him of his duty.

Valentino Sandro, Pole's house-steward, disapproved of a number of things, but chiefly of the inordinate number of his master's acquaintances and their habit of dragging 'il Signore' about from place to place and using his house as if it were their own. In particular he resented Priuli. 'Priuli came to our house to visit', he wrote to a friend, 'and stayed for a whole month. He has great love for my lord, but we are all tired of his way of life. While we were at Santa Croce he came to stay there and never ceased till he drew "il Signore" to his house at Padua and finally made him give it up and come to Venice. It is expensive enough to keep house anyhow, but much more to move about. And now the Bishop of Verona has sent "il Signore" 250 gold crowns, praying him accept them to buy horses to visit him at Verona!'

That Pole should now make Venice itself rather than Padua his principal place of residence was natural enough and, though he admitted his desire for the constant companionship of Contarini, Caraffa and Priuli, his decision was not uninfluenced by more objective considerations. At Venice he was in immediate touch with all Europe. Not only was the Venetian foreign service unrivalled, but the Republic remained, as a great financial and commercial centre, the meeting-place of the world, even though, with the increase of the Turkish power in the eastern Mediterranean and the discovery of new sea-routes, her dominance was starting to decline.

Pole's old friend, Dr. Richard Pace, was no longer at the English Embassy, but the new Resident, Edmund Harvel, soon succumbed to the Lord Reynold's charm and not only passed on to him all the public news from England but also despatched and received on his behalf his private correspondence. Harvel found it impossible to believe that Pole was seriously interested in affairs of state. 'He delights more in study than in life or glory which are always condemned by him,' Harvel wrote apologetically to Cromwell, 'and the sweetness of learning is so great in such a man so inflamed with virtue that only with difficulty can he be withdrawn from study.'

Nevertheless, Reginald thought it wise to entrust occasional letters to Michael Throckmorton who, of all his household, he trusted most.

That autumn an event occurred which profoundly affected Pole and his friends. Clement VII died. After a Consistory which lasted only a single day, Alexander Farnese, in the sixty-seventh year of his age and the fortieth of his cardinalate, was elected Pope and took the name of Paul III.

Farnese, no less than his predecessors, was a child of the Renaissance and, in the gardens of Lorenzo de' Medici, had learnt that love of beauty which had resulted in his building, during his cardinalate, the most perfect palace in Rome,[5] where he entertained Leo X. His sister, Julia, had been Alexander VI's mistress. He himself acknowledged a son and a daughter and his first act when he became Pope was to raise two of his nephews, aged sixteen and fourteen, to the Cardinalate. He made no secret of his wish for the Papacy. He was on the point of being elected Pope on the death of Leo X and again on that of Adrian VI and it was said of him that 'he could not live in charity with the memory of Clement VII who occupied the papal chair for twelve years during which he insisted it ought to have been his own'.

Yet, in spite of these things, Paul III became 'the Pope of the Reform'. His pontificate had been delayed until age had brought much wisdom and some sanctity. Above the battle, he understood the deepest needs of the Church and he made immediate preparations to summon an Ecumenical Council to undertake its reformation.

As a first step, he created Contarini (whom he knew only by reputation) a Cardinal, allowing him to remain a layman, but inviting him to take up his residence in the Vatican and initiate a reform comparable to that which Giberti had made in Verona.

Among the other new Cardinals were Gianpietro Caraffa and John Fisher, who was described in the *Diaria Pontificum* as 'John, Bishop of Rochester, kept in prison by the King of England'.

[5] The Palazzo Farnese is now the French Embassy.

13

Deaths and Entrances

John Fisher had been sent to the Tower, five months earlier, for refusing to take the oath which had been ordered by 'the Statute of the Supremacy and Matrimony', as the mass of new legislation was popularly and appropriately known. With him in the Tower, though kept apart from him, was Sir Thomas More, who had made a similar refusal.

Parliament, composed of Cromwell's carefully selected nominees and the King's placemen, in the few weeks of its 1534 sitting, obediently legalised a revolution. It forbade any appeals to Rome; abolished the bishops' oath of spiritual obedience to the Pope; retrospectively legalised Henry's marriage with Anne, declaring Princess Mary a bastard and making it high treason to deny the right of succession to Anne Boleyn's children; decreed that every Sunday a bishop should preach at St. Paul's Cross denying that the Pope was Head of the Church; vested the right of the visitation of monasteries in laymen appointed by the Crown; declared that Henry was 'Supreme Head on earth' of the Church in England, without the original saving clause 'as far as the law of God allows'; and finally, in an Act of Treason, extended the penalty of hanging, drawing and quartering not only to things said and done but to things thought, so that any appearance of opposition, real or fabricated, to the King's policy could be thus punished.[1] And, in putting these new laws into effect, Henry and Cromwell dispensed with the necessities of tested evidence by proceeding by Bill of Attainder—a procedure originally designed for dealing with criminals who had fled from justice and could not be produced in court, which had been found effective for the speedy removal of opponents during the Wars of the Roses.

When, at the beginning of April, Convocation was invited to renounce the Pope's supremacy and substitute Henry's, there was such a rush to apostasise that all the English Bishops except Fisher immediately signed their acceptance. Fisher epitomized the situation: 'The fort is betrayed even by those who should have defended it.'

They were followed obediently and with even more enthusiasm by the clergy and the monks. The Franciscans[2] predictably, led the way with the declaration that not only did they honour 'the chaste and holy marriage which lately had been contracted and consummated' between Henry and Anne but—with remarkable prescience—they also swore fidelity 'to whatever other wife our said King Henry may marry'. They agreed with the Dean and Chapter of St. Paul's that Henry was 'the one whom alone, after Jesus Christ our Saviour, we owe everthing' and the Bishop of London further emphasised the loyalty of the metropolitan see by actually preaching a sermon (his stammering and his uncouth voice had prevented him from ever preaching before) damning the Pope in such terms that Chapuys reported to the Emperor that 'the invectives of the German Lutherans against the Pope are as nothing compared with the abominable sermons heard in the English pulpits'.

The wholesale flight from the Faith was gratifying—though Henry himself insisted that the Supremacy had nothing to do

[1] Lingard's comment that 'it would be difficult to discover under the most despotic governments a law more cruel or absurd' seems just.
[2] The ordinary Franciscans; not, of course, the Friars Observant at Greenwich, several of whom were sent to the Tower.

with religion and his immediate circle realised only too clearly that it was indeed merely a consequence of the Matrimony—but the obstinacy of John Fisher robbed Cromwell's triumph of some of its savour. As long as one Bishop—and such a bishop—remained firm, there was no knowing what effect it might have on public opinion. Accordingly, Cranmer summoned him, though he was almost too weak to travel, from Rochester to London.

'There my Lord Canterbury put him in remembrance of the Act of Parliament wherein is provided an oath to be ministered to all the king's majesty's subjects for the surety of his succession in the crown of his realm. "Which oath", said he, "all the lords spiritual and temporal have willingly taken, only your lordship except. And therefore His Majesty holdeth himself greatly discontent with you and hath appointed us to call you before us and offer you the oath once again".'

Once again Fisher refused it as 'being so contrary to God's word'. The Bishop was thereupon 'sent to the Tower where he was closely imprisoned and locked in a strong chamber away from all company saving one of his servants, who, like a false knave, accused his master to Cromwell afterwards'.

On the same day, Monday, April 13, 1543, Sir Thomas More also refused the oath.

More would not give his reasons. He went so far as to admit: 'I never withdrew any man from the oath, nor never put, nor will, any scruple in any man's head.' If part of his refusal concerned the theological issue, that was not—as it was with Fisher —the whole matter. More was indeed prepared to argue against the Supremacy: 'In some things for which I refuse the oath, I am not bounden to conform to the council of one realm against the general Council of Christendom.' But this was a matter which might have been adjusted, for both Cromwell and Cranmer, aware of the scandal which More's imprisonment would cause in Europe, urged the King to allow Sir Thomas to take the oath in a modified form. When Henry, yielding to Anne Boleyn's 'importunate clamour', refused on the grounds that it might be taken 'as a reprobation of the King's second marriage' he went to the heart of the matter.

More wrote to a cleric who consulted him about his reason: 'As touching the oath, the causes for which I refused it, no man wotteth what they be, for they are secret in mine own conscience; some other, peradventure, than those that other men would ween and such as I never disclosed to any man yet, nor never intend to do while I live.'

Anne, remembering More's implied slander on her by his past refusal to attend her coronation, was easily able to interpret his present refusal to acknowledge her child as Henry's rightful heir. But, though she never ceased to urge his death, the secret was safe enough with him. The one-time Lord Chancellor—no less than the Princess Mary—could be trusted to keep his knowledge locked in his conscience.

Anne, however, realised how deadly, at that moment, was the danger. The very day before the arrest of Fisher and More she had arranged with Smeaton another occasion for intimacy and, in anticipation of the result, had told the King she was pregnant.[3] At all costs, with Jane Seymour in the ascendant, she must give Henry a son, if she too was not to be put aside like Catherine.

To Catherine, at Buckden, a Commission, headed by the Archbishop of York, was sent to gain her assent to the oath, though no one seriously supposed she would give it. The whole Act was read to her and the Archbishop pointed out that, as one of the King's subjects, she was, like any other, liable to trial for high treason, unless she acknowledged the right to succession of 'the fair issue already sprung from His Grace's marriage to Queen Anne; and more is likely to follow by God's grace'.

'I shall never quit the title of Queen,' retorted Catherine, 'but

[3] She had to admit in September that she was not. I have taken the date from Smeaton's admission of the adultery on April 26, 1534, to which Anne had 'procured and incited him' a fortnight earlier.

shall retain it till death. I am the King's wife and not his subject and therefore not liable to his acts of parliament. If you have orders to execute this penalty on me, I am ready. I ask only that I be allowed to die in the sight of the people.'

The Commissioners then administered the oath to Catherine's servants and, meeting with a wholesale refusal to take it, arrested several of them and returned to the King with their unsatisfactory news. Henry ordered that 'the old Princess-Dowager' was to be removed from Buckden to the safer castle of Kimbolton, half-a-day's ride away, and to be given new servants who were sworn to address her only as the 'Princess-Dowager'. Catherine on her part refused to accept any who denied her Queenship and was, in consequence, when she arrived at Kimbolton in the middle of May, reduced to four Spanish servants, who, as foreigners, were excused the oath. The Queen was confined to one room which she left only to go to Mass in the chapel or to walk in the narrow, walled garden which lay behind it.

With More and Fisher safely in the Tower facing, at some convenient moment, a Bill of Attainder, the usefulness of the Nun of Kent was at an end and, a week later, she and four of her principal associates were executed at Tyburn.

Elizabeth Barton's importance had never been more than as a possible trap for bigger game but, in this particular at least, the great ones had escaped. Cranmer, with the best will in the world, had failed to implicate them. Queen Catherine had refused to see the Nun; More, though he had seen her, had merely told her not to meddle with political prophesyings; Fisher, certainly, had listened to her tirades against the King and failed to report them, but, as she had previously said the same things to Henry himself, this could hardly be construed as concealment of treason; the Marchioness of Exeter, who had invited the Nun to her house, had only asked her prayers in a family trouble; and the Countess of Salisbury had seen her only as thousands of others had in the hey-day of her notoriety and had consulted her on nothing.

Before she was killed, the poor 'hypocrite Nun' did public penance and admitted that 'she never had a vision in all her life, but that all she ever said was feigned of her own imaginings only to satisfy the minds of them which resorted to her, and to obtain worldly praise'.

Margaret Pole had climbed slowly back to life and in the summer she was able to leave Montagu's care at Bisham. In spite of his entreaties to her to stay and of Geoffrey's offer of alternative hospitality at Lordington, she insisted on going to Warblington with a few of her own household. It was an assertion of will and an exercise in judgment.

For the first time in her life she had no duty to perform, no one except herself for whom to be responsible. The court was closed to her, by her own wish as much as by Henry's will. Catherine and Mary were beyond her help. Her world had shrunk to playing games with and telling stories to her nine-year-old grandson, Henry, Montagu's only boy—'the hope of our race', as she had called him when she thought she was dying and her mind was running loose among the dynastic preoccupations of her own youth.

She had too much time. She must, because of her nature, impose some pattern of action on the formless days and she had no intention of becoming a resented interference in either of her sons' households, however Montagu's Jane and Geoffrey's Constance might protest their affection.

So she went to make her new world in the Sussex countryside. First, as a thank offering for her recovery, she founded at Warblington a little hospital in which everyone who needed could get free treatment from her own surgeon, Richard Eyre, who, though a gossip and a grumbler, was a skilful doctor and was devoted to her. She knew how to manage him and when he complained, as he occasionally did with reason, that some of the humbler patients were more exacting than he thought their condition warranted, she would remind him of Christ's saying:

'Inasmuch as you have done it unto the least of these My brethren you have done it unto Me' and ask whether, in that case, any trouble could be too great.

Her second care—second in time but, to her, first in importance —was to gather round her a school of priests, to whom she gave the hospitality of a wing of Warblington Castle where they could live a semi-monastic life of prayer and study. She had discussed the matter with Montagu's chaplain and confessor, Father John Collins, at Bisham. He had pointed out that there were many good young secular priests, who had no vocation to the religious life in the stricter monasteries and no inclination to enter the lax houses, who might benefit greatly from such an arrangement. The idea appealed to her the more because it was to just such a one, Father John Helyar, that she had, just before her illness, given the living of Warblington, promising him that, when he had served for a year or two as parish priest, she would send him to the University of Paris to continue his studies. For the first of her company of priests she chose, on Father Collins's recommendation, an intellectual ascetic, Father John Crayford, whom she intended should succeed Father Helyar when he went overseas.

To the little church of the village, dedicated to St. Thomas of Canterbury, she made many benefactions, and when, at the end of October, news arrived in England that the new Pope had selected the name of Paul III, she provided a new church bell for the tower. It was embellished with the inscription 'Sancte Paule, ora pro nobis'.

Just before Christmas, Thomas Starkey arrived in Warblington from Padua, with news for her of Reginald. He informed her that her son had advised him to return to England now that his law studies were over and hoped that she would allow him to become her chaplain.

This was not strictly true. Certainly Starkey's studies were over and when he had announced to Pole that he was thinking of returning to England, Reginald had approved it as a means of getting first-hand knowledge of events at home, and had added that he was sure that his mother would, if Starkey wished, allow him to be her domestic chaplain until he had decided what he wanted to do. The difference might be slight enough, hardly more than a shift of emphasis from conventional politeness to a purposed intention, but, much to Starkey's surprise, Margaret seemed to be aware of his real motives.

'I cannot, Father Thomas,' she said, 'allow you to waste all the new learning you have acquired on an old woman living in seclusion. You should be at court, offering your services to the King.'

'If I cannot serve Your Ladyship,' he answered, 'there is no one I would rather serve. But—'

She interrupted, again anticipating his thought: 'The King will, I have no fear, honour my counsel thus far' and wrote a recommendation for him, asking Henry to consider him for the post of one of the Royal Chaplains.

Margaret, seeing Starkey after two years' absence, had no illusions. Whatever might happen, she did not want him at Warblington.

The King welcomed Starkey with undisguised enthusiasm. The priest happened to arrive at court in the middle of January, just before the day fixed—January 15, 1535—for the proclamation of the King's new style: 'Henry the Eighth, by the grace of God King of England and France[4], Defender of the Faith and Lord of Ireland, and Supreme Head on earth of the Church in England'. Henry, in spite of the subservience of Parliament and of Convocation, was still slightly apprehensive of the possible effect in the country as a whole when the public proclamation was made; and, comprehensibly, he was anxious to know Pole's reaction to recent events.

Reginald's integrity, ever since he had refused the Archbisho-

[4] The English claim, originally made by Edward III, to the kingship of France was monotonously maintained in official documents for centuries.

pric of York, had become, maddeningly and uncomfortably, Henry's touchstone of judgment. Pole could be neither bribed nor brow-beaten and the King, whose contempt for Cranmer was as great as his use of him, took a perverse delight in it. Reynold, after all was both his cousin and his 'creation'. And he obstinately refused to believe that he would not, in the end, become also his defender.

He questioned Starkey, as closely as Margaret Pole had done, about Reginald, his studies, his friends, his manner of life. Here the answers were simple enough and Starkey stressed Reginald's interest in the reform of the Church.

'What is his opinion of my causes lately defined here?' Henry shot at him.

'He desires above all,' Starkey replied, 'to do Your Grace true and faithful service.'

'That I do not doubt,' said Henry. 'What I am asking you is his opinion on my marriage and on the authority of the Pope.'

'That I cannot answer certainly, Your Grace,' said Starkey, 'but I am certain that, as far as his learning and judgment goes, he would use all the power and the knowledge which he has obtained by Your Grace's liberality to him to maintain whatever has been decreed by Parliament.'

Henry, though applauding Starkey's diplomacy, was not satisfied. 'Tell him I require his opinion of these two points, simply, honestly and without equivocation. I do not wish a great volume or book, but the most effectual reasons—whatever they may be— briefly and plainly set forth.'

'Your Grace wishes me to return to Italy with this message?'

'No,' said Henry. 'A letter will be sufficient.'

In his letter to Pole, conveying the request, Starkey added: 'All the rumours which came to you in Italy from men of corrupt judgments are utterly false; for although the King has withdrawn himself from the Pope's authority, he has in no point slid from the certain and sure grounds of Scripture, nor yet from the laws and ceremonies of the Church. Nothing is done here without due order and reasonable means. If I had found the false reports in Italy to be true, I would never have sought to enter his service.' And he concluded with the message that 'Mr. Secretary Cromwell's loving goodness to you gives place to no man's', a *bêtise* sufficiently startling to make Reginald immediately discount the rest. When he showed the letter to Contarini and Priuli they agreed that Starkey, whom they had disliked, was already either Cromwell's suitor or his tool or both.

Cromwell had climbed from power to power. Already Henry's principal Secretary, he was that January appointed the King's Vicar-General in all affairs of the Church and, in particular, Visitor-General of the monasteries, in preparation for fulfilling his promise to make Henry the richest prince in Christendom. He had prepared an elaborate plan based, on good Marsiglian doctrine, on the fact that Henry, as Supreme Head, was the owner of all Church property. By the dissolution of eight hundred or so religious houses and the confiscation of all their possessions, a first step was to be taken to transfer the Church's wealth to the Royal Exchequer. All the possessions of the smaller houses were to go to the King 'for the maintenance of his royal estate'; all the possessions of the larger monasteries, except ten marks a year for every religious who was a priest and five marks for every nun, was to go to the King as Supreme Head of the Church.

Cranmer who, as Archbishop of Canterbury, imagined that he had some responsibilities in the matter was promptly disabused. It was announced that Cromwell's appointment as Vicar-General was made necessary by the self-seeking, the indolence, the licentious bad example of those who claimed to govern the Church, by which the Bride of Christ had been so disfigured that her Spouse could hardly recognise her; and it was expressly enacted that neither the Archbishop of Canterbury nor any other ecclesiastic should have power to visit the monasteries.

The first blow fell on the holiest—on the Carthusians, whose dedication and sanctity no one had ever doubted. Cromwell's tactics were masterly. First the Order must be deprived of its leaders. Then those who were left must be intimidated in a way which would impress all other religious houses as well as the ordinary citizens. And there must be a show of reason. In the case of the Carthusians, Cromwell was sure that his reasonableness would fail. He had already sent them copies of Marsiglio which, having glanced at, they threw in the fire.

John Houghton, the Prior of the London Charterhouse, with two provincial Priors, and Richard Reynolds, a Brigettine of Syon who was reputed the most learned monk in England, were arrested and required to take the Oath of Supremacy. Refusing, they were brought to trial on April 28, 1535, for that 'traitorously machinating to deprive the King of his title as Supreme Head of the Church of England, they did on the 26th of April declare and say that the King our Sovereign Lord is not supreme head on earth of the Church of England'. As the jury, in view of the known piety and integrity of the accused, hesitated in their verdict, Cromwell, as Master of the Rolls, broke in on their deliberations and informed them in language which could not be misunderstood that unless they immediately returned such a verdict as the King's Highness demanded and expected, they themselves should, without trial and at once, suffer death.

After the verdict of guilty had been pronounced, the Religious were asked why they persisted in an opinion forbidden by the lords and bishops in Parliament. Richard Reynolds spoke for them all: 'I have all the rest of Christendom in my favour. I dare even say all this kingdom. Though the smaller part holds with you, I am sure the larger part is at heart of our opinion, although outwardly, partly from fear, partly from hope, they profess to be of yours.'

Pressed to reveal the names of those who agreed with him, Reynolds replied: 'All good men. I have in my favour all the General Councils, all the historians, the holy doctors of the

Church for the last fifteen hundred years, especially St. Ambrose, St. Jerome, St. Augustine and St. Gregory; and I am sure that when the King knows the truth, he will be very ill-pleased, or rather indignant, against certain bishops who have given him such counsel.'

The sentence for high treason was passed on them all and their execution at Tyburn fixed for May 4.[5] On that day, Sir Thomas More's daughter happened to be visiting him in the Tower and, looking out of his window, they saw the procession of death start. 'Lo, do you not see, Meg,' he said, 'that these blessed Fathers are now as cheerfully going to their deaths as bridegrooms to their marriage?'

Every attempt was made to render the scene at Tyburn impressive to the great crowd that had gathered there. Against all precedent, the condemned were hanged in their religious dress, to emphasise the connection between the monastic orders and treason. Against all custom, they were executed singly, instead of being hanged together on the large gallows, so that each might watch the mutilation of those who went before him and his courage thus be shaken. Against all traditional mercy, they were not allowed to hang until they were stupefied, but cut down at once so that they were fully conscious when they were castrated and disembowelled.

The occasion was attended by the notables of the court, including Anne Boleyn's father, the Earl of Wiltshire, the young Duke of Richmond and, masked but unmistakable, the King himself.

Immediately after the execution, Starkey wrote to Pole: 'At the last Parliament an Act was made that all the King's subjects should, under pain of treason, renounce the Pope's superiority; to which the rest of the nation agreed. Therefore they have suffered death, according to the course of the law, as rebels disobedient to the princely authority and persons who have rooted sedition in the community. I myself tried to prevail in argument with Reynolds, but nothing would avail. It seemed

[5] May 4 is now observed as the Festival of the English Martyrs.

that they sought their own death, of which no one could be justly accused. You may repeat this, as you think expedient, to those whom you may perceive to be misinformed.'

As the deaths of the priors had not had the effect of intimidating the Order, Cromwell ordered the arrest of three more Carthusians, one of whom was Sebastian Newdigate. Sebastian had been one of the wilder spirits at Court and a great favourite of the King. Suddenly he had changed his way of life and sought entry to the Charterhouse. No one had supposed he could endure the strict discipline and his sister, who considered it one of his more tasteless escapades, went to the Prior and told him so. For answer, the Prior had sent for the novice and his sister, recognising the change in him, went away abashed.

Cromwell's choice of Newdigate as a victim was not only motivated by his dislike of him—at court, Sebastian had pointedly not been of Cromwell's set—but it was also a test of the King. At the beginning of the imprisonment, Henry himself went to see Sebastian in the Tower and promised, if he would only renounce his vocation and return to court, that he would give him a fortune and load him with honours. When the young man refused, the King, to Cromwell's relief, interfered no further and Cromwell ordered a special form of imprisonment. The Carthusians were sent to Newgate to spend the seventeen days before their execution 'standing bolt upright, tied with iron collars fast by the necks to the posts of the prison, and great fetters fast rived upon their legs with great iron bolts; so straitly tied that they could neither lie nor sit, nor otherwise ease themselves, but stand upright; and in all that space they were never loosed for any natural necessity.'

'For the keeping of the King's subjects in more terror and fear'—as Cromwell headed one of his lists of things to be remembered—more important executions were decided upon. Fisher and More must die. Against Fisher the King's wrath had increased since his elevation to the Cardinalate, and he

173

wittily announced that he would send Fisher's head to Rome to wear the Red Hat.

On June 22, the Bishop, so weak that he had to be carried in a chair to the scaffold—'his long, lean, slender body nothing in matter but skin and bare bones, a very image of death'—was beheaded on Tower Hill. The full sentence for treason was modified at the last moment only because had he been drawn at the horse's tail to Tyburn, he would certainly have died on the way.

After the execution, the headsman 'took away the bishop's clothes and his shirt and left the headless body lying there naked upon the scaffold almost all day after. Yet one at last for pity and humanity cast a little straw upon the dead body's privities. And about eight o'clock in the evening, certain men vilely threw the body, all naked, flat upon his belly, without any winding sheet into a grave and so, following the commandment of the King, buried it very contemptuously.'

Fisher had announced to the bystanders at the scaffold: 'Christian people, I am come hither to die for the faith of Christ's Catholic Church. I desire you to help me with your prayers that in the moment of my death, I faint not in any point of the Catholic Faith for any fear.'

Exactly a fortnight later, Thomas More stood at the same scaffold. Henry had ordered him 'at his execution not to use many words'; Cromwell did not wish ordinary people to confuse punishment for high treason with martyrdom for the Catholic faith, and More was, above all, a brilliant advocate. More was content to obey. He merely asked everybody present to pray for him and to bear witness that he was suffering 'in and for the faith of the Holy Catholic Church'. The point was made even more surely by the brevity.

The executions had their intended effect at home, but abroad the shocked reaction was summed up in Erasmus's comment that the King of England had killed 'the wisest and most saintly

men that England had' and Cromwell was forced to busy himself with diplomatic explanations. He enquired from Edmund
Harvel how the news was received in Venice. He was told:
'It is considered to be extreme cruelty and all Venice is in great
murmuration to hear it. They speak a long time of the business,
to my great despair for the defaming of our nation, with the
vehementest words they can use.'

Cromwell replied by assuring the Italians that 'these rebels,
these enemies of their country, these disturbers of public peace,
these impious and seditious men were found guilty of high
treason. When, after long and mature deliberation, with absolute
unanimity certain laws and statutes were made in Parliament
for the common good of the kingdom, and in perfect accordance
with the true Christian religion, these men alone refused to
acquiesce. They sought how they might refute by juggling
arguments these holy laws. The most clement king could not
longer tolerate such atrocious guilt.'

From Kimbolton, Queen Catherine broke at last her long
silence and wrote to the Pope: 'Your Holiness knows and all
Christendom knows, what things are done here, what great
offence is given to God, what scandal to the world. If a remedy
be not applied shortly, there will be no end to martyred saints
and ruined souls. The good will be firm and suffer. The luke-
warm will fail if they find none to help them and the greater
part will fall away like sheep without a shepherd. I write frankly
to Your Holiness as one who can feel for me and my daughter
for the martyrdom of these good men, whom, it comforts me
to hope, we may follow in their sufferings though we cannot
imitate their lives. We await a remedy from God and Your
Holiness. It must come speedily, or the time will be past!'

At the same time the Pope received a letter from the French
Nuncio, reflecting the feeling at the court of France. It reminded
him that 'Reginald Pole, a relation of the King of England, but
of the White Rose, is at Padua. He is of great virtue and learning. If Your Holiness would give him Fisher's Hat, besides the

other advantages, it would seem to the people of England a Christian and worthy revenge on the King.'

The effect of the executions on the Poles in England was most critical in the case of Montagu. Because of his status he had been on the commissions which condemned the Carthusians as well as Fisher and More, and in none of the trials had he made any protest. He had accepted the fiction that the crime was high treason, and his limited and logical mind had contented itself with the reflection that, as it was undoubtedly, under the new law, treason to uphold the supremacy of the Pope, the martyrdoms were an unfortunate, but not illegal, necessity. Only when they were over and he had returned to Bisham and his confessor, Father Collins, did he find the truth inescapable. Certainly he still refused to admit it in words, but he had so serious—and physically inexplicable—a breakdown in health that for many months his life was despaired of.

Geoffrey Pole, on his part, pestered Chapuys daily, asking the Ambassador to arrange for him a passage to Spain and an interview with Charles V in Madrid so that he might urge the Emperor personally to undertake an immediate invasion of England. Chapuys eventually managed to dissuade him because, as he put it in a letter to Charles, 'the service he would do your Majesty is less than nothing compared with the cost of the injury he would bring upon himself and his friends'.

It was, however, at Warblington and on Margaret that the effect was most inescapable. The ninety-five-year-old Bishop of Chichester—that Robert Shirburn who had once been King Henry VII's envoy at the Vatican and had forged a Papal Bull appointing himself to the see of St. David's[6]—had written to Cromwell on St. Peter's Day, exactly a week after Fisher's execution: 'On this day, every abbot, prior, dean, parson etc. in the diocese has been ordered to preach and publish the Royal Supremacy and the abolition of the Bishop of Rome's authority.'

[6] *The Marriage made in Blood* p. 174.

In the little Warblington church, dedicated to the martyr, St. Thomas of Canterbury, Father John Helyar did, indeed, preach on the Supremacy, taking his text from the Gospel of the day: 'Thou art Peter and upon this rock I will build My church and the gates of hell shall not prevail against it', but the sermon was not one of which Cromwell would have approved.

Margaret, applauding the priest's courage, was at the same time apprehensive for his safety. Next day she informed him that the time had come for her to keep her promise to send him to study in Paris and arranged with Hugh Holland, a local ship-owner who traded in grain with the Low Countries, to take Helyar as a passenger on his next journey to the Continent.

Before he went, she had several conversations with him about the matters on all their minds. Margaret shared with her eldest son the instinct to obey the King for the good of the state and, in spite of her horror at the executions, to regard them as a political matter, not touching the fundamentals of religion.

'It is not, Father,' she said, 'as if the supremacy of the Pope is of so great an importance. Even I know that many wise and saintly men have disputed it. Sir Thomas More himself was one, in his earlier days; and the King was its defender. Had it been some greater point of doctrine, such as Our Lord's divinity or teaching regarding Our Lady, I would have agreed that denial was apostasy and those who died for it were martyrs. But this is a little thing of no certainty.'

'With respect, Your Ladyship, this is everything. All is in this. Take away St. Peter and his successors as guardians of the Faith, and no doctrine is safe. Our Lord, Our Lady, the Church, Heaven itself—all will be thrown down in the end.'

'I know the King. The Pope himself gave him the title of "Defender of the Faith". He would not permit such abominations.'

'So we may pray, but I fear otherwise. There will be many martyrs, Your Ladyship.'

Margaret objected to the use of the word 'martyrs'. Martyrdom was something that had happened a long time ago when Christians refused to sacrifice to pagan idols.

'I have known the King all his life,' she said. 'He is as good a Catholic as you or me, Father. Other kings have quarrelled with the Pope. This will be mended.'

'But until it is, Your Ladyship, it rends the unity of the Church.'

'I do not say that that is not a grave sin, and I pray, as you do, daily, that it may be mended. The wicked killing of the holy Bishop of Rochester, of Sir Thomas More, of the good monks—and, remember, Father, they were my friends—is a stain on Henry's soul. But I cannot account them martyrs, as the saints of old were martyred. I say no more than that.'

But Helyar would not let it rest. Two days later he returned to the matter and asked whether Margaret would accept the judgment of a saint who was himself involved in the early persecutions.

Margaret perforce agreed.

'Then listen, Your Ladyship, to the words of St. Denys the Great.'[7]

And he read to her a passage he had copied carefully from a volume of the Early Fathers which Father John Crayford was studying: 'That martyrdom which a man suffers to preserve the unity of the Church, so that it be not broken, is worthy in my judgment of no less commendation but rather of more than that martyrdom that a man suffers because he will not do sacrifice to idols. For in this case a man dies to save his own soul. In the other he dies for the whole Church.'

'Where did you find this?' she asked.

'It is in the library Your Ladyship has been gracious enough to provide for us to study. Father Crayford pointed it out to me.'

[7] St. Dionysius of Alexandria, a bishop of the third century, who lived through and recorded the great Decian persecution of 250 A.D.

'Then,' said Margaret, smiling, 'I must be content to accept such an answer. Or at least to consider it. But I do not wish you to be a martyr; so I shall ask Master Holland to catch the earliest tide he can.'

Meanwhile Starkey was writing another urgent letter to Reginald, bidding him in the King's name make haste with his judgment and urging him 'not to be like those here who stubbornly repugn to the common policy'.

That 'year of blood', 1535, ended with Christmas festivities at court more magnificent and hilarious than usual. Anne Boleyn was pregnant, and the King was further exhilarated by the death, a fortnight after Christmas, of Catherine.

She wrote him a last letter: 'My most dear lord, king and husband, the hour of my death is now drawing on and the tender love I owe you forces me, my case being such, to commend myself to you and to put you in remembrance of the health and safeguard of your soul which you ought to prefer before all worldly matters. For my part, I pardon you everything and I pray God that he will pardon you also. For the rest, I commend unto you our daughter Mary, beseeching you to be a good father to her. Lastly, I make this vow, that my eyes desire you above all things.'

When the news of her death arrived at court, Henry exclaimed 'Praise be to God!', summoned court officials to attend the interment at Peterborough of 'the right noble and excellent Princess, our dearest sister, the Lady Catherine, widow and dowager of the right excellent Prince, our dearest and natural brother, Prince Arthur' and, to emphasise that Catherine had never been his wife, dressed in yellow from head to foot, with a white plume in his cap, and, with undisguised enjoyment, continued the festivities.

Anne, when she received the news, was washing her hands in a golden basin, set in a rich cover. She exclaimed: 'Now I am indeed Queen' and gave the messenger both the basin and the cover as a reward for his tidings.

A fortnight later, however, entering a room unexpectedly, she surprised Jane Seymour on Henry's knee, returning passionately his caresses. The result of Anne's fury, indignation and alarm resulted in the premature birth of a boy—dead.

When Henry rated her for the loss of his son, she retorted: 'You have no one to blame but yourself. It was my distress about that wretch Jane Seymour.'

The King raged out of the room and announced to the courtiers in attendance: 'I was seduced into this marriage and forced into it by sorcery. That is why God will not permit me to have male children. That is why I want to make a new match.'

Mark Smeaton was becoming, from long immunity from suspicion, careless and Anne, from her emotional need of him, indiscreet in her favours. She gave him more and more considerable gifts, which he spent on jewels, dress and horses. Worse, he became insolent and overbearing and, after the manner of royal favourites, quarrelled with some of the courtiers, in particular with Sir Thomas Percy, the brother of the Earl of Northumberland, Anne's first love.

Anne, on hearing of this, sent for Percy and ordered him to make up the quarrel. Percy, though forced to obey, continued to bear such a grudge that he went to Cromwell, told him of the favour the Queen was continually showing to her musician and suggested that Smeaton could not have acquired by fair means all the money he was in the habit of spending.

Cromwell thanked him and asked him secretly to watch his enemy, with the result that, on April 29, Sir Thomas was able to report that he had seen Smeaton early in the morning coming out of Anne's apartments in the palace of Greenwich. Later in the morning, as Smeaton was returning to London, he was arrested and taken to a house in Stepney where he found himself facing the interrogation of Cromwell and a burly, truculent sadist, Sir William Fitzwilliam, Lord High Admiral of England, who had been an intimate of Cromwell ever since they had been together in Wolsey's household. Fitzwilliam put a knotted cord round Smeaton's head and started to twist it, while Cromwell watched amusedly and the musician screamed with pain.

The examiners realised that they would have no difficulty here and when Smeaton had made a full confession of events at court for the last three years, acknowledging not only his own relationship with Anne but also implicating Francis Weston, William Bryerton and Harry Norreys—though not Thomas Wyatt—as her lovers, Cromwell for his own purposes added the name of Anne's brother, George, Viscount Rochford. When Smeaton momentarily demurred at this accusation of incest, Fitzwilliam merely said: 'Subscribe, Mark, or you will see what will come of it' and Smeaton obediently signed.

Neither Cromwell nor Fitzwilliam believed the incest, but George Boleyn was already forming a party at court in opposition to Cromwell and, had he been allowed to survive his sister, he would certainly never have rested till he had avenged her. It was as well to get rid of him while the opportunity offered. As for a jury questioning so improbable an accusation—for brothers and sisters are apt to spend time together alone quite innocently—both Cromwell and Fitzwilliam remembered one of Wolsey's remarks to them: 'If the Crown were prosecutor and asserted it, juries could be found to bring in a verdict that Abel was the murderer of Cain.'

At their trial, Norreys, Bryerton and Weston pleaded 'Not Guilty'. Rochford defended himself against the charge of incest with such cogency, passion and eloquence that the betting among the people was ten to one that he would be acquitted. But to the added charge that he had used expressions showing that he doubted whether Elizabeth was Henry's child, he made no reply; and when he was handed a paper with a question on it which he was forbidden to read aloud he, knowing that nothing would prevent his judicial murder, proclaimed in a voice that could be heard in every corner of Westminster Hall: 'The

King is not able to have relations with his wife, as he is quite impotent.'

This answer, as Chapuys reported to Charles V, infuriated Cromwell who was preparing to have Elizabeth bastardised in law but who now had, comprehensibly, to insist that Henry was her father.

Mark Smeaton pleaded 'Guilty' and, from first to last, gloried in his love. Anne's version of events that fatal morning at Greenwich ran: 'Upon Saturday before May Day, I found him standing in the round window in my Chamber of Presence and I asked why he was so sad and he answered and said it was no matter and then I said: "You may not have me speak to you as I should to a nobleman, because you be an inferior person" and he answered "No, no, Madame, a look sufficeth me and so fare you well".' This had a tenuous connection with the truth in that he had had a tantrum of jealousy about his aristocratic rivals which his mistress had done nothing to placate. And when death came he paid the price of his 'low degree'. The others were merely beheaded. He had to suffer the terrible death for high treason. But even on the scaffold he refused to retract his love.

When Anne heard of it, she said: 'I fear his soul will suffer for the false witness he hath borne', but as she also asserted that she had never spoken to him for three years until that morning, which everyone at court knew from observation to be palpably untrue, her remarks carried little weight.

Anne herself was tried by a specially-selected jury of peers presided over by her uncle Norfolk, who was not altogether displeased to get rid of her. Her father offered himself, also, as a juror, but even Cromwell's stomach was turned by that indecency and Wiltshire's subservient services were declined.

The verdict was not in doubt, but before she died she had one more service to perform for Henry. She must co-operate in having her marriage annulled. As the process against

Catherine had started by the arrangement that Wolsey should call the King and Queen before him, so now the formula was repeated. Cranmer summoned Henry and Anne to Lambeth and in the under-chapel of the archiepiscopal palace, after a two-hour hearing, he solemnly pronounced the marriage invalid on the grounds of Henry's previous connection with Mary Boleyn. Henry, at forty-five, was still a bachelor, with three bastards, Richmond, Mary and Elizabeth.

And, before she died, Anne had one more thing to do on her own account. There was one sin and one sin only that troubled her conscience. When Lady Kingston, the wife of the Lieutenant of the Tower, came into her room, Anne locked the door and ordered Lady Kingston to sit in the Chair of State.

'It is my duty to stand,' said Lady Kingston, 'and not to sit at all in your presence, much less upon the Seat of State of your majesty the Queen.'

'Ah! Madame,' said Anne, 'that title is gone. I am a condemned person and by law have no estate left me in this life. But, for the clearing of my conscience, I pray you sit down.'

'I have often played the fool in my youth,' said Lady Kingston, 'and, to please you, I will do it once more in my old age' and sat down on the Chair of State.

Anne then fell on her knees before her and with tears in her eyes said: 'I ask you to bear witness that I would kneel humbly like this before the Princess Mary, my step-daughter, and ask her forgiveness for all the wrongs I have done her. You are my proxy for her, for there is no other; and until I have done this, my conscience cannot rest.'

Lady Kingston answered: 'I know the Princess Mary well and I can swear that, in her name, I can give you forgiveness, Madame. Which I do most joyfully.'

Next day, at nine in the morning, the sound of a Tower canon announced that Anne Boleyn was dead, her head cut off by an expert swordsman who had been brought over from Calais.

Cranmer, hearing it, remarked to a Scottish divine who was visiting Lambeth: 'She who was a Queen on earth is now a Queen in Heaven.'

Henry, dressed as a bridegroom, on the sound of it hurried to Jane Seymour, whom he married next day.

When the news of these events reached Venice, Reginald Pole put the finishing touch to his long-awaited reply to Henry and sent it to England by the trustworthy Michael Throckmorton.

14

The Book and its Consequences

The King had been explicit enough in what he wanted from Reginald. 'He does not wish for a great volume or book,' Starkey had written, 'but the most effectual reasons briefly and plainly set forth.' He desired them on two points only—the Marriage and the Supremacy; and he would prefer to see Pole dead than that he should 'for any worldly promotion or profit dissemble with him'.

That the answer was a book which ran to 280 folio pages was unfortunate but, in the circumstances, inevitable. Not merely was Henry's request less simple than it seemed, but between its arrival and Pole's reluctant completion of the task things had happened. The Carthusians and Fisher and More had been killed. Queen Catherine had died. Her successor and supplanter had been executed. The King had now a third wife whose marriage-lines were unquestionably valid and who was said to be sympathetic to the Catholic cause.

Further, to complicate matters, the King had kept sending Reginald copies of the propaganda supporting the Supremacy which he had had written by accommodating theologians as the price of their bishoprics. Edward Foxe's—he was given the see of Hereford—came first, followed quickly by Richard Sampson's (who was rewarded by Chichester on Shirburn's death) and rounded off by Stephen Gardiner's of Winchester. They all purported to show that the Pope was not Head of the Church and that Henry was.

Reginald had no difficulty in understanding why the King should have had them written and disseminated in England, where the ignorant might well be impressed by a trio of episcopal lucubrations, but he was puzzled as to why Henry, who was himself a good enough theologian to estimate them at their true value even if he used them for his own ends, should send them to him. He presumed that he was meant to answer them. This would considerably lengthen his reply.

Finally, bedevilling all, were his personal feelings for Henry. Despite the disillusion and revulsion which the King's proceedings had occasioned, he was still bound to him by affection and gratitude. When Montagu, recovered from his illness, wrote to tell him of the King's continuing favour to him, Reginald replied truly enough: 'I count whatever is good in me, next to God, to proceed from His Grace's liberality in my education, which I esteem a greater benefit than all the promotion the King ever gave to any other.' And to the Emperor he wrote that, despite everything, Henry was 'endowed by God with all qualities and parts which constitute a great and religious prince'.

Conflicting emotions bred procrastination. For six months Pole had talked a great deal, thought more but written nothing. Eventually he had left Padua for Venice, where he took a great house on the Grand Canal and, on September 4, 1535, started the 'letter' whose object was now clear to him. He must so deal with the theological issue as 'to try to render the Barque of Peter safe against piratical attacks' and to Henry himself he must tell the truth in love. He must be Nathan to Henry's David. As a friend and spiritual adviser, he must urge him to repent and make what atonement he could for his misdeeds. The King, who had, after all, forgiven him for his plain-speaking that day he had been offered the Archbishopric of York and who knew that, despite his own views, he had carried out the mission for him in Paris, would surely understand.

Having once started *A Defence of the Unity of the Church*, Pole had worked relentlessly throughout the bitter Venetian winter and at last was able to despatch it. In a covering letter, he explained that he had carried out the King's command but 'how it will satisfy you, only He knows in whose hand are the hearts of kings'.

But many besides the Almighty had little doubt how the book would be received. Contarini and Priuli, to whom he showed parts of the manuscript, implored him to moderate his language; to which he replied that flattery had been the root of the whole trouble and that Henry must be told the truth. To Henry himself he admitted that 'never was a book written with more sharpness of words, nor again more ferventness of love'.

Henry might perhaps be forgiven for resenting the first and doubting the second.

The theological section, defending the Primacy of Peter, might have been not only what Henry expected but what he himself might have written in the days when he became *Defender of the Faith*. He could even approve the mild witticism at the expense of Sampson's name—'no Samson but Goliath', the enemy of the chosen people—but he was irritated by Pole's exact knowledge of the circumstances: 'He is a Judas. He has sold himself for a small price; he wanted the Bishopric of Norwich and he only got Chichester.'

But it was the portrait of himself that threw Henry into so towering a rage that, after reading it, he began to make extensive and careful plans to have Pole assassinated.

'I can only lament', Reginald wrote, 'that you should imagine God had called you to build up the Church in England. Are titles given for nothing that men should call you, the robber and persecutor of the Church, the "Head of the Church"? Your father was a penurious man, but even he founded a few monasteries for the care of the poor; but who can cite any good deed of yours? What are your public works? Pleasure-houses, built for your own gratification, ruined monasteries, wrecked churches. During twenty-six years you have wrung more money out of your people and clergy than the kings, your predecessors, during five hundred years. I know. I have seen records of the accounts. You have destroyed your nobles on the most frivolous pretences. You have filled your Court with worthless men to whom you have yielded up everything . . .

'What have you done, during the past three years, but set everything to work to rob your own daughter, who for twenty years has been recognised as your heir, of her rights and to make her appear as a bastard? What father ever tried to deprive his rightful daughter of her inheritance and to give it to the child of a concubine?'

As regards Anne, Pole went straight to the unanswerable point which the tactful had been scrupulous to avoid. If Catherine was within the forbidden degrees, so was Anne and for the same reason. 'Was not the wife you chose for yourself the sister of one you had first seduced and then kept for a long time as your mistress? At the very time you were trying to prove a papal dispensation to be invalid, you sought for a dispensation to marry the sister of your former mistress!'

Yet these things were of small importance compared with Henry's major crimes. 'What shall I say of the butcheries which have made England a slaughter-house of the innocent? The gracious Bishop of Rochester, the unparalleled More, the learned Reynolds and so many others have been the victims of your senseless and wicked fury. All nations mourned when they heard of these tragedies. Is England another Turkey to be ruled by the sword? Were the Emperor already in arms against the Turk and on the point of setting out, I would follow him and cry: 'Turn about and pursue a worse enemy of the Faith and a greater heretic than may be found in Germany. My oppressed country calls you".'

That there had been bad Popes, Pole was the last to deny.

What he himself had seen in Rome, had indeed, made him pledge himself to the reform of the Church. But both the hypocrisy and the illogicality of Henry's position irritated him. 'If a bad pope is no successor of St. Peter, if only those pastors are legitimate who have the virtues of the Apostles, the Church has already ceased to exist, for who could compare in sanctity with the Apostles? Among ten bishops, one is generally unworthy.' Morally depraved bishops were bad enough, but what about a morally depraved King? Can Henry, of all people, be the Pope's successor as supreme head of the Church? In a burst of biting contempt, Pole, after again rehearsing Henry's varied wickednesses, flung at him: 'And you are the man who pretends to hold that the Pope, on account of his moral deficiencies, cannot be Head of the Church!'

Pole left no doubt that he knew the risk he was taking in speaking as he did to the new Supreme Head: 'Those who have tried to teach you, you rewarded with death; those who came to heal you were put to death; so what chance have I with my exposition of the truth?'

Throckmorton delivered the book to Starkey, who asked him eagerly for news of the household in Venice. Throckmorton told him as little as possible.

The tenth of June was the feast day of St. Margaret of Scotland. Margaret Pole had a great devotion to her name-saint, who was also her ancestress and whose daughter had been educated at the Benedictine nunnery of Romsey, which she occasionally visited on her journeys in Hampshire.

On this day in 1536, however, she went to that other Benedictine abbey, St. Mary's at Winchester—known familiarly as Nunnaminster—where her grand-daughter, Mary, Geoffrey's child, was a pupil.

There were reasons for her visit apart from the fact that she always liked to spend that day in Benedictine surroundings where, because of St. Margaret's benefactions to that Order, the feast was likely to be splendidly observed; and, in these days when no one knew how far the consequences of Cromwell's attack on the religious houses would reach, she feared that the splendour of devotion would, at any moment, die. Also, she would be able to see Geoffrey who had promised to be at Winchester and who had not visited her at Warblington for some months. For another, her friend, the Abbess,[1] Elizabeth Shelley, had been visited by Cromwell's Commissioners in May and now wanted her advice as to how to save the great house from falling victim to his rapacity.

Dame Elizabeth Shelley had been, in a sense, the victim of her own ingenuity. At the time of the enquiry into the annual values of all the religious houses her Treasurer, who was a brilliant accountant, had made it appear £179. The Commissioners, checking it, made it £330. No one was reprimanded, for, to the Commissioners, it merely meant that their haul would be greater than had been expected and, on her side, the Abbess, who had originally commended her Treasurer, could hardly reverse her judgment. But they now discovered that the only abbeys and monasteries to be touched were those with a value of less than £200 a year, so that, had the true figure been entered, Nunnaminster would—for the time being at least—have been safe.

The Abbess was now relying largely on the efforts of her brother, Sir William Shelley, who was a Judge of the Common Pleas and a personal friend of King Henry, to save the house. But she saw no harm in additionally enlisting the efforts of the parents of the twenty-six 'children of lords, knights and gentlemen' who were being educated there and very obviously the Countess of Salisbury, who, with the death of Anne Boleyn, would surely return to favour, was an important ally.

The journey to Court, whither Henry had recalled her, was

[1] I am indebted to Dr. John Paul whose monograph in *The Hampshire Field and Archaeological Society* is, as far as I know, the only life of Dame Elizabeth Shelley for calling my attention to her connection with Margaret Pole.

another reason for Margaret to visit Nunnaminster. At sixty-three she found travelling, which once she had welcomed, a burden and, after the thirty-mile journey from Warblington, it was good to spend a day and a night in the comfort of the guest-apartments of the Abbey.

Peace of mind, however, she was not to find. There to greet her were not only Geoffrey and his wife, but Montagu, who had ridden post haste from London.

'Son Montagu,' she said surprised, 'I had not expected you to join us, though I am glad of it. If only Reynold were here, it would indeed be a family festival to honour my saint.'

'Your beloved Reynold'—Margaret winced at her eldest son's sudden bitterness of tone—'is wise to be in safety. If he were here I doubt not he would lose his head. He has endangered all ours.'

And he told her how the King had summoned him to his presence and raged at him about Reginald's book, reading to him certain passages which had so appalled him by their outspokenness that he had only just prevented himself falling on his knees to beg Henry's forgiveness on his brother's behalf.

'He has bidden me write to Reynold to summon him home that he may discuss the matter with him. He wishes you to do so also and will order it when you come to court.'

'You will do so?'

'Of course. I have no choice. Nor, my Lady Mother, have you if you are wise.'

'Reynold will not come.'

'So we may pray; and trust he is like the fox in the fable who saw too many beasts go into the lion's den and none come out to adventure himself. But it is not he but we who are put in jeopardy. So we must dissemble.'

'There was treason in what he wrote?'

'Treason ten times piled on treason—as the law now runs—and insult beyond your imagining.'

'And ingratitude for all the King has done for him?'

'That underlies all. And for that I shall reproach him with a will.'

'I too,' said Margaret, 'shall find that lends honesty to what I may have to write. Reynold should have remembered Henry's goodness to him even if he was in conscience bound to reprove the King's proceedings.'

'Thank God,' said Geoffrey, 'that I am not drawn into this.'

'Rather pray God you may not be,' retorted his brother. 'Who knows how far this will reach?'

London, when Margaret arrived, was *en fête*, honouring the new Queen. Yet the citizens, happy that Anne was dead and obediently accepting Jane, reserved their deepest loyalty for Princess Mary. The rumour had reached them that Jane Seymour had begged Henry on her knees to restore Mary to court and to favour and now, as the Countess of Salisbury's coach made its way to Westminster, they swarmed round it till it was brought to a standstill.

'The Princess,' they cried. 'Let us see her. Long life to her.'

Margaret realised that the crowd assumed that she had brought Mary with her, so long had Governess and Princess been inseparable in public.

'I thank you on her behalf,' she called to the people, 'and I promise you she will be here anon on the King's order.'

When she told this to the King, he smiled at her graciously and said: 'Your promise, my Lady, but interprets my own intention and it is my pleasure to fulfil it without delay.'

Though she knew him so well, she found it difficult to gauge his mood. On the surface, he was again recognisably the prince of his early promise. Though he was forty-five and lame and corpulent with lack of exercise and bore a life-marked face whose eyes and mouth were a warning, he radiated something of the buoyancy and magnanimity of the golden youth who long ago had given her back her inheritance. She attributed the change in him, insofar as it was good, to his happiness in his new marriage and, insofar as it was evil, to the pain he was suffering. She knew that, six months earlier, Henry had fallen so badly in the lists, with his armoured horse crushing his leg, that everyone thought it a miracle he was not killed. He had lain for two hours without speaking and, despite all the subsequent attention of his doctors, his leg had not only not healed but was now ulcerating. The continuous pain of it, thought Margaret, whose rheumatism had taught her something of pain, might go far to explain his impatience and his sudden bursts of rage and even, perhaps, his lapses of judgment.

She might have judged less charitably had she known of his outburst to the French Ambassador the day after he had received Pole's book that he intended to root out the White Rose, though she might have dismissed even this, in her present mood, as a harmless flash of anger.

She was, in fact, so sure of Henry—whom she had after all known all his life—that she herself broached the subject of her son's writing.

'I hear from Montagu, Your Highness,' she said, 'that Reginald has been a cause of great offence to you. I am sure that it was unwitting.'

'He chose his words with too great care for that,' retorted Henry, 'but we both know that his honesty sometimes leads him to too much bluntness.'

'At least I dare aver he had Your Highness's good at heart. There is no one who holds you in greater affection and loyalty.'

'So he said,' said Henry. 'That I accept and for this reason I am anxious to discuss it with him face to face. I would ask you, my lady, to lend your entreaties to mine that he should return home as soon as possible. In Italy he has heard too many slanders.'

Michael Throckmorton—who had managed to get out of England only by promising Cromwell that he would act for him as a spy on Reginald—arrived in Venice with the packet of letters at the beginning of July. Pole turned first to his mother's letter, which opened by giving him her love and blessing but, in its continuance, did not mask her disapproval. 'My hope to have comfort in you is turned to sorrow to see you in the King's indignation,' she wrote. 'I trust you will take another way to serve our master as your duty and his many kindnesses to you demand. Otherwise you will be the confusion of your mother. I do not cease to pray for you and now ask God that He will give you grace to serve your prince truly or else to take you to His mercy.'

Montagu was more outspoken. He reminded his brother that their family had been 'clean trodden underfoot' until the King showed 'his charity and mercy' and set them nobly up again. From the King Reginald had 'received all things' which made his present conduct all the more 'unnatural'. The present religious differences would be healed. 'I cannot conceive that any laws made by man are of such strength that they may be undone by man, for what seems politic at one time at another time proves the contrary.'

Reginald reflected that Montagu was, after all, a courtier and could not be expected to see things in the light of absolute principles or of theological distinctions. As he continued to read, he saw that the same thought had occurred to the writer. 'Let no scrupulosity embrace your stomach,' Montagu warned him. 'Learning you may well have, but undoubtedly neither prudence nor pity and you show yourself in danger of running from one mischief to another.'

Thomas Starkey wrote heatedly: 'If you remember at all my nature, my deeds, and my duty, you may perhaps partly understand how your bloody book pricked me and how sorry I was to see the King so irreverently handled. Leave your fantasies and you will find that the King's heart is much sooner won than lost.'

Henry's own letter, though critical, was in fact the mildest. The King merely thanked Pole for the book, while demurring at its conclusions, and asked him to return to England as soon as possible so that he might discuss it with him.

Throckmorton, in confirmation of the fury which the book had provoked on all sides, told his master that, in order to escape from England, he had had to pretend to become Cromwell's spy.

'Then, Michael, I will find some other messenger to take my answers back.'

'It will be better, sir, that I take them if you will give me also some news that I can deliver my Lord Cromwell to colour the pretence.'

'No doubt we can find some.'

'When will your Highness wish me to leave?'

'Not for a week at least. They are difficult letters to write.'

The Venetian summer increased the difficulty. To escape the sweltering heat, Reginald set out next day for a farm near Padua where he could, in solitude, make his decision.

At the same time, in England, Henry took measures against Pole in Parliament which obediently enacted that, 'as divers seditious and contentious characters, being imps of the Bishop of Rome, do in corners and elsewhere, as they dare, instil the continuance of his pretended authority', the penalties of high treason were extended to cover any who by their writing upheld the papal supremacy. That simplified matters considerably in dealing with Reginald the moment he set foot in England.

The same month, another Succession Act was passed. Mary and Elizabeth were both bastardised and the succession settled on the children of 'His Highness's most dear and entirely beloved lawful wife Queen Jane'. Yet, as it was problematical whether there would be any children, Henry was given the power to leave the throne, in the event of his death, to any one he chose, as he might leave any other piece of his personal property.

The purpose of this was quite clear. He intended to leave

it—unless Jane bore him a son—to Richmond, who was now seventeen. When the young man died of consumption a week after the Act was passed, there were not wanting those who saw in it the continuance of the curse on all the King's male issue. Montagu, indeed, said as much to his brother Geoffrey, who agreed with him; but their mother reprimanded them sharply for speaking so foolishly. The important thing, Margaret said, was that now Princess Mary was the only possible heir and that Henry would have to take her back into favour.

For the King, despite his promise, would not, though he had visited his daughter and sent her gifts, allow her back to court until she acknowledged the Supremacy. Throughout May and June, ill with anxiety, troubled with her usual sleeplessness, racked with neuralgia, Mary had somehow found strength to resist the relentless bullying of Cromwell. But now that her half-brother's death had revolutionised the political situation, Chapuys counselled submission. God, he said, looked more closely at men's intentions than at their acts and an oath exacted by threats would be in no way binding on her conscience. And so, at eleven o'clock one night, she at last put her signature to the paper her father had sent her to sign. She acknowledged him 'Supreme Head of the Church in England'; she repudiated 'the Bishop of Rome's pretended authority' and she admitted that her mother's marriage with Henry 'was by God's law and man's incestuous and unlawful'.

And once the paper had gone to the King, she never, all her life, forgave herself.

As, days later, she poured out her grief and self-scorning to her old Governess, Margaret did her best to comfort her. She adduced all the reasons for drawing a casuistical line between politics and religion with which she herself intended to face Reginald should he decide to return and argue; she endorsed Chapuys's judgment that an oath under duress is no oath; she assured Mary—though with less confidence than she assumed—

that Catherine, now surely in Paradise, would approve her action. But the Princess would not be comforted.

Nor did Margaret convince herself. Strangely, as it seemed to her, the more she urged it the less she believed it. The very simplicity of the issue, as it had been presented to Mary, forced her to see where Reynold stood. Unnecessary invective apart, it might have needed a lengthy book indeed to propound the formal arguments, with their religious, constitutional, legal and moral implications, which justified the curt negatives—that Henry was not the Head of the Church and that his marriage to Catherine was not invalid. Margaret saw only dimly that everything hung on the affirmative—that the Pope, whoever he might be and however unworthy he might be, was God's Vice-regent—but at least she remembered that it was for this that Fisher and More and the Carthusians had died and, though she was not yet prepared to accept it unreservedly for herself, she began to see the meaning of John Helyar's: 'All is in this.' Reynold might be more in the right than she had allowed.

In his letter, which arrived in August, he reminded her that she had, from his earliest youth, dedicated him utterly to God's service. 'This dedication now, Madam my mother, I require you to maintain. Do not let the injury of withdrawing from that service be ever found in you towards my Master and yours, but touching yourself and me both, commit all to His goodness, as I doubt not that Your Ladyship will. Remember how we spoke when we looked at the wall at Warblington.'

She remembered that day when they were discussing whether or not to put the motto, *Spes mea in Deo est*, on the south wall of the garden near the sundial. Geoffrey had urged that the motto proclaiming that 'in God is my trust' had been used so profusely in the decoration of the house that its use on the garden wall verged on the ridiculous; but Reynold had vehemently defended its appropriateness near the sundial as a reminder that Time without a belief in God's over-ruling providence was a thing to be dreaded and feared.

'This shall be to me,' the letter ended, 'the greatest comfort I can have of you to whom I send my love and my duty.'

Pole's missive to the King, well-intentioned though it may have been, was not calculated to mollify him. 'I learn by Your Grace's letter,' it began, 'that you expect not a letter but me in person. There is nothing I desire more and it is you alone who prevent it. For me to come to England now would be to cast temerariously away my life which I am bound to keep to God's pleasure.'

He reminded Henry that he had written the offending book with extreme reluctance and only because the King had ordered him to. And 'here is the difficulty in a prince. Who will tell him his fault? And if such a one is found, where is the prince who will hear him?' But in this case God had provided a faithful subject in a safe place where he could speak at liberty. 'My whole desire is was and ever shall be that Your Grace may reign long in honour, in wealth, in surety, in love and estimation of men.' And now that God had rid the King 'of that domestical evil at home who was thought to be the cause of all your errors, and with her head, I trust, cut away all occasion of such offences as did separate you from the light of God, this is the time, Sir, to call to God that, your ancient years now growing upon you, you may finish your time in all honour and joy'.

It was not so much the letter as the information which Throckmorton brought with him to convince Cromwell he was spying for him that fanned Henry's hatred. This was that the Pope had summoned Pole to Rome to advise him in the preparations for an Ecumenical Council and that he intended to make him the Cardinal of England in place of the martyred Fisher.

Nothing, it was true, was finally settled and Pole had promised Throckmorton that, should the matter of the Cardinalate be taken further, news of it should not reach England until he was safely back in Italy, lest the King's vengeance should fall on him. But the very fact that Pole was, at the same moment as he was refusing to go to England at the bidding of the King, preparing to go to Rome at the bidding of the Pope, was sufficient to provoke one of Henry's insensate rages. It also disturbed Pole's family more than anything else he had done.

For Margaret, the focus shifted again. This was another simplification. Reynold, given a straight choice of obediences, had chosen wrongly. This she could not forgive. She wrote that, if he obeyed the Pope's summons, she would disown him. Montagu put it even more forcibly and at his suggestion she called her household at Warblington together and told them 'she took her son to be a traitor and for no son, and that she would never take him otherwise'. But her voice contradicted her words and none of them believed her.

Reginald had already set out for Rome when Throckmorton overtook him at Verona and delivered the letters. Their effect was such that for several days he was uncertain whether to continue the journey. At last he made his fateful decision and wrote to Contarini: 'The more numerous and more terrible the letters are I receive from England as to the King's disposition towards me, the more needful it is that I should trust for my safety entirely to the Pope for whose authority I incurred the King's displeasure. The King certainly thought that those letters would prevent my coming to Rome and he would have been right had not Divine grace sustained my resolution.

'Of these letters, one was from Cromwell, written in the King's name, full of all kinds of threats. Another, which moved me deeply, was from my mother and my brother, written in such a miserable strain that I almost succumbed. I certainly had begun to change my plans, as they so earnestly besought me not to go on this journey against the King's will: otherwise they would renounce all ties of nature between us. I did not see how to avoid this blow, aimed at my very vitals, except by a change of plan, for which I intended to ask leave of the Pope, nothing doubting his kindness.

'But I have now seen that my perseverance will redound all the more to the glory of Christ when neither the King's threats nor love of parents can make me swerve.'

He had chosen as his mother, whatever she might say now, had taught him to choose.

He continued on his way to Rome, but before he reached it he received more news from England. Yorkshire and the neighbouring counties had flamed into revolt and, under the banner of the Five Wounds of Christ, the common men of England were marching to London to restore the Faith.

15

The Banner of the Five Wounds

'The dangerest insurrection that hath ever been seen,' as Cromwell—against whom it was mainly directed—called it, began on Sunday, October 1, 1536, when the Vicar of Louth in Lincolnshire preached a sermon, rousing his congregation to defend their faith. By the Friday, a 'people's army' of ten thousand men occupied Lincoln, but because it had no effective leader, disintegrated before the army under the Duke of Suffolk which Henry (himself staying in London to superintend the strengthening of the Tower lest Suffolk should be unsuccessful) sent against them with specific instructions to 'with all extremity burn and kill man, woman and child, to the terrible example of all others'.

Across the Humber, in Yorkshire, there was, however, a leader. There the revolt started at Beverley, led by a young barrister, Robert Aske, who issued a proclamation for all men to assemble on Skipworth Moor and take an oath to be faithful to the King's issue and noble blood, to preserve the Church from spoil and to be true to the Commonwealth (a careful euphemism for getting rid of Cromwell). This proclamation was nailed to the door of every church in the county and the first three demands were the destruction of the heresies of Wyclif and Luther; the repeal of the Act of Supremacy and the restoration of the Pope's authority in spiritual matters; and the confirmation of the privileges and rights of the Church by act of Parliament.

Aske said that, speaking for himself, 'unless the Bishop of Rome was head of the Church in England as heretofore he would die in that quarrel', and the first verse of the Pilgrims' Song embodied the whole matter:

> Christ crucified!
> For Thy wounds wide,
> Us commons guide,
>   Which pilgrims be
> Through God His grace
> For to purchase
> Old wealth and peace
>   Of the spirituality.

With the Five Wounds of Christ as their banner and the Pilgrimage of Grace as their name, 'all the flower of the North', thirty-thousand strong, marched south and the royal forces, under Norfolk, dared not try conclusions with them.

Norfolk, after he had served the King to the best of his ability by presiding over his niece's trial and execution, had hoped for some signal mark of royal favour. Instead, much to his mortification, he had been virtually banished from court and, for the last three months, had been sulking at his manor of Kenninghall in Norfolk. When the Lincolnshire rising had broken out, the King had pointedly given the command to Suffolk. But the danger was now too great and Henry had no option but to recall Norfolk, who was not only his most experienced soldier but, as the hero of Flodden, had still a name to conjure with in the North.

Norfolk immediately saw that his only hope of success lay in persuading the Pilgrims to parley. He would have to make concessions but, in the same letter as that in which he described the rebels as 'all the flower of the North', he assured Henry that he need have no qualms about any promises he might make to them: 'Sir, most humbly I beseech you to take in good part whatsoever promises I shall make to the rebels (if any such I shall make) for surely I shall observe no part thereof.' Henry naturally agreed to this and at a meeting with the Pilgrims' leaders on the bridge at Doncaster, Norfolk promised in the King's name to reform all the abuses they had specified (including the restoration of the monasteries), to give a free pardon to all the Pilgrims and to hold a Parliament at York, where it would not be overshadowed by Cromwell and the court. Norfolk himself swore that he was heart and soul with the Pilgrims and arranged to accompany Aske to the King to lay the petitions before him. On this assurance, in spite of the opposition of the Durham contingent which did not trust Norfolk and wished to advance at once and wipe out the Royal army—which would have been easy enough—Aske persuaded the Pilgrims to agree to a truce. By the beginning of December, they had all dispersed to their homes.

A fortnight after the start of the Pilgrimage, Reginald Pole, accompanied by Priuli, Giberti and Caraffa, arrived in Rome where the Pope received him with great honour and gave him apartments in the Vatican next to those of Contarini. The friends were reunited to devote themselves to plans of reform.

The news from England, however, suggested a new and separate mission for Pole himself. 'Signior Reynold Pole,' a Papal diplomat in France wrote, 'could do service to God by going to England. He could do much among the people there who are mostly alienated, if not from the King, at least from all his ministers.'

The Pope, impressed by these considerations, determined as a first step to create Pole Cardinal of England as successor to the martyred Fisher. By Contarini and Giberti and Caraffa and Priuli, the suggestion was welcomed. No one could be more worthy of such an honour and such a responsibility than their friend. But Pole, when the Pope approached him on the matter, was horror-stricken.

'At such a time as this, Your Holiness,' he protested, 'it would destroy any influence I might have in England.'

'How so?' asked Paul.

'It would make me appear tied too closely to Your Holiness, and making a deliberate defiance of Henry.'

'Cardinal Contarini and the Bishop of Verona are not of that opinion.'

'In all other things I would submit to their judgment, Your Holiness; but not in this. I know my own people. I most humbly beg Your Holiness, for the sake of the Church, not to give me this honour.'

'And for your own sake?'

'That too. I am not worthy of it.'

'Others think differently and I am of their opinion.'

'Yet, even if I were, I would still beg Your Holiness to leave me in obscurity for the sake of my family in England. I fear they are already in danger because of the book I have written.'

Paul found this difficult to understand. He could not believe that the King of England would hold the family responsible for Reynold's opinions; but Pole managed to persuade him that Henry, in his present mood, might do anything and the Pope was sufficiently impressed to promise to defer the Cardinalate. Then suddenly and inexplicably, he changed his mind.

Three days before Christmas, the Pope's Chamberlain went to Pole's apartment to tell him that, on holy obedience, he was to prepare himself to receive the Cardinalate at once. To emphasise the point, the Chamberlain was accompanied by a barber who had instructions to put Pole's tonsure in order. With Pole was Priuli, who made a note of the episode: 'Since my good lord did not expect such a thing, he was extremely confused and showed by his face his displeasure; but because time pressed and there was no room for a reply, like a lamb before the shearer, he showed himself obedient.'

Later that day, Reginald was created Cardinal, taking his

title from the church which was originally known as 'the Church of the Bandage.'[1] According to tradition, St. Peter, having escaped from the dreaded Mamertine Prison where Nero had confined him, was hurrying towards the Appian Way by which he intended to make his way to safety and leave Rome for ever, when, at this point, the bandage wrapped round the wound caused by his prison chains fell off. On the Appian Way itself, he met Jesus and exclaimed in surprise: 'Where are you going, Lord?' and was answered: 'Back to Rome to be crucified again.' Peter, understanding, turned round and went back to the city to face his martyrdom.

At the reputed place of Peter's vision, the chapel of *Domine Quo Vadis* had been built, but had fallen into disrepair from neglect. Pole, pondering the strange relevance of St. Peter and his end to his own career at the moment, wished to restore *Domine Quo Vadis* before he set out, as he had now determined to set out, for England and death. But it would take too long, nor was he rich enough. Instead, he built a little circular chapel about a hundred and fifty yards from the church, at the next fork in the road—which, some contended, was the real place of the vision.

On February 7, 1537, the Pope at a secret consistory, made Pole Papal Legate to England. Reginald accepted his task: 'Long ago, Your Holiness, I determined to offer my life in this matter. Now it is a duty. I ask Your Holiness's prayers for my country and myself.'

The one thing necessary was speed. Pole must be at York for the parliament which was to meet there in the spring. To ensure this, would the Pope arrange with the Emperor and the King of France for him to have a safe-conduct through their dominions? He planned to set out for Flanders in a week's

---

[1] The church was in existence in the earliest times and is referred to as 'the Bandage' (*fasciola*) four centuries before it was changed to Ss. Nereus and Achilleus when it was rebuilt in the eighth century, and by which title it is now known.

time. The Bishop of Verona, who was said to be *persona grata* with King Henry, would accompany him officially and, of course, Alvise Priuli privately. He would set out on Ash Wednesday.

On Shrove Tuesday, Throckmorton arrived in Rome with letters from England. The Bishop of London, on behalf of the clergy, accused Pole of having been seduced by the fair words and promises of the Bishop of Rome and 'for the vain-glory of a Red Hat you make yourself an instrument of his malice who would stir up rebellion in the realm'. Starkey, in one of his long and argumentative tirades, asked him to repudiate his Cardinalate: 'We should be glad to hear that by utter refusal you would show your love for His Highness. If you do not, you declare yourself open enemy to the King and his realm, as in such case he will and must accept you.' On behalf of the Privy Council, Pole was reproached for 'incredible ingratitude towards the King and country and such unseemly and irreverent behaviour as no mortal enemy could have contrived and forged the like'.

To these letters, Throckmorton added the private information that it was generally expected that, as soon as it was convenient, the King would break his word and proceed against the Pilgrims who, having disbanded, were now defenceless. It was true that a Parliament was promised at York and that Henry had further placated the northerners by promising to have Jane Seymour crowned in York Minister; but no one seriously believed that it would happen.

'Then,' said Pole, 'I must make the more speed to be there. It is proper that all should know that His Holiness approves of the manly and Christian demonstration the people are making.'

By the time Throckmorton had arrived in Rome, the King's vengeance on the Pilgrims was already a reality. Norfolk had returned to the North and hundreds of arrests were made. On February 24, when Pole had only just got beyond Bologna, Norfolk wrote to Henry that he had chosen seventy-four ordinary men in Cumberland and, as an example, had had them hanged in their own villages 'on trees in their own gardens'. He apologised that the numbers were so small and explained that he had to proceed by martial law, as juries would not have convicted one in five. 'And, sir,' he concluded, 'though the number is nothing so great as should have suffered, yet I think the like number hath not been heard of put to death at one time.' He still hoped for more and when he had finished in Cumberland, he would proceed to the other counties 'and thence into Yorkshire to begin again there'.

Henry wrote back his approval, confirmed that 'the course of our laws must give place to martial law' and ordered: 'You shall without pity of circumstance cause the monks to be tied up without further delay or ceremony.' Cromwell had suggested that the Pilgrimage, which had been for the defence of the monasteries, was a convenient excuse for their more speedy and thorough destruction.

On April 10, Pole made a state entry, as Legate, into Paris. Stephen Gardiner, Bishop of Winchester, who was the English Ambassador, had been instructed by Henry to demand of Francis that he should arrest Pole and send him to England. The French King replied that, as the Legate had a safe-conduct, arrest was impossible but that he should be asked to leave within ten days.

Henry, enraged, then sent his 'one-eyed minion', the 'Vicar of Hell', Sir Francis Bryan, to demand Pole again and to remind King Francis that the treaty between England and France did not recognise safe-conducts. But, by this time, the French King was with his army and Pole had left Paris for Cambrai. Bryan was furious. As the Nuncio in Paris put it in a letter to the Pope: 'Not having succeeded in bringing the Legate to England into the catalogue of the martyrs, Bryan is very desperate and discontent with the French and bragging that, if he found the Cardinal alone in the midst of France, he would kill him with his own hand—and similar big words. This shows clearly the mind of the English King and that he fears Pole more than any-one else.'

The independent Archbishopric of Cambrai being neutral territory, Henry wrote to Gardiner and Bryan that, 'as we would be very glad to have Pole trussed up and conveyed to Calais', they might enlist men 'capable of such an enterprise' to kidnap him. To make such a course more attractive, the King offered 10,000 English gold pieces for the Cardinal alive or dead and a party from Calais set out to earn it. The leader of the gang, however, had to write disappointedly to Cromwell: 'The man you wot of doth not come out of his lodging, nor intends to as far as I can learn.' Priuli had seen to that.

The Prince-Bishop of Liége, to whom the Pope had particu-larly commended Pole, then offered his fellow-Cardinal the hospitality of his see, but suggested that Reginald, for safety's sake, should travel the hundred miles between them in disguise. This Pole refused to do. For one thing, as he was Legate, it would compromise the dignity of the Holy See; for another, his whole purpose in remaining as near as he could to England was to give some encouragement to the 'poor good men' of the North by showing that their plight was the concern of the Pope, whose ambassador he was. It was as ambassador, not as a kidnap-ped traitor, that he must appear in England. But ambassadors—especially legates, 'the highest embassy used among Christian princes'— did not disguise themselves for purposes of their per-sonal safety.

But by this time—it was the middle of May—the 'poor good men' of England had been finally crushed. Norfolk had dealt with the North to Henry's satisfaction in both branches of his policy. There had been over two hundred executions and the monasteries had been attended to: 'If it be your pleasure to have the houses of Bridlington and Jervaulx suppressed, I will ride there and employ men who will see to your profit. Jervaulx is covered with lead and as for Bridlington there is none like it, worth £3,000 or £4,000, and standing near the sea it can be easily carried away.' There were now over 20,000 religious or homeless beggars on the roads.

The leaders of the Pilgrimage had been sent to London and tried and condemned for 'conspiring to deprive the King of his title of Supreme Head of the English Church'. Twelve were executed but there was some dissatisfaction among the Londoners and Henry, rather than incur blame for too great severity, ordered the public killings to stop and the remaining prisoners were left to die privately in prison from the plague, which was raging in the capital. Aske himself was well guarded for subsequent execution in York.

On Montagu the King's breach of faith had a decisive effect. He had, though with misgivings, taken the Oath of Supremacy. He had ridden north with Norfolk against the Pilgrims. He had dissociated himself from the views of his brother Reynold, both publicly and privately. But at last he was disillusioned.

'There was a time,' he said to Geoffrey, 'when nothing could be more firmly trusted than a King's word. Now they do not consider a promise a promise but merely a policy to blind the people.'

'We must blame Cromwell for that,' Geoffrey answered.

'The King and Cromwell are of the same nature. As long as they can live at their own pleasure, they care nothing what becomes of the realm. There is now no one at Court but flatterers and no one serves the King but knaves.'

'You have served him yourself well enough in the past.'

'I was brought up with him, but I never liked him. I always thought that one day he would go mad. He has never made a man but he has destroyed him again, either by displeasure or by the sword.'

'Like Wolsey.'

'Yes. And Wolsey would have been an honest man had he had an honest master.'

'What touches us most,' said Geoffrey, 'is what he may do to the new Cardinal our brother.'

'Thank God Reynold is safe from him,' said Montagu.

Geoffrey looked at his brother. He was still not quite sure of him. It was Montagu, after all, who had insisted on writing the angry letters to Reynold; Montagu who had made their mother speak against him to the household at Warblington; Montagu who on his knees had apologised on his behalf to Henry. Geoffrey, as the youngest son, understood that Montagu, as head of the house, was bound by certain responsibilities which he had escaped; but he was always uncertain how far his eldest brother's dynastic duty corresponded to his real feelings. Nor was their mutual understanding helped by Montagu's disapproval of Geoffrey's general irresponsibility. If, now, Geoffrey was suspicious of the suddenness of Montagu's apparent *volte face*, Montagu equally was apprehensive of Geoffrey's possible indiscretion in a dangerous crisis.

'Have you heard what they are saying at court?' Geoffrey asked.

'What are they saying?' replied Montagu, who knew perfectly well.

'I had it from Lady Darrell that Cromwell has sent his man, Peter Mewtas, across the sea to shoot Reynold.'

'He has chosen the right knave,' said Montagu, 'but Reynold is less simple than Aske.' It was Peter Mewtas who had taken the King's dishonoured safe-conduct to Aske and persuaded him to come to London.

'Are you with me in sending a warning to Reynold?' said Geoffrey.

'If you can see some certain way to do it,' answered Montagu, 'without making things worse.' Then, remembering that Geoffrey was always in debt, he added: 'If you need any money, I will let you have it; but you need not tell me all your intention, so that, if it comes to the pinch, I can deny knowledge of it on oath.'

Geoffrey, realising that this was probably the first time that Montagu had completely trusted him, rode post-haste to Chichester, where he found Hugh Holland about to take a cargo of grain to Nieuport.

'My brother the Cardinal is in those parts,' said Geoffrey. 'Will you do an errand for me to him?'

When Holland agreed, Geoffrey gave him a message: 'Commend me to my brother and tell him I would I were with him and will come to him, if he will have me. Make him see that here everything is crooked; God's law is turned upside-down, abbeys and churches are overthrown and he himself is proclaimed a traitor. Tell him that men are sent from England to destroy him and that Cromwell himself has sent Peter Mewtas to kill him with a hand-gun or otherwise as he sees best.'

Holland promised to deliver the message carefully, but the day before he sailed Geoffrey suggested a slight alteration in plan: 'How say you, Hugh, if I go over with you myself and see that good fellow?'

'Oh, no, sir,' Holland replied with unnecessary alacrity. 'My ship is fully loaded and my mariners would be suspicious if you were aboard.'

'Well, then,' said Geoffrey, reflecting gloomily that no one, from the Imperial Ambassador to the captain of a trading vessel, ever seemed to show much enthusiasm for his help, 'remember what I have said to you and fare you well.'

When Holland arrived at Cambrai, the Cardinal was on his way to Liége, travelling, as he had insisted, as Legate and protected by the Emperor's safe-conduct—Charles V's reply to Henry's suggestion that he would supply 4,000 foot-soldiers and their pay for ten months for the Emperor's army in exchange for Pole.

Reginald was at Alne Abbey, on the outskirts of the city, when his brother's messenger overtook him. When Holland had delivered his message, he merely said: 'Is Cromwell so anxious to kill me? I trust it will not lie in his power.' After Holland had given him an account of things in England, he sent messages to his family. To his mother he sent his love and asked her blessing. 'I trust,' he said, 'that she will be glad of mine also.'

Momentarily Hugh Holland's stolid face betrayed him. He had been present at Warblington when Margaret had announced that she considered her son a traitor. Pole noticing the change of expression divined the cause of it. He too was aware of the episode but had dismissed it from his mind as being an action imposed on her by political necessity. Now he wanted to reassure her that he understood it and that his trust in her was unshaken. Since he could not give this as a direct message, he chose a method which she would understand. But, inevitably, Holland did not and was shocked when the Cardinal added: 'And tell her that if I thought she held the opinion that any other than the Pope was Head of the Church, mother of mine as she is, I would trample on her.'

'I am to tell her that?'

'That is my message to her. To my brother Montagu, give my commendation and remind him of our motto: "I trust in God." '

'And what am I to say to Sir Geoffrey, sir?'

'Give him my love and advise him not to meddle with anything but to let well alone.'

Reginald realised what danger Geoffrey had put himself in by merely sending Holland to warn him. This affectionate solicitude was, since Reginald had been officially proclaimed a traitor, high treason.

Next day, Pole continued his way to Liége, where he arrived on June 1 and was pontifically received with great honour. He was given the old palace as his residence. 'They take him there for a young god,' Cromwell's agent wrote angrily to his master.

'I will make Mr. Traitor Pole eat his own heart,' said Cromwell.

On July 12, Robert Aske was laid upon a hurdle and drawn through the main streets of York, where it was market-day. He

212

was then brought out on a scaffold which had been erected on the top of the Clifford Tower, so that the whole city might watch his death. He had been promised that he would be allowed to hang till he was dead in return for an acceptable confession. He told the listening crowd that 'the King's Highness was so gracious a lord to all his subjects that no man should be troubled for any offence comprised within the compass of his gracious pardon'. For himself he admitted that 'he had greatly offended the King's Majesty in breaking the laws whereunto every true subject is bounden by the commandment of God'.

In one sense this was no more than the confirmation of his original mistake when, at that first parley with Norfolk, he trusted the word of a faithless king and, laying aside the Pilgrims' badge of the Five Wounds, had declared: 'Henceforth we will wear no badge nor sign but the badge of our sovereign lord.'

With Aske's death, the banner of the Five Wounds was banished from popular memory as a treasonable device. But at Warblington, Margaret Pole, having received and understood her son's message, took from the chest in which she had put it the tapestry she had worked long ago when it had seemed possible that Reginald would marry Princess Mary. The silks had not lost their lustre. The gold of the marigolds of Mary shone the brighter among the purple of the pansies of Pole. And, in the backing of the Five Wounds, the vivid red was like newly-spilled blood.

16

Jane Seymour gives Henry an heir

Ten days after Aske's execution, Henry bestowed on Cromwell the highest order of chivalry, the Garter.

To his spy, Richard Moryson, who had returned to England from Pole's household when the Cardinal had left Venice, Cromwell now entrusted the task of vilifying Pole, who, he admitted, 'came somewhat too late into France at the last commotion; if he had come in season, he would have played an hardier part than Aske did.' In the hysteria was a hint of relief.

Moryson, in what Henry welcomed as a 'pretty book', described his one-time benefactor as 'the archtraitor whom God hateth, nature refuseth, all men detest, yea, and all beasts too would abhor if they could perceive how much viler he is than the worst of them'. The Cardinal's true friends are those who wish him dead, for only so can he escape 'the gripes, the wounds, the tossing and turmoiling, the heaving and shoving that traitors feel in their stomachs'. God leaves him alive 'only because thy life hath many more torments much more shame in it, more than any cruel death can have. What greater shame can come to thee than to be the dishonour of all thy kin, a comfort to all thine enemies, a death to all thy friends? O Pole, O whirlpool, full of poison, that wouldst have drowned thy country in blood, thou art now a Pool of little water and that at a wonderful low ebb.'

The Cardinal's only comment was: 'I have read his writings more with pity than with indignation because they show nothing but the miserable servitude of his mind.'

Now that any hope of his legation being received was at an end, Pole was anxious to leave Liége and return to Rome as soon as possible. But he could not do so without the Pope's permission and, in the interim, he was grateful for the respite. More than once he said to Priuli: 'How we must thank God for this time of quiet!' His only regret was that Contarini was not with them.

Priuli, writing to Contarini, described their manner of life: 'In the morning everyone remains in his room until an hour and a half before dinner, when we assemble in the private chapel for the recitation of the Office. The Bishop of Verona is our Master of Ceremonies. After Office, we hear Mass and dine at mid-day. During dinner there is a reading from St. Bernard and conversation. Then some two hours pass in agreeable and useful talk until an hour and a half before supper, after which we sing Vespers and Compline, and the Legate, who finally allowed himself to be persuaded thereto, every alternate day lectures on the Epistles of St. Paul, beginning with the Epistle to Timothy, to the great satisfaction of Giberti and everyone. Shortly after the lecture comes supper; then we boat on the river or walk in the garden, discussing various topics.'

Meanwhile, Michael Throckmorton was in England, still trying to induce Cromwell to go to Liége to discuss things with Pole face to face, and promising on his master's behalf that Pole would renounce his cardinalate if the King would return to the Papal allegiance. When it became clear that so Utopian a solution had no practical relevance, Throckmorton left Cromwell under no illusion that his spying for him was a pretence and fled from England. Cromwell, after imprisoning his brother, Sir George Throckmorton, as an act of vengeance wrote bitterly to Michael: 'I might have judged that that detestable traitor your master, with his shameful ingratitude, unnaturalness and conspiracy, could have but even a servant such as you are. You and your master have both shown how little fear of God resteth in you as you work treason towards your prince and country. You have bleared my eyes once; you shall never deceive me a second time.'

In his fury, as he dashed off page after page of invective, Cromwell revealed his intention of destroying Pole's family. 'Pity it is,' he wrote, 'that the folly of one brainsick Pole—or, to say better, of one witless fool—should be the ruin of so great a family, who shall feel what it is to have such a traitor as their kinsman.' As for Reginald himself, he can be killed at any moment: 'Whensoever the King will, His Highness may bring it easily to pass that he shall think himself scarce sure of his life, even though he went tied at the Pope's girdle. There can be found ways enough in Italy to get rid of a traitorous subject. Do not let him think that, where Justice can take no place by process of law at home, she may not seek other means abroad.'

Cromwell ended by threatening Throckmorton's own family: 'If you were natural towards your country or your family you would not shame all your kin. This I am sure of, that the least suspicion shall be enough to undo the greatest of them. I desire God that you and your master may acknowledge your detestable faults. God send you both to fare as you deserve; that is, either to come to your allegiance or else to a shameful death.'

Throckmorton was with Pole in Rome when the letter reached him. The Cardinal had entered the city on October 18, having been forced to travel 'clean out of the common way' to escape relays of Henry's assassins. The first news he received was that, a week earlier, Henry had at last been given an heir. Once more the balance of politics had changed.

Jane Seymour had chosen for her motto: 'Bound to obey and serve.' It showed considerable self-knowledge. She was the very pattern of placid obedience. Having watched her predecessor's stormy passionate career (she was only two years younger than Anne), Jane opted for oblivion. Anne's excoriating remarks were still remembered and quoted at court. Jane was so careful of utterance that she contrived to say, during her Queenship, nothing sufficiently significant to be worth recording. Only once did she try to influence Henry, when on her knees she pleaded with him to restore the abbeys dissolved during the Pilgrimage of Grace. He said: 'Get up and don't meddle with my affairs.' She obeyed.

Her large face, with its small features, was faintly reminiscent of a sheep, but it was of alabaster whiteness. By marrying her, the Supreme Head gained one brother-in-law whose name was Smith and another whose grandfather was a blacksmith at Putney; but Henry though 'within eight days of the publication of his marriage, having twice met two beautiful young ladies, he said and showed himself somewhat sorry that he had not seen them before he was married', found in the very insipidity of Jane's devotion the certainty he needed to mend the self-respect that Anne had so mangled. Against 'that witch' he still raved, swearing that more than a hundred men had been her lovers and even accusing his newly-created bishops of telling her that 'it was allowable for a woman to ask for aid in other quarters, even among her own relatives, when the husband did not satisfy her desires'.

The shadow of Anne seemed to lie across Henry's potency and three months after his marriage to Jane he confessed to Chapuys 'that he felt himself growing old and doubted whether he should have any child by the Queen'. A month later, Princess Mary was received back into favour and recognised once more as heir to the throne 'in default of issue by the present Queen and none is expected on account of the complexion and disposition of the King'.

Jane, five years older than Mary, had always been her firm friend even though, during the last year or two, it had been impossible to show it. Now she made it her especial care to reconcile the King and the Princess. When Mary came back to court, she gave her a valuable diamond ring and induced Henry to give her 'a check for about a thousand crowns for her pocket-money'. Courtiers noticed that whenever the King was not present, the Queen, to prevent Mary having to follow her through a door, would take her hand and pass through it side by side with her.

That Christmas—it was the Christmas of 1536 when Pole was made Cardinal in Rome and in London Peter Mewtas had been sent to lure Robert Aske to his death by a safe-conduct—the King, the Queen and the Princess rode from Greenwich to Westminster in state. In Fleet Street, in spite of the bitter cold which had frozen the Thames, stood ecclesiastics in copes of gold, with crosses and candlesticks and censers swinging to cense the royal company as it went to St. Paul's for High Mass. From the north door of the Cathedral, down the hill to London Bridge, stood priests from every parish in London, each with their finest church crosses and candles and censers. They were flanked by members of all the City Companies 'standing in their best liveries with their hoods on their shoulders'. A stranger to England would not have known that there had been any change in the religious scene. It was all as it had been. The new Queen was as devout a Catholic as the Princess, her step-daughter; and the King was Defender of the Faith.

Even Pole had admitted that there was 'nothing much at variance with the Catholic standard, except that authority is ascribed to the King—a thing which it is difficult to say whether it is more foolish or impious. The mercy of God has protected the faith of the people'. The Supremacy was, after all, a matter of politics. It was perhaps unfortunate that the Carthusians, Fisher, More, Pole, the Pilgrims, the Pope and the rest of Christendom thought otherwise; but Henry was quite clear on the matter. Moreover, he was determined to show the world that he remained a devout Catholic.

He had dissolved Parliament in the spring, just before Anne's execution. As soon as a new one assembled, he intended to put things beyond doubt by an act, punishing by burning as heretics any one who denied Transubstantiation or who advocated Communion in both kinds and by hanging as felons any who questioned the necessity of confession, the efficacy of masses for the dead, the celibacy of the clergy and the vows of chastity of the religious. Meanwhile, for himself, he was a pattern of devotion. His troublesome knee made kneeling an agony and Cranmer, anxious to help him, told him that it would be in order to sit while he was receiving Holy Communion. 'If I could get not only on the ground but under it' the King answered, 'I should not consider I was doing sufficient honour to the Most Holy Sacrament.'

In the circumstances, Cranmer found it impossible to introduce the doctrinal reforms which, both as a potential Lutheran and a secretly-married Archbishop, he wished the Supreme Head to enact in his church, or even to insist on small changes which would acclimatise the people to greater ones. Such simple things as forbidding fasting on Fridays and the observance of such immemorial feasts as Corpus Christi and All Souls were ignored. Sadly Cranmer wrote to Cromwell: 'My lord, if in the court you do keep holy days and fasting days, when shall we persuade the people to cease from keeping them?' But both Cranmer and Cromwell knew that, as long as Jane was Queen, there was no chance of effective change.

That Christmas season found Henry in unwonted spirits. For one thing, it was the first anniversary of Queen Catherine's death and he felt it incumbent on him not only to rejoice but to show his rejoicing. The Twelfth Night revels were unparalleled. He ate and drank magnificently. At night he managed to bed with Jane.

In March, to celebrate the Queen's pregnancy, there was a public *Te Deum* and another in July, which could be interpreted both as a public intimation that Jane, whom Henry for safety's sake was keeping surrounded by doctors in private, still did well, and as a thanksgiving for the execution of Aske.

Hampton Court was chosen for Jane's lying-in. It was a difficult birth. Henry, asked which, should it come to a choice, he wished saved, the mother or the child, replied without hesitation: 'The child by all means, for other wives can easily be found.'

At two o'clock in the morning of Friday October 12—the Eve of St. Edward the Confessor—the son whom Henry had craved for nearly thirty years was born. Once more *Te Deum* was solemnly sung in all the churches; bells rang, the Tower cannon fired, bonfires blazed, there was feasting in the streets 'with fruit and wine'. On Monday, the child, who was named Edward, was baptised by torchlight in the chapel of Hampton Court. Cranmer performed the ceremony and Princess Mary was the boy's godmother, giving him, as one of the presents, the golden cup that Wolsey had given her at her own christening.

Jane was very ill. She was carried to the chapel, as etiquette demanded, on a pallet decorated with the crown and arms of England worked in gold thread and furnished with four pillows of crimson and gold. In spite of her velvet mantle furred with ermine, she felt very cold, though she had a high fever. Nine days later she was dead.

There was, of course, a crop of rumours, the principal being that the King had caused her death 'when she was in severe labour in a difficult child-birth by having all her limbs stretched for the purpose of making a passage for the child, or (as others stated) having the womb cut before she was dead, so that the child ready to be born might be taken out'.

And the concealed but intense hatred for the King among the ordinary people spilled over on to his heir. At the funeral of a child in London, the priest for some reason became suspicious, because of the great crowd of idlers who were attending it. He opened the shroud and found that it was not a child but a wax image, evidently intended to represent the baby prince, with two large pins through its heart. The story spread like wildfire and when Jane died it was rumoured that Henry and Edward were also dead.

In the circumstances, it was considered imperative to have a funeral of more than usual splendour, though the King himself, whose horror of death increased with age, left Hampton Court immediately, after having ordered 1,200 Masses to be said in London churches for the repose of Jane's soul. She was embalmed and, for eighteen days, lay in state in the chapel at Hampton Court where, every day, requiem mass was said 'with all ceremonies, with censings and with holy water'.

On November 12, the magnificent funeral procession set off from Hampton Court to Windsor. Immediately behind the hearse, upon which stood the wax effigy of Jane in her robes of state, with a sceptre of gold in her right hand, her fingers covered with rings of precious stones and her neck with jewelled ornaments, rode Princess Mary on a horse trapped to the ground with black velvet. She was representing her father as principal mourner. At her right hand rode Lord Montagu.

Cromwell, watching them, decided that the time was now propitious to strike. As long as Jane had lived, the Poles were protected by the mere fact of the Queen's friendship with Mary. Now that that shield had gone, there was nothing to save them.

When the long ceremony was at last at an end and Queen Jane safely interred in the vault in St. George's Chapel at Windsor, Cromwell wrote to his spy, Gervaise Tyndale, who was still in Lincolnshire (where he had done excellent work in informing against many who had taken part in the Pilgrimage of Grace) and ordered him to go to Warblington.

17

Gervaise Tyndale goes to Warblington

Sir Geoffrey Pole was the first to feel the royal displeasure. After the Queen's funeral, he went to do his usual duty at court, 'but the King would not suffer him to come in'. In some perturbation he rode to consult his brother who was at his house at Bockmore in Buckinghamshire. It was here, at their father's family manor, that they had spent a little of their boyhood together—Geoffrey, a spoilt precocious child of four; Montagu, a swaggering sixteen preparing for his service at court. Their father's recent death had made Montagu boyishly punctilious about his responsibilities as head of the house and to Geoffrey in particular he had seemed a second father. Those early, ineradicable impressions made Geoffrey in times of tension instinctively seek the protection of Bockmore, when Montagu was in residence, in preference to his unsympathetic wife and seven children at Lordington.

Montagu, when his brother told him of his rebuff said: 'Geoffrey, it is a sign that God loves us that He will not suffer us to be there. None rule about the court but knaves.' And he broke into one of those diatribes against the King that had now become a habit with him: 'Supreme Head he may be, but, for all that, he has a sore leg that no poor man would be glad of and, for all his authority next God's, he will not live long.'

That night Montagu dreamt that the King was dead and woke Geoffrey to tell him so. 'God grant it is a portent. Then we can deal with Mr. Cromwell,' he said.

But it was not true and it was Cromwell who was about to deal with them.

Gervaise Tyndale went to Warblington early in the spring of 1538. Following the plan which had proved so successful for Richard Moryson in Venice, he arrived ill and destitute. The Countess of Salisbury, who was in residence, was immediately sympathetic and put him in the care of the doctor, Richard Eyre. Tyndale's health was quickly restored, but he showed no inclination to leave the company of that well-meaning gossip. From Eyre alone, he decided, he could collect most of the information his master needed.

Tyndale differed from Moryson and most of Cromwell's other spies in that he was actuated by certain principles. He was fanatical in his Lutheran beliefs—as indeed his earlier actions at Grantham had shown—and the execution two years earlier of his famous kinsman, William, had made him an obsessive proselytiser. William Tyndale, working in the Low Countries on his version of the Bible, had been arrested and, by order of the Emperor, had been tried for heresy and, on condemnation, strangled at the stake and his dead body burned in the state prison near Brussels. Gervaise, with a martyr in the family was now determined at all costs to encourage the reading of 'God's Holy Word'—as it was to him—and the fact that Margaret Pole was equally determined that none of her tenants at Warblington should be infected by a dangerous and heretical mistranslation of Holy Writ—as it was to her—lent to their disagreement a certain dignity which was absent from the squalid betrayals of Moryson and his kind.

Tyndale, indeed, impressed, as it was impossible not to be,

by the Countess's piety and charitable goodness, tended to blame others for her theological shortcomings. 'There is a company of priests,' he wrote to Cromwell, 'in my lady's house which do her much harm and keep her from the true knowledge of God's word.'

The priests, on their part, led by Father John Crayford, who was now the parish priest, wanted nothing so much as to be rid of Tyndale and when he announced his intention of opening a school in the neighbourhood he found even more decided opposition than he had done at Grantham.

The matter came to a head in the middle of June and was occasioned by the circumstance that the little church at Warblington was dedicated to St. Thomas of Canterbury.

The Supreme Head had decided that it was necessary to re-write history. The majesty of the law, the terror of the numerous executions, the fear engendered by the army of spies might have cowed the nation into acquiescence; yet the present was still menaced by the past. Magnificently at Canterbury Thomas Becket still defied King Henry and the pilgrims at the shrine took on the appearance of a protest.

Henry therefore issued a summons addressed 'to thee, Thomas Becket, sometime Archbishop of Canterbury' charging him with treason, contumacy and rebellion and giving him thirty days to answer the indictment. As, at the end of that time, the shrine remained undisturbed by Becket's resurrection, sentence was pronounced against him that his bones should be publicly burnt to admonish the living of their duty by the punishment of the dead and that his shrine and all the offerings made at it should be forfeited to the Crown.

Consequently a Commission for the destruction of the shrine arrived, under a strong military guard which could deal with any popular rioting; the shrine was broken open with a sledge-hammer, the bones duly burnt and the ashes scattered to the winds, while the jewels and gold of the shrine were carried off in two coffers on the shoulders of eight men, and twenty-six carts removed the accumulated offerings to God and St. Thomas. The wonderful jewel known as the 'Regale of France', which King Louis VII of France had presented three and a half centuries ago, Henry had set in a ring for his own thumb.

To Cromwell's practical mind, the satisfactory booty was sufficient excuse, were any needed, for the play-acting of the condemnation; but to Henry the condemnation itself was of prime importance. He issued a Royal Proclamation.

'Forasmuch,' it ran, 'as it now clearly appeareth that Thomas Becket was killed in a riot excited by his own obstinacy and intemperate language and was afterwards canonised by the Bishop of Rome as the champion of his usurped authority, the King's Majesty has thought it expedient to declare to his loving subjects that he was no saint but rather a rebel and a traitor to his prince. Therefore His Grace straitly chargeth and commandeth that henceforth the said Thomas Becket shall not be esteemed, named, reputed nor called a saint, but 'Bishop Becket', and that his images and pictures throughout the whole realm shall be put down and avoided out of all churches and chapels and other places; and that henceforth the days used to be festivals in his name shall not be observed, nor any service, office, collects and prayers in his name read, but erased and put out of all books.'[1]

The most popular of St. Thomas's feasts was that at the beginning of July, which commemorated the removal of his bones from their original resting-place in the crypt of Canterbury Cathedral to the Shrine fifty years after his death. The 'Translation of St. Thomas' was always celebrated with particular splendour at Warblington and Father Crayford was

[1] In consequence of the severe penalties attached to this decree, it was rigorously carried out and a calendar containing the name of St. Thomas unerased is a great rarity. The dedication of the churches to him was usually changed simply to 'St. Thomas' and left to be assumed to be St. Thomas the Apostle. The church at Warblington was rebuilt—it was a Saxon foundation recorded in Domesday Book—within a few years of Becket's martyrdom in 1170 and was one of the earliest dedications.

making the usual preparations for the feast when Tyndale came up to him, as he was discussing things with a group of villagers in the churchyard, and accused him of defying the King by keeping the now-forbidden festival.

The parish priest retorted that he had received no personal instructions from his Bishop and, though he had heard rumours of the King's proceedings against St. Thomas, he had no intention of making any changes until he was ordered to by proper authority.

'You can take my word for it,' said Tyndale.

One of the villagers, a devout spinster, screamed: 'The word of a heretic!'

In a moment all was in uproar and a youth who was one of Tyndale's secret supporters went to find the village constable lest the schoolmaster should be set on by the angry parishioners.

Tyndale, however, quivering with righteousness, stood his ground, called Father Crayford a knave and said that he should consider reporting the matter. During the momentary lull produced by this threat, he shouted: 'I know well enough what is going on in these parts. I know how that treasonable knave, Hugh Holland, under pretence of being a merchant man, goes overseas with letters to Master Pole, the traitor Cardinal, so that all the secrets of the realm are known to the Bishop of Rome.'

The constable arrived in time to hear this admission and, turning 'in a great fume' on Tyndale with: 'This countryside was a happy place before such fellows as you came to find fault with our good priests', ordered him to go home. Fortunately Richard Eyre had come out to see what was afoot and, hearing his guest shout at the top of his voice matters which he had told him secretly in the strictest confidence, hurried him into the house.

The entire village, of course, was perfectly aware of Hugh Holland's visits to the Low Countries. At least a dozen of the younger men were waiting to go over with him on his next trip to enlist in the Emperor's army. Ever since one of the

Countess's servants, John Stappill, had taken this step and 'come home like a jolly fellow apparelled in scarlet and a hundred crowns in his purse', the more adventurous had decided to seek a similar fortune. If they could not get service with the Emperor, they would go to Cardinal Pole, 'and there we shall be sure to be retained'.

But for this knowledge to be used in a threatening way by a 'foreigner' from Lincolnshire (who, in any case, was not of an endearing temperament) was in the nature of a crisis. Or so, at least, the constable thought. The more the good man considered it, the less he liked it. Had the Countess been in residence, he would have immediately gone over to the Castle to consult her. But she was in London. The only person he could report to was Sir Geoffrey, for whom he had little respect. Also, it would mean riding over to Lordington and temporarily leaving the welfare of Warblington in the hands of his unsatisfactory deputy. In the end, however, he decided that it was his duty to go, whatever the inconvenience.

Geoffrey received the information hysterically. His alternating anger and fear, the constable thought, were out of all proportion. Her Ladyship would have been far calmer in far worse circumstances.

There was, however, some excuse for Geoffrey for a reason of which the constable was naturally ignorant. Not quite a week earlier, after he had left Montagu at Bockmore, he had decided to leave England with the next fair wind, 'for safe-guard of his life'. The only difficulty was his chronic shortage of money. As Hugh Holland still refused to take him, he needed ready cash to pay his passage on some other boat. To resolve the awkward situation, he went over to Chichester to see Dr. George Croftes, the chancellor of the cathedral there, who, he knew, had also thought of emigrating to escape the new ecclesiastical measures. Croftes lent him twenty nobles and wished him God-speed.

Next morning, however, Croftes sent him an urgent letter

saying that 'he had the most marvellous dream that night that ever he had in his life and that he saw Our Lady appear to him and she pledged him that it should be to the destruction of Sir Geoffrey and all his kin if he departed the realm'. Geoffrey was sufficiently impressed to abandon his plan and return the money.

Now, when the Warblington constable came to warn him that a hostile stranger was aware of the comings and goings in the harbour, with all the danger that that knowledge implied, Geoffrey's first thought was that, had he paid less attention to clerical dreams, he could have been safe on the Continent, making his way to Reginald. The need for immediate action, however, quickly cut across his regrets. If, as seemed only too likely, Tyndale was a government spy, the first necessity was to forestall him. Peremptorily he ordered the constable to return to Warblington and tell Richard Eyre and Hugh Holland that they would be required to ride to London with him next day.

Cromwell, when he was informed that Sir Geoffrey Pole was requesting an interview on a matter of some urgency, was not unduly surprised. He granted it at once, and listened with every appearance of sympathy while Geoffrey explained that he had thought it wise to come direct to His Lordship to acquaint him of certain false rumours which were circulating in Warblington.

Cromwell's little gimlet-eyes remained hard but his mouth smiled as he said, assuming the bluff man-to-man attitude which was second nature to him on such occasions: 'We cannot but be divided, Sir Geoffrey, in the matter of your brother, but, as I do not credit you with his faults, so you, I trust, will not impute injustice to me.'

'It is because I do not that I have presumed to disturb you for what may seem a trifling matter,' said Geoffrey, relieved, and gave him an account of the matter with even more than his usual volubility. He explained that Hugh Holland, who had once been in his personal service but was now a grain-merchant trading with France and the Low Countries, had indeed taken letters overseas; but they were letters of a personal nature to Father John Helyar, sometime parish priest of Warblington, who, by the Countess of Salisbury's bounty, was studying at the University of Paris. Hugh Holland confirmed this.

Cromwell, looking at Holland's stolid face, was sure that he was lying but decided that he was the only man there worth considering and wondered whether to impound him, were he willing, for his own service. All he said was: 'John Helyar? The name has a familiar ring' and motioned to one of his secretaries, who started to study a pile of papers.

Geoffrey continued his narration. He told Cromwell how a stranger in Warblington, who had been in the care of Richard Eyre, the surgeon, had misunderstood certain things Eyre had told him in conversation and had enlarged them into what might well be construed as treason. Richard Eyre, penitent and terrified, admitted to a certain indiscretion in his talk, but vehemently denied that he had said anything that could be so interpreted. If he was loquacious, it was because entertaining small-talk was part of a doctor's stock-in-trade to put patients at their ease.

Cromwell understood perfectly. The building of false rumours on the slenderest foundation of fact was one of the dangers which beset every statesman. Privately, he assessed Eyre as a male-gossip, that most dangerous of characters to his friends, and wished that there were more of his kind about to make the task of his spies easier.

The secretary put a paper before Cromwell, who interrupted Geoffrey with: 'I see that this John Helyar's goods were seized as forfeit to the King's Majesty because he spoke traitorous words before he fled overseas.'

Geoffrey, seconded by Holland and Eyre, protested that Helyar was the most loyal of subjects. They were surprised beyond measure when Cromwell said, scribbling a note which he passed to the secretary: 'Then, as an earnest that I do not doubt your word in this or in any other matter you have spoken of, his goods shall be restored to him.'

Geoffrey was fulsome in his thanks. As the three made their way to the Countess's house by the Dowgate, he congratulated himself on the rightness of the course he had taken in appealing direct to Cromwell.

Margaret was, when she was told of it, by no means so sanguine. She turned angrily on Eyre.

'Before I left Warblington, did I not tell you to turn Tyndale out? Did I not warn you he was a heretic bent on stirring up trouble?'

'Your Ladyship,' replied the doctor, 'I did indeed give him your message.'

'And what was his answer?'

'He said that he would not leave either for lord or lady until he was in better health.'

'Yet,' said Margaret, 'he seems to have recovered it rudely enough.'

'He has left now,' said Geoffrey.

'One of the first sayings I taught you,' replied his mother, 'concerned a horse and the stable door. But what cannot be amended must be endured. Have you told your brother of this?'

'I came straight to London. There was no time to go to Bockmore.'

'Montagu must be warned,' said Margaret.

'If your Ladyship pleases,' Hugh Holland said, 'I will ride there immediately.'

'Tell my brother I will be hard on your heels, Hugh,' said Geoffrey.

It was, however, two days before Geoffrey set out for Bockmore, after having seen his mother, accompanied by Eyre, off to Warblington. Margaret intended to assure herself personally that Tyndale was no longer there and had threatened, if he was, to withdraw her support of the hospital.

On the London road, about twelve miles south of Bockmore,

Geoffrey met a small band of soldiers, accompanied by one of the Royal officers, on their way to the capital. With them was a prisoner, 'with his hands bound behind him and his legs bound under his horse's belly'. It was Hugh Holland. Cromwell's note to his secretary had not been to secure the return of Father Helyar's lands but to order that Holland was not to be let out of sight. He had been followed to Buckinghamshire and arrested almost as soon as he had spoken to Montagu.

'Why, Hugh,' exclaimed Geoffrey, trying to mask his fear with a pun, 'where are you bound to go?'

'They have not told me, Sir Geoffrey,' Hugh answered, 'but you would be wise to keep on your way lest you follow me too soon.'

At Bockmore, Montagu told Geoffrey the circumstances of the arrest—'it was not without a good scuffle and had I had more of my men at the house Hugh would have got away'— and Geoffrey in turn recounted to his brother the events that had led up to it.

'You were a fool to dare Cromwell,' was Montagu's comment.

'I saw no other way,' said Geoffrey, 'and he was not ungracious.'

Montagu stared at his brother, reluctant to believe him such a simpleton. 'You will stay here with me until this blows over,' he said. 'Have you kept any letters from Reynold?'

'One or two,' admitted Geoffrey. 'Have you not some?'

'I burn everything as soon as I have read it,' said Montagu, 'and if you are prudent you will do the same in future.' Then, apparently changing the subject: 'Does your wife know Father Collins?'

'He has never been to Lordington. How should she know him?'

'He is going there now. Give me your signet ring.'

'Why?'

'That she may know the message is truly from you.'

Calling his chaplain, Montagu bade him ride at once to

Lordington, show the ring to Lady Constance and see that she burnt every letter that could be found.

When Father Collins returned, having burnt all correspondence, whether incriminating or not, there was a long discussion as to what was best to do. The chaplain counselled taking no action; Montagu considered appealing direct to the King on the grounds of old friendship and faithful service; Geoffrey was prepared to face Cromwell once more; but they all agreed that it would be wisest to be in London where they could learn more quickly what was being done.

In London, however, torture had broken the silence of Hugh Holland. Geoffrey was arrested and sent to the Tower on the charge of having corresponded with his brother, the Cardinal, without first showing his letters to the King.

18

'To make him eat his own heart'

Cromwell was in no hurry, Montagu, though apparently free, could not escape. He was surrounded by spies and, should he make any attempt to leave the country, he could be immediately arrested and his action construed as treason. As for Geoffrey, the longer he was on the rack of suspense, threatened with the practical rack which had broken Hugh Holland, the more easily he would be persuaded to proffer required evidence. He was kept in close confinement in the Tower, on an inadequate diet, for fifty-eight days before he was summoned for the first of the seven examinations and fifty-nine interrogatories which Cromwell had prepared for him. Their object was to make him implicate the rest of his family. Just before they started, his wife was allowed to visit him. Horrified by his condition, she wrote to warn Montagu that he had been driven to frenzy and was in a fit state to become the instrument of their ruin.

Margaret, from Warblington, wrote to her eldest son: 'Son Montagu, I send you, from my heart, God's blessing and mine. The greatest gift I can send you is my prayers to God for His help, of which, I perceive, you have great need. And as to the case I am informed you stand in, my advice is to refer you to God first and so to order yourself both in word and deed as to serve your prince, as far as is within your power, without disobeying God's commandment. Pray daily to God that He will enable you to do this or else will take you to His mercy.'

For Geoffrey she could do nothing, except, proudly, to trust him. When her daughter-in-law warned her of his state of mind and added: 'I pray God, Madame, that he do you no hurt one day,' she replied quietly: 'I trust he is not so unhappy that he will hurt his mother.' And her faith was justified. In all the things that Geoffrey, driven almost over the edge of sanity, was made to say, he uttered no word which could be twisted, even by Cromwell, to implicate her.

At the end of his first examination, Geoffrey, realising that he was not, in his enfeebled state, strong enough to hold out against torture, tried to kill himself, but the knife missed his heart and he succeeded only 'in hurting himself sore'.

Meanwhile, investigations were proceeding in the neighbourhood of Warblington at an unexpectedly high level. The brutal Lord Admiral, Fitzwilliam, who had recently been made Earl of Southampton, was at his seat at Cowdray. One autumn day, while he was hawking, a poor man approached him to ask a favour. The man's wife had been committed to prison by the local magistrate, John Gunter, for saying that Sir Geoffrey Pole would have sent a detachment of men overseas to his brother, the Cardinal, if he had not been sent to the Tower.

On hearing Pole's name, Fitzwilliam's irritation at being interrupted in his pleasures changed to the liveliest interest and he promised to investigate the matter immediately. The reports of Geoffrey's intention were traced to the Harper of Havant, Laurence Taylor, who said he had the information in the first place from Richard Eyre of Warblington.

The magistrate had not troubled further to examine the Harper, but had allowed him to go to fulfil a professional engagement at a local wedding. When the Lord Admiral heard this, he turned in fury on the unfortunate J.P. whom he accused of criminal disloyalty. Gunter, 'with tears and sobbing' admitted that he had not understood the importance of the

234

matter but would make what amends he could by finding the Harper. Within twenty-four hours he had traced him and delivered him to the Admiral. The magistrate accompanied him in person and attempted to reinstate himself in Southampton's good graces by reporting extensively some of his own confidential conversations with Geoffrey Pole.

Furnished with so much and so detailed knowledge, Southampton betook himself to London to help Cromwell in examining Geoffrey. He knew enough to be able to make the prisoner think he knew everything and could play the common trick of making a desperate man believe that, while he might possibly save himself by confession, he could certainly save no one else by silence.

On November 4 Montagu was arrested and sent to join Geoffrey in the Tower. There was also arrested their cousin, the Marquis of Exeter, who had once said: 'I like well the proceedings of Cardinal Pole, but I like not the proceedings in this realm and I trust to see a change.' Montagu himself was charged with High Treason, under the recent act, for dreaming that the King was dead.

The following week, Henry decided to stage a public display of his orthodoxy. As Supreme Head, clad in white silk, he presided over the trial of a priest who had denied Transubstantiation. The King, when the priest threw himself on his mercy, condemned him out of hand and ordered Cromwell, as Vicar-General, to sentence him to be burnt alive at Smithfield.

Southampton, accompanied by the Bishop of Ely, made his way to Warblington to interrogate Margaret Pole. Though neither of her sons had implicated her, the Admiral had little doubt that he could make her implicate herself.

She answered the questions put to her quietly and with immense dignity. 'We travailled with the Lady of Salisbury all day, both before and after noon till almost night; but for all

235

we could do she would confess nothing,' the Admiral wrote to Cromwell.

Next day they tried again. They were alternately sympathetic and insulting, 'traitoring her and her sons to the ninth degree'. The result was the same. They reported that 'such a woman had never been heard of, she was so earnest and so precise and so manlike in continuance'.

The third day they returned to the attack. Was it not true, for instance, that she had heard from her other sons of the failure to assassinate the Cardinal? Certainly. And was she not glad?

'For motherly pity I could not but rejoice.'

They asked her whether she would have welcomed his return as the Pope's Legate.

'I have often wished to see him again in England with the King's favour, though he were but a poor parish priest,' she said.

So it continued. Everything was so 'sincere, pure and upright on her part', the Commissioners reported, 'that we must needs think one of two things of her; either her sons have not made her privy nor participant of the bottom and pit of their stomachs, or else she is the most arrant traitress that ever lived'.

They had perhaps forgotten that she was, by right, a Plantagenet ruler who had had more experience of statecraft in her girlhood than they had had all their devious lives. But they realised at least—and told Cromwell—that 'we have never dealt with such a one; we may call her rather a strong and constant man than a woman'.

The only thing that troubled Margaret was when she was told that she must leave her home at Warblington immediately and go to Southampton's house at Cowdray as a prisoner.[1] 'She

[1] In the standard work, *The Pilgrimage of Grace*, the authors, M. H. and R. Dodds, who are not particularly sympathetic to the Poles, remark: 'It is no wonder that the thought of being left in the keeping of such a man appalled even so brave a lady.' Fitzwilliam was, if possible, a worse character than Cromwell, but has not impinged so much on history. Readers are referred to his portrait by Holbein.

seemeth thereat to be somewhat appalled,' the Admiral wrote, 'and it may be that she will then utter somewhat when she is removed.'

She did not, but while she was under house-arrest at Cowdray, where she was treated with the utmost disrespect by the Admiral and his wife, Warblington Castle was systematically ransacked and, in an old coffer in the sewing-room, was found the tapestry Margaret had worked so long ago.

Here was clear proof of high treason. The Countess was obviously involved in fomenting the Pilgrimage of Grace for the purpose of deposing the King in favour of Princess Mary who would then marry Reginald Pole. What else could the Five Wounds and the pansies of Pole entwined with the marigolds of Mary mean?

The line of the prosecution was now clear. Henry epitomised it in a letter to the King of France whom, he had heard, Reginald Pole was on his way to visit.

'Weeping crocodile tears,' wrote Henry, 'he will, if it be possible, pour forth the venom of his serpent nature. He with divers other traitors, being of his kindred, hath conspired the destruction of our person, of Prince Edward our son, and of the Lady Mary and the Lady Elizabeth, our daughters.'

King Francis, however, was more impressed by another letter which he received at the same time from his own ambassador in London, begging to be recalled because he 'has to do with the most dangerous and cruel man in the world, who has neither reason nor understanding left'.

The Pope moved at last. The final straw was the King of England's challenging insult to the memory of St. Thomas of Canterbury. In the Bull of Excommunication, *Cum Redemptor,* Paul III proclaimed that, far from amending his ways, as he was given three years' grace to do before he was cut off from the Church, Henry 'has broken forth into new crimes and, not contented with the cruel slaughter of living priests and prelates, has exerted his savagery even on the dead. After causing St. Thomas, for the greater scorn of religion, to be summoned to trial and declared a traitor, he commanded his bones to be burned and the ashes scattered to the wind; thus surpassing the ferocity of any heathen people who, even when they have conquered their enemies in war, are not accustomed to outrage their dead bodies. Esteeming that even by this means he had not done sufficient injury to religion, he has spoiled the monastery of St. Augustine from whom the English people received the Christian faith; and, like as he has changed himself into a brute beast, so he has chosen to honour brute beasts as his companions by bringing animals into the monastery,[2] the monks having been expelled.'

To Reginald Pole, the Pope entrusted the diplomatic mission by which he hoped to make the excommunication effective. The King of France and the Emperor were, at last, at peace with each other. This state of affairs meant the decline of the King of England's influence, since Henry's foreign policy had consisted of allying himself either with Francis or with Charles, depending on which monarch would give him the better terms. Now that amity reigned on the Continent, England was of no account; and it would be possible for Charles and Francis, merely by a trade agreement prohibiting all commerce with Henry, to bring about a situation in which Henry would have been compelled to make peace with the Church and atone for his transgressions as the condition for keeping the Throne.

Even if Pole, as Cardinal-Legate of England, had not been the obvious choice as emissary to the Emperor with these proposals, the Pope felt under an obligation to offer him the opportunity to bring about the punishment of his family's persecutor. Soon after the news of his brothers' arrests had arrived in Rome, Pole sought an audience with the Pope; but Paul, remembering how unwillingly Reginald had left his life of retirement at Venice, how he had come to Rome only at the Pope's express

[2] The place was turned into a deer park and, later, into a pig farm.

command 'in virtue of holy obedience', how he had tried to avoid the cardinalate and had protested that it might harm his family, was stricken with remorse and refused for the moment to receive the Cardinal because, he said, he could not bear to look him in the face.

When, eventually, Pole set out for Toledo where the Emperor was (and where Henry's ambassador, Anne Boleyn's old lover, Sir Thomas Wyatt, was devoutly wishing that the preachers would 'stop discoursing about the burning of the Bishop's bones'), the Pope insisted that Reginald travelled as a layman, with only a few attendants, to escape Henry's assassins.

It was at Piacenza, where he arrived on January 9, 1539, that Reginald found letters telling him that, a month earlier in England, his brother Montagu and his cousin Exeter had been beheaded on Tower Hill and that, on the same day, Hugh Holland, George Croftes and Father John Collins had been hanged, drawn and quartered at Tyburn. Geoffrey Pole was still in the Tower. He had made a second attempt at suicide by trying to suffocate himself with a cushion.

Priuli tried to comfort the Cardinal as best he could.

'They died,' said Reginald, 'for God's cause, the most noble and glorious of any. I trust my mother is safe, though she, too, would gladly die for it.'

In England, Cromwell had received a congratulatory letter on the executions from Hugh Latimer, the Bishop of Rochester in succession to John Fisher. It ran: 'Blessed be the God of England whose minister you are. I heard you say once of Cardinal Pole that you would make him eat his own heart, which you have now, I trust, brought to pass, for he must needs eat his own heart and be as heartless as he is graceless.'

Richard Moryson was entrusted with the task of blackening the reputation of the dead men. Their wickedness, he wrote, was simply due to the fact that they were Papists, for anyone who believed that the Pope was the Head of the Church 'may well lack power or stomach to utter treason, but he cannot lack a traitorous heart'.

Cromwell further advised Henry to use a well-tried method of uniting all dissidents and stifling criticism—the suggestion that England was to be attacked by force of arms. In commissions for musters, for seamen, in every kind of official letters and missives, liege subjects were informed that 'that most pestilent idol, the cankered and venomous serpent, Paul, Bishop of Rome' was endeavouring 'by aid of the archtraitor, Reginald Pole' to move foreign princes to invade England and 'with mortal war, fire and sword to exterminate and utterly destroy the whole nation and generation of the same'.

As a lighter touch, Henry devised a spectacular entertainment for Londoners—an aquatic combat between two galleys on the Thames. One carried the Royal arms, the other the Pope's and several Cardinals' hats. They fought a long time, but the King's galley was victorious and threw the Pope and the Cardinals into the water. The French Ambassador thought it 'of poor grace and still less invention', but the Londoners loved it.

19

The Countess goes to the Tower

Despite the burdens of Church and State, the King's main preoccupation at the moment was matrimony. He intended to take a fourth—or, as he would have put it, a second—wife. To make it clear that he was now a widower, he had appeared in mourning for Jane Seymour even at the Christmas festivities, so that no one could escape the difference between that and the joyful attire he had adopted at the deaths of Catherine and Anne.

His problem was whether he should now ally himself with France or with the Empire. His preference was for France in the person of the twenty-three-year-old widow of the Duc de Longueville, Mary of Guise. He was sufficiently amorous of her to press his suit with the French Ambassador, to whom he explained: 'I am big in person and have need of a big wife.'

Madame de Longueville, however, preferred Henry's young nephew, King James V of Scotland.[1] The Ambassador, who, about to be relieved of his duty at the English court as he had requested, allowed himself a certain freedom of comment, suggested the Duchess's younger sister as a substitute: 'Take the young one; she is still a virgin and you would be able to have her at your measure.'

[1] Whom she married and by whom she became mother of Mary, Queen of Scots.

Henry then proposed that he should hold a large house-party near Calais at which other candidates could be assembled for his inspection.

The Ambassador explained that this was not the way things were ordered in France. Why did not Henry send some one he could trust to make a report?

'By God,' said the King, 'I trust no one but myself. The thing touches me too near. I wish to see them before deciding.'

'Perhaps, sire,' retorted the Ambassador, 'you would like to try them one after another and keep the one you found most agreeable. Is not that how the Knights of the Round Table used to treat the ladies of this country in olden times?'

Henry wished he could punish the Ambassador for the all-inclusive insult, but had to content himself by threatening that he might marry 'on the Emperor's side'.

The Imperial candidate was one of the Emperor's nieces, Christine, the widowed Duchess of Milan, who was sixteen. Henry sent his court painter, Hans Holbein, to make a portrait of her,[2] after his envoy had informed him: 'She is not so pure white as the late Queen, whose soul God pardon; but she hath a singular good countenance, and when she chanceth to smile there appear two pits in her cheeks and one in her chin, the which become her right excellently well.'

Henry approved her and to his proposal she answered officially: 'What should I say? You know that I am at the Emperor's commandment. I am his poor servant and must follow his pleasure.'

Unofficially she remarked: 'Had I five heads, His Majesty of England might have one.'

Negotiations dragged on until Henry, complaining that the Emperor 'was knitting one delay to the tail of another', was forced to realise that Charles, no more than Francis, wanted his friendship. To this extent at least, Pole had succeeded in

[2] This portrait has this year (1968) been cleaned and can be seen (in the National Gallery) as Henry VIII must have seen it.

closing the Catholic ranks against him. With extreme reluctance, making it quite clear that it was merely a disagreeable political necessity, the King allowed Cromwell to negotiate a marriage among the Lutheran princes of Germany. Cromwell chose Anne of Cleves, who was twenty-three. 'Everyone,' he told Henry, 'praises her beauty, both of face and body, and says she excels the Duchess of Milan as the golden sun does the silver moon.' The French Ambassador's remark that she was plain to the point of ugliness, Henry dismissed as evidence of his chagrin.

In the April of 1539, Henry called a parliament to put the seal of approval on his policy towards the Poles. The composition of the Commons was Cromwell's masterpiece. He appointed practically every member in order that Henry might have a 'tractable' House. It was the climax of his career. He had fulfilled his promise. Church and State were the obedient tools of an incredibly wealthy king whose absolute power over his subjects extended to the ability to execute them, without proper trial, on any excuse—and even for their dreams. The new parliament passed a comprehensive Bill of Attainder, retrospectively branding as traitors those who had already been executed and including in the same condemnation the Countess of Salisbury, Cardinal Pole and Henry, Montagu's sixteen-year-old son.

Before the introduction of the attainder, Henry was assailed by a slight doubt. He was aware that his actions were now being sourly scrutinised by the rest of Christendom and he did not wish to depart too flagrantly from legality. He therefore enquired of the judiciary whether it was in order for one who was able to appear in his defence to be condemned by Act of Parliament without being called on to appear. As such proceedings were originally intended to deal with those who were beyond the reach of the King's courts, he had no doubt of the rightness of including 'the traitorous Cardinal' in the Attainder, but was it proper to give his mother, who was obviously available, no chance to defend herself?

Henry had reason to be concerned about this. Against Margaret, there was no evidence whatever except a piece of needlework. Moreover as she was, apart from his children, his nearest living relative, he might expect considerable execration for his treatment of her from all Christendom.

The judges, aware of the answer Henry wanted and yet retaining shreds of professional conscience, decided that it was 'a dangerous question' but ruled that, if the prisoner were condemned by Parliament, 'it could not come in question afterwards whether he were called or not called to appear'.[3]

It was enough. When the Bill of Attainder came to the Lords, Cromwell exhibited the needlework as evidence of Margaret's intention to dethrone the King. She was condemned in that, additionally, she had 'confederated herself' with Montagu and Reginald Pole, knowing them to be traitors and common enemies of the King and had traitorously aided, maintained and comforted them.

She was taken from Cowdray and put in a damp cell in the Tower of London where Henry hoped she would sicken and die of natural causes to save him the odium of having her executed.

Geoffrey, although included retrospectively in the attainder, had already been pardoned and released. Broken in body and mind, he crawled back to Sussex where he made attempt after attempt to see his mother while she was still at Cowdray, but was always prevented by Southampton, who threatened to have him rearrested unless he left the country. At last he decided to do so; but, before he went, there was one action which would give him some relief. He waylaid the magistrate, John Gunter, who had 'dealt unkindly with him in his trouble by uttering things they had communed in secret' and 'did so sore hurt and wound him' that the magistrate nearly died.

[3] It may be of interest that academic historians see in this only, to quote Sir Kenneth Pickthorn, 'one of the steps by which the court of parliament becomes the sovereign legislature'.

Geoffrey then managed to get taken aboard a Flemish ship and according to the Chronicler, 'passed over to Flanders, leaving his wife and children. Thence he found his way to Rome and throwing himself at the feet of his brother, the Cardinal, he said: "My lord, I do not deserve to call myself your brother, for I have been the cause of our brother's death." The Cardinal brought him to the feet of the Pope and procured forgiveness and absolution for his sin. Then the Cardinal sent him back to Flanders with letters to the Bishop of Liége, who treated him with all honour and allowed him a ducat a day and food for himself, two attendants and a horse.'[4]

That Margaret Pole did not die in the Tower was due partly to her own resilience, partly to the efforts of the Keeper, Thomas Philips, a kindly man who had himself once been a prisoner for a brief spell and who had known the Countess when he had a minor post on the Welsh Marches and she was with Princess Mary at Ludlow. He relaxed her captivity as far as he dared, allowed her grandson, Henry, to visit her occasionally and, after a few months, appealed to the Privy Council for more clothes for her, 'for she wanteth necessary apparel both for to change and also to keep her warm'.

It was from the cold that she suffered most. From her earliest years, ever since she had been taken as a child into the vault in which her murdered father lay buried in Tewkesbury Abbey, cold had been for her the very symbol of death. She had seen to it always that her houses were full of sunshine and warmth. It might have been better, she thought, if she had steeled herself to endure the cold rather than dispel it. She offered her enforced endurance of it now as an additional penance for her sins.

She was not sure in what her particular sinfulness had consisted. In the last days at Warblington, Father Helyar—and later Father Crayford who had succeeded him as her confessor

---

[4] Geoffrey lived in Liége for the next twelve years. He was eventually amnestied and returned to England where he died in 1558, the same year as Reginald.

—had warned her against pride. They seemed to mean, when she sought further enlightenment, an unwavering trust in her own judgment. She could not deny it, but she told them, not as an excuse but as a simple statement, that after sixty years' experience of the vicissitudes of court at the very centre of events, her judgment was likely to be as trustworthy as anyone else's.

In the dilemma which Henry had forced on them all, she had tried always to act as she had advised Montagu to act, to be, as Thomas More had put it, 'the King's faithful servant, but God's first'. She was sure that her friends, More and Fisher and the Carthusians and Father Reynolds of Syon were not traitors; but she was still not certain that they deserved the name of martyrs. For herself, if it should be her lot to die as they had—which in the circumstances was possible—she would certainly die in the same Faith, rejecting Henry's temporary megalomania about the Headship of the Church, but she would not consider herself therefore entitled to the great name of 'martyr'. Martyrdom, in spite of all that Reginald and others might say and all that her theologians at Warblington might quote from the Fathers, meant a great deal more than that.

If she blamed herself for any particular shortcoming, it was for a certain lack of prudence. Not in day-to-day matters or in the general conduct of life, but in not taking note of a pattern of fatality. She saw it now with the utmost clarity—how as soon as her uncle, King Edward IV, had tried to make the throne safe for his son, he had proceeded against his brother, Margaret's father, who was the true Plantagenet heir: how, as soon as the usurping Tudor, Henry VII, had tried to make the throne safe for his son, he had proceeded against Margaret's brother, who was the true Plantagenet heir. Here in the Tower, her father, Clarence, and her brother, Warwick, had spent their last days before they were killed as a dynastic safeguard. Why had she not seen that when Henry VIII at last had a son, he would act no differently but proceed against her son, Montagu, who was the true Plantagenet heir? The moment Jane Seymour's child was born, Margaret should have urged—commanded—Montagu to leave the country.

It needed her loneliness to allow her to see the pattern clearly, but in the Tower it was repeating itself in horrifying detail. Just as Henry VII had reduced her brother to a childish simplicity by depriving him of the rudiments of learning, so Henry VIII was now treating her grandson. Young Henry Pole was forbidden to have a tutor (which Exeter's son was allowed), and was subjected to longer and longer spells of solitary confinement. When, by the kindness of the Keeper, he was allowed to visit her, she did her best to correct it, lavishing on him all the love and care that was possible in such fugitive circumstances; but, though she tried to give him her strength as once her own grandmother, Cecily, had strengthened her, she had to watch the boy's gradual deterioration and face the fact that the hope of her house was doomed. She could only pray that he would be allowed to die mercifully.[5]

In her cold diminished world, Margaret still heard something of what proceeded on the great stage outside. She could have heard more, for the Keeper was ready enough to tell her; but she knew too well how spies could listen to twist the simplest words to a prisoner's hurt and she soon made it clear that she was not disposed for gossip. Even when she heard that Cromwell had lost the King's favour and was facing a Bill of Attainder, she did not agree with the Keeper's remark that, so hoist on his own petard, it was a judgment on him.

'The judgment of men,' she said quietly, 'belongs to Christ, who knows the hidden things of the heart.'

Cromwell's downfall was the result of the Cleves marriage. When Henry first saw his new bride, he was 'so marvellous astonished and abashed' that he could hardly speak. He found

[5] Henry Pole's fate—except that he never emerged from the Tower—is unknown. He was probably starved to death.

words, however, to describe her to one of his intimates as a 'Flanders mare' and ask explosively: 'Why should wise men make such reports as they have done? I see nothing in this woman as men report of her. I like her not.'

He turned to Cromwell: 'What remedy?'

Cromwell explained that there was, unfortunately, none. Already he faced an alliance of Francis and Charles. If he refused to marry Anne of Cleves now she had come to England, he would alienate all the German Lutherans and be without a friend or ally in Europe.

'Is there none other remedy,' Henry groaned, 'but that I must needs, against my will, put my neck in the yoke?'

Cromwell reiterated that there was none.

On his wedding-morning, the King informed his minister who, by now, was becoming slightly apprehensive on his own behalf: 'My lord, if it were not to satisfy the world and my realm, I would not do what I must do this day for none earthly thing.'

Next morning Cromwell waited on him again, hoping that the bridal night had brought some improvement in the situation. How did he now like the Queen?

'From the first,' said Henry, 'I liked her not well, but now I like her much worse, for I have felt her belly and her breasts and thereby, as I can judge, she should be no maid; which struck me so to the heart when I felt them that I had neither will nor courage to proceed any further.'

Obviously, whatever the cost, Anne must be got rid of. Cranmer was called on for his usual duty and in due course pronounced the marriage null and void on the ground of 'a defect of intention in the sacrament of matrimony, His Majesty the King having gone through the form of it under the impulse of his political necessities, against his true desire and without inward consent'.

Four days after the archiepiscopal judgment, Cromwell who, for three months had been Earl of Essex—a supreme example of

Henry's habit of lulling before he struck—was executed, not on Tower Hill but at Tyburn on account of his plebeian origin. The charge was High Treason.

The same day, Henry married his fifth wife—a small vivacious, red-headed girl of seventeen, Anne Boleyn's cousin, Katharine Howard, who was already (though naturally unknown to him) experienced in love. He called her his 'rose without a thorn'.

Two days later the King, whose habit of confusing religion and matrimony had not diminished with the years, thought it advisable to remind his people of the path of credal orthodoxy. At Tyburn he hanged three Religious for denying the Supremacy and at Smithfield he burnt three Lutherans for denying Transubstantiation.

'It was wonderful,' wrote the French Ambassador, 'to see adherents of the two opposing parties dying at the same time, and it gave offence to both. And it was no less strange to hear than horrible to see, for the obstinacy and constancy of both parties and the perversion of justice.'

Immediately after Christmas, Henry began to make preparations for an impressive Progress in the north, where he could present the new Queen to the people.

In the general atmosphere of rejoicing, he did not forget Margaret Pole. At the beginning of March, the Queen's tailor was given an order for certain apparel for the Countess, and in April—a year after Thomas Philips had asked for them— there were delivered for her at the Tower 'a night-gown furred, a kirtle of worsted and petticoat furred, another gown of the fashion of night-gown of saye, lined with satin of Cyprus and faced with satin, a bonnet with a frontlet, four pairs of hose, four pairs of shoes and a pair of slippers'.

The cold was over.

20

The morning of May 27, 1541

The day after Ascension Day, May 27, 1541, the Countess was woken at six in the morning and told that it was the King's will that she should die within the hour. Henry had suddenly changed his mind and determined to clear the Tower of traitors before he set out for the North.

She thought it 'very strange' but dressed as quickly as she could in her new clothes. As soon as she was ready, she was carried out in a chair, not to the usual block on Tower Hill but to a remote corner of the Tower precincts at East Smith-field Green where a few people had been summoned to watch her end. The French Ambassador, who was among them, noted that there were so few 'that till evening the truth was still doubted, for those here are afraid to put to death publicly those whom they secretly hate'.

There had been no time to erect a scaffold. There was only a low block, used for decapitating dead bodies, set on the ground. Nor was the ordinary executioner in attendance. He had been sent ahead to the North lest the King should require his services there. In his place was a terrified youth of seventeen who was unaccustomed to killing.

Margaret, who seemed to have an access of strength as she got down from the chair, spoke regally to the little crowd, asking their prayers for her soul. She also asked them to pray for the King and the Prince and the Princess. To Mary she sent her especial love and the message: 'Blessed are they who suffer persecution for justice' sake.'

She was told to lie down at the block.

She replied: 'So should traitors do and I am none. I have committed no crime. I have had no trial. My head never committed treason: if you will have it, you must take it as you can.'

It was not difficult to force her. She was nearly seventy and had been imprisoned for two years. The inexperienced young headsman—reported Chapuys, who, like his French colleague, was there as an official spectator—'literally hacked her head and shoulders to pieces in the most pitiful manner'.

When the news arrived in Italy, Reginald, after opening the letter, went into his private oratory and for an hour faced his grief alone. When he returned, he had regained 'his wonted serenity of countenance'.

'Until now,' he said, 'I had thought God had given me the grace of being the son of one of the best and most honourable ladies in England and I gloried in it. Now He has vouchsafed to make me the son of a martyr.'

Priuli, when he had realised the meaning, 'was struck as one dead'.

Reginald said: 'Let us rejoice, for we have another advocate in Heaven.'

ROME
THE FEAST OF BLESSED MARGARET POLE, 1968.